Eloquence of Chaucer's Women:

The Wife of Bath, Criseyde, and Prudence

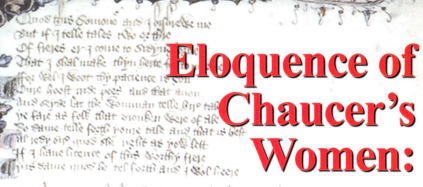

NOJI Kaoru

Hon-no-Shiro
Otowa-shobo Tsurumi-Shoten
Tokyo

Eloquence of Chaucer's Women:

The Wife of Bath, Criseyde, and Prudence

NOJI Kaoru

Eloquence of Chaucer's Women:
The Wife of Bath, Criseyde, and Prudence

by NOJI Kaoru

©2017 by NOJI Kaoru

All rights reserved.
No part of this book may be reproduced
or transmitted in any form or by any means
without permission in writing from the publisher.

ISBN978-4-7553-0405-7

Introduction

With respect to the image of women in medieval society and literature, the antinomic conflict between Eve and the Virgin Mary must be confronted. Eve was the first sinner, who was responsible for the Fall of Man. She is often used as the exemplar of sexual temptation, whom clerics should avoid. She bears always an evil and bruised image within Christian tradition. This is often counter-balanced by the typology of the Madonna. She is the Mother of Jesus Christ, the Blessed Virgin, pure and sacred. She is worshiped as an ideal woman. These ideas are based on the contradiction between adoration and contempt for women in medieval Christian society, which leads to the notions of misogyny (hatred of women) and misogamy (hatred of marriage).

Geoffrey Chaucer was in his age the most renowned story-teller and skillful narrator. He portrayed a large variety of women in his works. It is clear that women and the relationships between man and woman, husband and wife are Chaucer's favorite subjects in his story-telling. The poet created his women following this medieval literary convention; however, his particularly keen insight is subtly reflected in his characters. He offers some of his female characters the ability to express their own thoughts and feelings. They freely use their own words and speak fluently and eloquently. As in the famous question asked by the Wife of Bath, 'Who painted the lion?', women in literature have almost always been created and developed by male authors. Chaucer grants them 'eloquence' and makes them speak spontaneously.

That most of Chaucer's female characters are much more attractive ii Introduction

than his male characters has long been affirmed. It has been suggested that one facet of their attractiveness lies in their eloquence. Prior studies, however, have not taken up their eloquence as a main theme and have not fully discussed the matter. This dissertation focuses on that very point—the eloquence of Chaucer's women—and analyzes the essence of their speeches and rhetoric, and examines how and why he developed them; in consequence, there will be brought to light not only Chaucer's intention in creating eloquent women and one aspect of his personal view of women but also a fuller understanding of his imaginative literature in general will emerge.

Is Chaucer really friendly toward women? If searching for an answer to this question means an approach with a feminist reading, the standpoint of this thesis is indeed feminism. Prior to modern feminist arguments, the sixteenth-century Scots poet Gavin Douglas referred to Chaucer as women's friend. Yet the question stubbornly casts some doubt on the question, "Is he really?"

As early as 1915, G. L. Kittredge suggested that the contemporary political and social catchword "feminism" is not inappropriate in considering Chaucer's fourteenth century ethos.[1] In the 1960s, D. W. Robertson influentially argued that medieval literature must be approached on its own terms and in relation to its own uniform orthodoxies. Among the hierarchies, it assumes is the doctrine that the female is subordinate to the male. To Robertson the Wife of Bath is "a literary personification of rampant "femininity" or carnality."[2] From this point of view it is certainly impossible to call Chaucer a pro-feminist.

At the end of the 1980s, the exploration of gender stereotypes played an important role in the work of David Aers and Sheila Delany, although they situated themselves in the tradition of Marxist criticism rather than in that of feminism. Then book-length studies of gender in Chaucer appeared one after another: Carolyn Dinshow's *Chaucer's Sexual Poetics* (1989), Priscilla Martin's *Chaucer's Women* (1990), and Elaine Tuttle Hansen's *Chaucer and the Fiction of Gender* (1992).

In the second half of the 1990s, influential studies on Chaucer's gender issues appeared, such as Angela Jane Weisl's *Conquering the Reign of Femeny* (1995), Anne Laskaya's *Chaucer's Approach to Gender in the Canterbury Tales* (1995).

In those prominent Chaucerian feminist studies, the Wife of Bath and Criseyde have been fully discussed by many scholars. Yet, not enough attention has been paid to Dame Prudence, who is one of the most eloquent speakers among Chaucer's characters and the poet himself narrates her as a pilgrim in *The Canterbury Tales* (henceforth *CT*). This dissertation discusses the most notable three types of women who speak eloquently in insisting on their opinion. They are completely different from each other with regard to their appearances, personalities, and positions: a widow, a lover and a wife. They are three representative types.

In discussing eloquence, a very brief survey of the historical back-ground of rhetoric is useful. According to James J. Murphy (2005):

> Marcus Tullius Cicero (106–43 B.C.), whose works were proved to be the most popular medieval source of Roman rhetorical theory, had defined rhetoric in his *De inventione* (87 B.C.) as "eloquence based on rules of art" and further declared it to be a "branch of political science." For Cicero the aim of eloquence was to persuade an audience by speech. (1)

iv   Introduction

It goes without saying that Greek rhetoric, already in the 5th century B.C., was a specialized field of study in its own right, distinguished from poetic (literary works and studies). Thus Aristotle could deliver a series of lectures outlining the definition and parameters of literary tragedy and, besides, lectures discussing the rationale for and techniques of rhetoric, rhetoric as a discipline being focused on oratory.

When Greek culture waned, the Roman power was in the ascendancy; poetic fell into abeyance and the Romans who were concerned with the advancement and security of their empire built on the Greek foundation of rhetoric and greatly expanded the techniques pertinent to oratory as political persuasion. For well over a millennium rhetorical theory and practice constituted one of the primary areas of concentration for Roman and later systems of education.

Chaucer was neither a rhetorician nor was he, in all probability, particularly well informed about rhetoric—any more, that is, than his ordinary literate fellows. As much rhetoric as he knew, he doubtless picked up as one aspect of the common knowledge of the day shared by literate people. What is worth noting is his application of rhetorical techniques—that is to say, essentially oratorical techniques—to literary works.

It was natural that Chaucer, like every educated 14th century English poet, would have availed himself of the devices of rhetoric. In Chaucer's works, rhetorical terms and devices can be found everywhere:

> "Telle me this now feythfully,
> Have y not preved thus symply,
> Withoute any subtilite
> Of speche, or gret prolixite

Of termes of philosophie,

Of figures of poetrie,

Or colours of rethorike?   (*The House of Fame*, 853–59)[3]

God woot that worldly joye is soone ago;

And if a rethor koude faire endite,

He in a cronycle saufly myghte it write

(*The Nun's Priest's Tale*, 3206–08)

It moste been a rethor excellent

That koude his colours longynge for that art,

If he sholde hire discryven every part. (*The Squire's Tale*, 38–40)

Chaucer uses technical rhetorical terms such as "rethorike," "colours," and "figures," which means 'metaphor.' These terms can be found in *Boece* and *The Clerk's Tale* and *The Franklin's Prologue*.

There is an amusing degree of irony, itself one rhetorical device, in recalling that the Wife of Bath's story is orally delivered; that is, it is a verbal statement now embedded by Chaucer in a literary work and it takes the basic form of the five parts of rhetoric as described by Cicero in his *De inventione*: (1) *inventio*, or the discovery of valid arguments that render one's case plausible; (2) *dispositio*, or the placement of such arguments in their proper order; (3) *elecutio*, or language appropriate to the arguments; (4) *memoria*, or firm control of matter and words; and (5) *pronuntiatio*,or use of the voice and body suitable to the subject matter and style.[4] *The Wife of Bath's Tale* (henceforth *WBT*) is analyzable in just that way, except that because this is a merely literary telling the audience cannot see her body language; she is after all, anyway, riding a horse; nor can her voice be heard except as memory assures us basically how she would control her voice and delivery. Chaucer might have described body language and voice but that did not seem necessary in developing the heart of the matter. Thus rhetoric offers both an enabling and controlling structure.

Geoffrey Chaucer was born between 1340 and 1345 in London. He is of course widely considered one of the greatest English poets of the Middle Ages. He was from a wealthy but not an aristocratic family. His grandfather and father were prosperous wine merchants and deputies of the king's butler. The Chaucer family had moved from Ipswich to London in the early 14th century, where it was possible for a merchant's family to become 'gentry' within two or three generations, or even less. Chaucer was a highly educated man. He probably went to school at St. Paul's grammar school. He was literate and had a great knowledge of Latin and French.

He started his public career as a page to Elizabeth, Countess of Ulster, and wife of Edward III's third son in 1357. He also worked as a courtier, a diplomat, and a civil servant, as well as working in the king's service. He often made diplomatic journeys to Italy, France, and Spain between 1360 and 1381. In the Hundred Years War with France, he was captured in 1360 and finally ransomed for £16 which was paid by Edward III himself. He made a journey to Italy with a trading mission in 1372–73. He visited France again in 1381 to make a marriage arrangement between King Richard II and a daughter of the French King. From 1374 to 1386 he was Controller of the Custom (the export tax on wool, sheepskin and leather). Chaucer was appointed Justice and Justice of the Peace and Knight of the Shire of Kent (1385–86).

Having come from bourgeois society, Chaucer was familiar with the court life. He also had an 'international' mind. In France and Italy, he was influenced by many great contemporaries, such as Deschamps, Froissart, Machaut, Boccaccio, Dante and Petrarca. He translated the French poetry, Guillaume de Lorris's *Le Roman de la rose* (henceforth *Roman*) into *The Romaunt of the Rose* (henceforth *RR*) and learned of the allegorical world of courtly love. *The Book of the Duchess* is a dream vision, showing John of Gaunt's love for his wife, Blanche, which had an influence on Machaut and Froissart. In Italy, Chaucer would have had an opportunity to read Boccaccio, Petrarca, and Dante. He composed *Troilus and Criseyde* (henceforth *TC*) based on Boccaccio's *Il Filostrato* (henceforth *Fil*). *CT*, which consists of 17,000 lines of verse and 2,000 lines of prose, has as its sources various literary works of classical and medieval Europe. The poet created his literary works from a great variety of perspectives. It goes without saying that he has long been studied from innumerable points of view by hundreds of scholars.

This dissertation takes up the three eloquent women—the Wife of Bath, Criseyde and Prudence—and analyzes their skills of eloquence and the significance of their speech in order to explore Chaucer's real and hidden intentions in creating such characters and one part of his view of women. Chapter I explains his relation with some women in his actual life. Section 1 explores the women in his family tree who were deeply involved with him and searches for their influence on him and the creativity of his composition. Section 2 treats Chaucer's wife Philippa and their marital life in order to identify some hints about his special interests in marriage and women. Section 3 investigates the most mysterious and shocking enigma in his life: the case of Cecily

viii   Introduction

Champain. Chapter II describes the portrayals of the three women and discusses how Chaucer describes the features and personalities of each of them. Chapter III analyzes the eloquence of the Wife of Bath in her Prologue and Tale. Section 1 examines her excuses for remarriage by her claiming advantageous appeal to the Bible. Section 2 discusses her ways of controlling her first three husbands and the effect of her continual complaints and attacks on those husbands. Section 3 considers the conflicts with the two "badde" husbands and the meaning of the reconciliation with the fifth husband at the end of her Prologue. Section 4 examines the sovereignty of women and a feminized man in the female-dominant world developed in *WBT*, which shares a common theme with her Prologue regarding the domination in marriage of a husband over a wife. Chapter IV discusses Criseyde's eloquent speeches in the three scenes. Section 1 treats her first speech when she permits herself to fall in love with Troilus. Section 2 examines her long and eloquent speech to persuade Troilus that they have to part. Section 3 discusses in her final speech why she chooses to stay with the Greeks and her betrayal of Troilus after all. Chapter V analyzes Prudence's lengthy speeches that are divided into three parts. Section 1 explores her way of amending her husband's anti-feministic thoughts. Section 2 demonstrates how her logical and flawless arguments instruct her husband. Section 3 explains the last part of her ideas and explores how her eloquence works to persuade him. Chapter VI summarizes Chaucer's three eloquent women and explores why he offers particular words to his female characters and how they utilize their words for their own purposes. Section 1 compares the Wife of Bath and Criseyde and discusses differences and similarities between them. Section 2 examines Prudence in comparison with the Wife of Bath and Criseyde. The final section clarifies Chaucer's intention in creating these eloquent women and their importance in his literary works.

Chaucer, as a court poet, does not always occupy a socially dominant position. He is, in a sense, a marginal being, just as women are in patriarchal society. He sometimes appears very friendly to women, but his judgment of women is clearly double-edged and is sometimes severe. He subtly reveals his true feelings for and against women or toward patriarchal society under cover of his women characters. Chaucer's ingenious devices underline the exquisite touch of their eloquence.

Abbreviations

CT	*The Canterbury Tales*
Fil	*Il Filostrato*
GP	*The General Prologue*
Mel	*The Tale of Melibee*
PBA	*Proceedings of the British Academy*
Roman	*The Romance de la rose*
RR	*The Romaunt of the Rose*
TC	*Troilus and Criseyde*
Troilus	*Troilus and Cressida*
WBP	*The Wife of Bath's Prologue*
WBT	*The Wife of Bath's Tale*

CONTENTS

Introduction i

CHAPTER I

Chaucer and the Women in His Life 1

    I-1 The Women in His Family 5

    I-2 Philippa, His Wife, and Their Marital Life..................... 9

    I-3 Cecily Champain and the Case of *raptus*...................... 18

CHAPTER II

Chaucer's Portrayals of Women.................................. 31

    II-1 The Portrayal of theWife of Bath 31

    II-2 The Portrayal of Criseyde 42

    II-3 The Portrayal of Prudence.. 61

CHAPTER III

The Wife of Bath's Eloquence in Her Prologue and Tale.... 69

    III-1 Eloquence in Her Excuses for Remarriage...................... 69

    III-2 How to Control Three "goode" Husbands 78

    III-3 Marital Conflicts with Two "badde" Husbands 83

    III-4 The Sovereignty of Women in *The Wife of Bath's Tale* 93

CHAPTER IV

Criseyde's Eloquence 101

    IV-1 Falling in Love with Troilus 102

    IV-2 Leaving Troilus 120

    IV-3 Remaining with the Greeks 135

CHAPTER V
Prudence's Eloquence 153

V-1 The First Part of Her Argument 155
V-2 The Second Part of Her Argument 161
V-3 The Third Part of Her Argument 177

CHAPTER VI
Chaucer's Intention in Creating Female Eloquence 195

VI-1 The Wife of Bath and Criseyde 195
VI-2 Prudence vs Criseyde and the Wife of Bath 199
VI-3 The 'Meaning' of Eloquent Women 202

Conclusion 209

Notes 213
Bibliography 217
Afterword 225
Index 227

Eloquence of Chaucer's Women:

The Wife of Bath, Criseyde, and Prudence

Chapter I

Chaucer and the Women in His Life

Geoffrey Chaucer was not only a man of letters. His life records cast light upon his career as a courtier, diplomat, and civil servant, as well. His social position enables one to grasp something of his biography, at least in rough outline. Though the records are nothing but public documents, they provide some clues for understanding Chaucer's actual life. To trace some part of that life, *Chaucer Life-Records* published by Martin M. Crow and Clair C. Olson (1966) is indispensable. The 493 articles are contained in the book. They are mostly legal documents such as records of expenses, payments of annuities, witness statements, pleas of debt, and house leases. As the materials are official, none of his private information about his childhood, educational background, or other personal details is given (Evans 2005: 9). Compared with English poets in the later centuries, very little of Chaucer's personal life is known. As an English poet in the middle ages, however, relatively a great deal of his life records has been found, considering that the Gawain-poet is anonymous and William Langland's personal history is obscure.

As Ruth Evans (2005, 10) has it, a biographical reading was regarded as almost a theoretical crime in literary criticism about twenty five years ago. That is, literary works and the author's personal experiences were not to be connected. But this does not mean that the author has no relation

[1]

to the works or that considering the author's life is worthless. Authors are complex figures so that Geoffrey Chaucer is "made up not only [of the] poetry (and prose) that he left us, but also of a variety of other texts: the life-records and all of the academic and popular supplements (biographies, portraits, scholarly articles and books, films, musicals, images, e-discussions, and even novels) that form the dense network of meanings and representations that we now recognize as 'Chaucer'"

My viewpoint is that Chaucer's life and his works are sometimes inseparable. This chapter surveys Chaucer's life, especially regarding the women who were deeply involved in his life. In the first section, Chaucer's family line is investigated in order to consider his family background. The second section introduces Chaucer's wife Philippa in order to give consideration to their marital life. The last section treats the most mysterious and scandalous episode in Chaucer's life records: the Cecily Champain case. His personal experiences and circumstances with women help to understand how some women characters in his works had been created and upon what his view of women had been based.

Chaucer and the Women in His Life 3

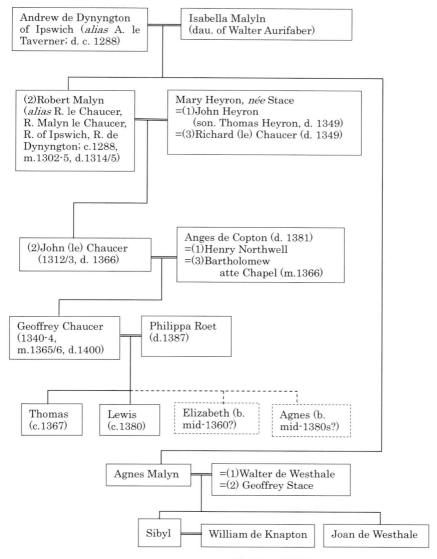

(1), (2), and (3) indicate the order of marriage

4   Chapter I

Personal Relations in The Chaucer's Family Tree

Andrew de Dynyngton of Ipswich: Geoffrey Chaucer's great-grandfather, a taverner in Ipswich.
Isabella Malyn: Geoffrey Chaucer's great-grandmother.

Robert Malyn (*alias* Robert le Chaucer): Geoffrey Chaucer's grandfather, a vintner in London, who took the surname, Chaucer from his master.
Mary Heyron: Geoffrey Chaucer's grandmother, maiden name is Stace.
John Heyron: Mary's first husband, a pepperer in London.
Thomas Heyron: son of John and Mary Heyron, a vintner.
Richard (le) Chaucer: Mary's third husband, a vintner, probably a cousin of Robert Chaucer or a relative of Robert's master, John le Chaucer.

Agnes Malyn: Geoffrey Chaucer's great-aunt.
Walter de Westhale: Agnes's first husband.
Geoffrey Stace: Agnes's second husband, who is a brother of Mary Heyron.
Sibyl: The daughter of Agnes and Walter de Westhale.
William de Knapton: husband of Sibyl.
Joan de Westhale: daughter of Agnes and Walter de Westhale.

John (le) Chaucer: Geoffrey Chaucer's father, a vintner.
Anges de Copton: Geoffrey Chaucer's mother.
Henry Northwell: Agnes's first husband.
Bartholomew atte Chapel: Agnes's third husband.

Geoffrey Chaucer: The person himself.
Philippa Roet: Geoffrey Chaucer's wife.
Thomas Chaucer: son of Geoffrey and Philippa Chaucer. John of Gaunt is suspected as father.
Lewis Chaucer: son of Geoffrey Chaucer and Cecily Champain, as a result of the *raptus* case (?).
Elizabeth Chaucer: daughter of Geoffrey and Philippa Chaucer. John of Gaunt is suspected as father.
Agnes Chaucer: daughter or granddaughter of Geoffrey Chaucer.

I-1 The Women in His Family

The Chaucer family originally came from Ipswich, Suffolk, where Geoffrey's great-grandfather, Andrew de Dynyngton, also called Andrew le Taverner, probably owned a tavern in the late 13th century. He married Isabella Malyn, a daughter of Walter Aurifaber, and begot a son named Robert le Dynyngton, also known as Robert Malyn, Robert Malyn le Chaucer and Robert le Chaucer (c.1288–1314/5). Robert moved to London and established himself as a successful vintner (Pearsall 1992, 12).

The family name Chaucer is not the name that had been succeeded to over generations. It was the poet's grandfather, Robert, who first announced himself as Chaucer. Lister M. Matheson (1991, 171–89) explains how Robert adopted the surname. Although the name in the Old French chaucier is translated as either "shoemaker" or "stoking-maker, hosier," Robert probably started his merchant career as an apprentice of a mercer in London. His master, called John le Chaucer, was engaged in fabrics trading. He was involved in a violent fight and died of his wounds in 1302. In his will, the master bequeathed his three daughters and his apprentice, Robert, certain sums of money for mercantile purposes. It may well have been appropriate for Robert to adopt his master's surname le Chaucer on this occasion.

Robert le Chaucer, in or before 1307, married Mary or Maria, the widow of John Heyron (Heron). Robert and Mary had a son, John Chaucer who was born in 1312/3 and grew up to be Geoffrey Chaucer's father. His father Robert probably named the son after his master, John le Chaucer. Robert died some time before 1316 when John was still an infant (Skeat 1899, xi). Robert's wife and Geoffrey Chaucer's grandmother, Mary, thus married three times in her life. Her first husband, John Heyron, was a pepper merchant in London. He was a close associate of John le Chaucer, Robert's master. Robert and Mary would have known each other prior to their marriage. Mary already had a son from her first husband. The boy was named Thomas Heyron, who also became a vintner. The third husband, Richard le Chaucer, was also a vintner. He might well have been either a relative, probably a cousin of Robert le Chaucer (Skeat 1899, xi) or a relative of John le Chaucer (Matheson 1991, 181). Richard and Mary married in 1323, some years after the second husband's death. The poet's father John Chaucer was raised by Richard and Mary.

When John was eleven or twelve years old, in 1324, he was kidnapped by two of his relatives. One of those was Robert's sister, John's aunt, Agnes Malyn, who first married Walter de Westhale, and the other was Geoffrey Stace. They conspired to abduct John Chaucer. The surname Stace was Mary le Chaucer's maiden name. Geoffrey Stace would undoubtedly have been her brother. Later, he became the second husband of Agnes. They contrived to marry John to Agnes's daughter Joan Westhale in order to obtain the property and lands which John would be supposed to inherit from his own father Robert le Chaucer. John and Joan must have been cousins. The attempt to force their marriage was unsuccessful. John's aunt was imprisoned in the Marshalsea and fined as much as £250. This is an extravagant penalty considering that one could live on £5 a year even in the 15th century. The sum was paid in full to John Chaucer by the time he was eighteen years old (Howard 1987, 5). In 1326, two years after the abduction, Mary and her third husband Richard declared themselves the legal guardians of John Chaucer, who was the heir of the properties owned by his father Robert le Chaucer. They pleaded the custody of the heir and land of Robert until John became of age—over fourteen years-old (Skeat 1899, xi). The purpose of kidnapping is usually for extracting for a ransom. But John's aunt, Agnes, and her second husband Geoffrey Stace abducted John Chaucer not for a ransom but for the properties of Agnes's brother, Robert Chaucer. They might well have tried to secure Robert's properties which his son John was to inherit. In my opinion, in this sense, Richard le Chaucer was not Robert's cousin, as W. W. Skeat states, but his master John le Chaucer's relative, as Matheson insists. Agnes Malyn probably tried to keep her brother's properties from Mary and Richard le Chaucer who were from outside of her family. At any rate what she and Geoffrey Stace did was at least ill-advised and it cost them too much.

John Chaucer became a more successful vintner than his own father. By 1337 John was established as an active member of the London merchant community. He was appointed deputy to the king's chief butler at the port of Southampton where he would check shipments of wine from Bordeaux to the king's cellars (Pearsall 1992, 14). He gave up the position in 1349, probably because he was busy dealing with the family properties which came into his hands. The Black Death ironically made this family wealthier. He inherited immense properties from several relatives killed by the plague of 1348–49, which depopulated the country by a third. According to Howard (1987, 7), John Chaucer "owned buildings and land in London and Middlesex, a brewing establishment, twenty-odd shops outside the city wall of London at Aldgate, ten and a half acres nearby, and various properties in Middlesex and Suffolk." Both John's stepfather, Richard le Chaucer and his half-brother Thomas Heyron died in 1349, the year of the first and the most fatal pestilence.

8   Chapter I

Thomas appointed John Chaucer his executor in his will which was proved in the Hustings Court on April 7, 1349. John Chaucer inherited the lands designated in the deed in the same year (Skeat 1899, xiv).

John Chaucer married Agnes Copton in the late 1330s. The Coptons were equal in rank and wealth to the Chaucers. Agnes's father John de Copton was killed when she was very young. She inherited the estate of her uncle Hamo de Copton, a coin maker, who worked in the Tower of London, when he and his only son died in the plague. A part of the properties came to the Chaucers through Agnes. Like some other women in the Chaucer family, Agnes married three times. She seems to have married a certain nobleman named Northwell before she married John Chaucer. She had a son from Northwell and may well have had a connection at the royal court through him (Howard 1987, 7). John Chaucer died in 1366 when he was fifty-four. Only a few months after, his widow remarried with Batholomew atte Chapel, citizen and vintner in London.

Owing to the two generations, Geoffrey Chaucer's grandfather and father, the family had been prosperous merchants who were quite influential and prestigious in the area of trading and came to have connections with the royal court. They were unquestionably well-off bourgeois. Their marriage would have been a convenient conjunction for both families. In Chaucer's family tree, the remarkable fact is that Chaucer's grandmother as well as his mother were widows when they married the Chaucers. They would have possibly brought some amount of dowry and properties inherited from their former husbands. As they had remarried, they would become wealthier and wealthier. Matsunami (1985, 19) infers that a living model of the Wife of Bath would be close at hand in Chaucer's own family and that it would not be possible for

Chaucer to depict such a woman as the Wife based on nothing but his imagination. The Wife of Bath became a widow five times and was so well-off as to make a pilgrimage several times to many countries. She spiritedly enjoyed her life and with toughness, waiting for the next husband. A woman such as she was neither exceptional nor peculiar but might easily have been familiar to Chaucer.

I-2 Philippa, His Wife, and Their Marital Life

In order to understand how Chaucer personally viewed women and marriage, his marital experience with Philippa, how and when they met and the nature of their interpersonal relationship, need to be taken into account. The earliest historical records of the two happened to be discovered only as late as 1851 on some scraps and fragments used as cushioning on the cover of a manuscript which was bought by the British Library. The fragmentary records are the payments and gifts from 1356 to 1359 by Elizabeth, Countess of Ulster and wife of Lionel, second son of Edward III (Crow and Olson 1966, 13–18). Her attendants' names frequently appear in those records: Philippa Pan and Galfrido [Geoffrey] Chaucer. It is well-known that Chaucer was in the service of the Ulster household presumably as a page of Elizabeth. But Philippa's identity has been much discussed. "The most attractive theory," Fisher (1977, 956) claims, "is that 'Pan' is a contraction of 'Panneto,' one form of the name of Sir Paon de Roet, father of Philippa Chaucer and Katherine Swynford, who was mistress and eventually (1396) wife of John of Gaun, Duke of Lancaster, third son of Edward III."

Philippa's father, Sir Gilles de Roet, came from Roet in Hainault, northern France, where he served in the household of Marguerite, Empress of Germany and Countess of Hainault, Queen Philippa's sister. When Queen Philippa came to England to marry Edward in 1328, he accompanied her. He already had a son and three daughters. The son, Walter, was in the retinue of the Black Prince, first son of Edward III. The eldest daughter, Elizabeth, also called Isabel, was put in a convent in 1349, when she was only thirteen then. Philippa and the youngest Katherine were raised by the queen. At some point, Sir Gilles de Roet went back to Hainault and returned to the service of Marguerite. He left their children in England.

When the two younger sisters grew up, the queen sent them out to her sons' households. The youngest sister, Katherine, was placed in the household of Blanche, Duchess of Lancaster. Her marriage was arranged in 1366 or 1367 with Sir Hugh Swynford, who was one of John of Gaunt's retainers. Philippa was in the service of Elizabeth, Countess of Ulster, until the Countess died in 1363. Philippa Roet and Geoffrey Chaucer were sure to have met at the court of Elizabeth in their youth.

Geoffrey and Philippa must have married in or before 1366, because Philippa Chaucer was given a life annuity of 10 marks (6£. 13s. 4p.) as a demoiselle to attend Queen Philippa by the King on September 12th 1366 (Crow and Olson 1966, 67). The last record of her annuity is dated June 18th 1387. If she had died in that year, their marital life would have lasted for over twenty years. They were separately in the service of the King and Queen. Chaucer had diplomatic missions under Edward III and was sent to France in 1368 and 1370, and to Italy for six months during 1372–73. Philippa also occasionally traveled with Queen Philippa. After the queen passed away in 1369, Philippa Chaucer served in the household of John of Gaunt as an attendant of his second wife, Constance of Castile, probably when they married in 1371. Philippa received an annuity from John of Gaunt for service rendered the Duchess in 1372. Philippa would have spent most of the time attending on the Duchess Constance at her court. Geoffrey and Philippa would not have been able to lead their marriage life together, or rather they mostly would have lived separately.

It is not known whether the Chaucers were well-matched or completely mismatched. The several historical documents concerning Chaucer's children cast a mysterious and questionable shadow over their marital life. It is widely known and generally believed that Chaucer had two sons: Thomas and Lewis. Thomas Chaucer was born in c. 1367 soon after his parents married and to become a retainer of the house of Lancaster, John of Gaunt. Thomas was one of the most prosperous men and a prominent person as a public servant in the early 15th century. His only daughter, Alice, had been married and widowed twice, which was not so unusual in those days and in Chaucer's family. Her third husband was William de la Pole, Earl of Suffolk, later Duke of Suffolk, in 1448. She had no children of her own.

Thomas had a great success in life and advanced rapidly to a high position in society. Furthermore, his daughter Alice rose to the aristocracy. As many scholars point out, the exceptional patronage of John of Gaunt to Thomas has given rise to a conjecture. That is, Thomas might have been a son of John of Gaunt and Philippa Chaucer. It is possible to presume that Gaunt would have entrusted his son and mistress to Chaucer. Being a retainer of Gaunt, Chaucer would have agreed to bring up the boy as his own son. As evidence that Thomas was Gaunt's illegitimate son, John H. Fisher (1977, 958) indicates that Thomas had

12   Chapter I

changed his coat of arms from the Chaucerian to the de Roet arms of
his mother. As early as the 16th century, Thomas's birth was regarded
as questionable. The Renaissance editor of Chaucer, Thomas Speght,
suspected that Thomas was Geoffrey Chaucer's son in his "Chaucer's
Life" in 1598. Speght noted that the tomb of Thomas Chaucer was in
Ewelme church, Oxfordshire. The tomb is decorated with the coat of
arms of Roet (Thomas's mother) quartering those of Burghersh (Maud
Burghersh was Thomas's wife) not those of his father, Chaucer (Pearsall
1992, 51, 279–80).

Lewis, another son, was referred to by Chaucer himself at the
beginning of *A Treatise on the Astrolabe*, 1391:

> Lyte Lowys my sone, I aperceyve wel by certeyne evydences
> thyn abilite to lerne sciences touching nombres and proporciouns;
> and as wel consider I thy besy praier in special to lerne the tretys
> of the Astrelabie. . . .
> This tretis, . . . wol I shewe the under full light reules and naked
> wordes in Englissh, for Latyn canst thou yit but small, my litel
> sone.   (*A Treatise on the Astrolabe*, 1–28)

Although the poet's direct address to "my little son Lewis" seems to
establish that Geoffrey Chaucer had a son named Lewis, some scholars
had tried to take him for Chaucer's godson, the son of Sir Lewis Clifford,
who was the poet's close friend.[5] And this is because they do not want to
admit the possibility that Lewis might not have been a son of Geoffrey
and Philippa but of Cecily Champain (Pearsall 1992, 216–17). The
details of the Chaucer-Cecily case will be discussed in the later section
of this chapter. Regardless of scholars' concerns, a newly discovered

document in which the names of Thomas and Lewis Chaucer are listed together provides proof of the connection of Chaucer family. The documents concerning the payments to Thomas and Lewis Chaucer as men at arms for service at Carmarthen, Wales in 1403 state that:

> In the Retinue Roll of William Lovenay, keeper of the great wardrobe, is a long list of the men at arms and the archers who formed the garrison of the royal castle of Carmarthern in 1403. One group, with the payment they received, is as follows:
> *Thomas Chaucer,—Treverek, Willelmus atte Lee, Ludowicus* [Lewis] *Chaucer, homines ad arma*, with twelve archers (*sagittarii*) —£14. 0*s*. 0*d*.   (Crow and Olson 1966, 544)

The purpose of this scroll was to pay wages to the men-at-arms. What is important about this document is that it mentions both Thomas and Lewis Chaucer. They were undoubtedly publicly recorded as sons of Geoffrey and Philippa Chaucer, apart from the question as to the actual identity of their father or mother.

Different from Thomas, nothing is known about the life of Lewis Chaucer, except the following two bits of information. One is that he was ten years-old when his father wrote *A Treatise on the Astrolabe* for him in 1391 as the poet addressing him as in the prologue "thy tendir age of ten yeer" (24). The other is that Lewis would have been sent to Oxford and put to school there. The colophon of the 15th-century manuscript of the Treatise (MS Cambridge Dd. 3. 53) states that this treatise was compiled by Geoffrey Chaucer for his son, Lewis, who was in Oxford under the instruction of the philosopher N. (error for R.) Strode (Benson 1987, 1092). Ralph Strode was a fellow of Merton College, Oxford in

14   Chapter I

1359–60, a logician, a philosopher, and a poet as well. He was a friend of Chaucer and a neighbor in London as of 1383, and he died in 1387. Strode probably was not a tutor of Little Lewis. The description of Strode in the colophon states that he was educated. Chaucer's statement in the Treatise that he had given an astrolabe to Lewis, marked for the latitude of Oxford (8–10) supports the idea.

The Chaucer Life-Records yields us the two records which lead to the conjecture that Chaucer had a daughter named Elizabeth and that John of Gaunt might have been involved with her birth. One states that "Elizabeth Chausier was nominated Nun in the Priory of St. Helen in London, 1377":

> A privy seal warrant, dated 27 July, 1 Richard II (1377), addressed to the lord chancellor, instructs him to make out letters patent under the great seal nominating Elizabeth Chausier to be received as a nun in the priory of 'Saint Eleyne' in London. The letters patent to this effect, directed to the prioress and convent of 'St. Elen' in London, bear the same date.
>
> (Crow and Olson 1966, 545)

George Williams (1965, 45–47) declares that Elizabeth Chaucer was born in the summer of 1367, right after her parents married in September of 1366. As mentioned above, Philippa received an annuity of 10 marks at that time probably for her wedding. The other is that "Warrant by John of Gaunt 12 May 1381, for Expenses and Gifts when Elizabeth Chaucy was made a Nun in Barking Abbey":

> On 12 May, 4 Richard II (1381), at the Savoy, John of Gaunt issued

a warrant to Sir William Oke, the clerk of his great wardrobe, instructing him to pay out of the issues of his receipt the sum of £51. 8s. 2d. for various expenses and gifts for Elizabeth Chaucy at the time she was made a nun in the abbey of Barking.

An entry from Register Braybroke, fol.cccxlvi, states that in 1397 Elizabeth Chausir, a nun at Barking Abbey, took a vow of obedience to a new abbess in the presence of the bishop of London. The spelling of the surname as 'Chausir' in this entry suggests that the Elizabeth Chausier and the Elizabeth Chaucy named in the records above were probably the same person. Various scholars have conjectured that she may have been a daughter of Geoffrey Chaucer. (Crow and Olson 1966, 546)

Barking Abbey was one of the oldest and richest convents in England. What is more remarkable here is the fact that John of Gaunt paid the extravagant sum of money for Elizabeth Chaucer. If he had nothing to do with her, why did John of Gaunt pay such a huge amount of money? F. N. Robinson (1986, xix) suggests that Elizabeth Chaucer may have been a sister of Geoffrey. But if Elizabeth were Chaucer's sister, there would be no persuasive reason why John of Gaunt paid the money "for various expenses" and gave her gifts. It would be easier and more natural to conjecture that John Gaunt was involved with her birth. That is, Elizabeth Chaucer was a daughter of Philippa Chaucer and John of Gaunt. It is uncertain whether Elizabeth was born before or after Thomas. They would have been born within a year or so of each other.

John M. Manly (1959, 52) and Howard (1987, 93) suggest that Chaucer may have had another daughter called Agnes who would have been named after Chaucer's mother. At the coronation of Henry II in

16   Chapter I

1399, she was listed as one of the damsels in waiting along with Joan Swynford, probably the daughter of Katherine Swynford and John of Gaunt. If she was still a damsel, namely, a young unmarried woman, her birth could have been dated in the mid-1380's. Howard (1987, 93) points out that "she might have been the poet's grandchild." In this case Philippa might have lived in Lincolnshire. There is a record in the form of a memorandum that she was admitted to the fraternity of Lincoln Cathedral in 1386 in a ceremony celebrating the admission of John of Gaunt's oldest son, the future king, Henry IV. She was considered to have died in the following year, because her annuity was not paid in 1387.[6] It would be almost impossible for this couple to have a child in the mid-1380. Because they must have lived separately, each of them would have gone his and her own way, and their married life might well have broken down.

The biographical records relating to Chaucer, Philippa, and their children seem to bear witness that Chaucer's matrimonial relationship with Philippa might not have been happy and enjoyable. Their marriage itself would have been basically a mismatch. Although Chaucer's father was a prosperous merchant, Geoffrey himself was probably neither a rich young man nor a land owner when he first met Philippa. He was neither of high birth, nor in a prestigious position at court. In the King's household, Chaucer was a newcomer "vallctus," (yeoman) from 1367 to 1374 and promoted to "armiger" (esquire) in 1368 at least a year after he married. On the contrary, Philippa was from a noble family, attendant on a royal household for a long time. She was a lady serving Queen Philippa and the daughter of a knight, Sir Gilles de Roet, "Guienne [Aquitaine] King of Arms," that is the keeper of the records of the noble family tree in Aquitaine, France (Howard 1987, 91).

One of the most convincing explanations of their marriage is that, as Williams (1965, 46) declares, "Gaunt (who had a contemporary reputation as being notably amorous as a young man) got Philippa with child, and persuaded (or hired, or forced) Chaucer to marry her." Philippa's sister, Katherine Swynford, had been John of Gaunt's mistress for over twenty five years, while she had four illegitimate children. When they married in 1396, John of Gaunt legitimated them. As Sir Hugh Swynford, Katherine's husband, and John of Gaunt's retainer, had no choice against his master, Chaucer would have been obliged to accept him.

In addition to the annuities, John of Gaunt sent Philippa some special gifts on various occasions. In 1373 she was given a buttonhook and six silver-gilt buttons as a New Year's gift, which would cost as much as ten marks. At a new year in 1380 Philippa received a silver-gilt goblet, which was worth 31s. 5d. In March, 1381 and in May, 1382, John of Gaunt gave her costly silver cups (Crow and Olson 1966, 88–91). Those valuable gifts to Philippa could show John of Gaunt's remarkable favour to her. The records sustain the idea that Philippa was his mistress.

What did the marriage mean to Chaucer's life? On the one hand, supposing his wife to have been John of Gaunt's mistress, and the daughter and the son his bastards, and that Chaucer covered the secret, his marriage would have been a miserable disaster. On the other hand, medieval marriage put more emphasis on the profit of the families rather than on individual emotions. The nobility of Philippa's family was united with Geoffrey's prosperity. In this sense, Chaucer might well have married Philippa because this matrimony brought him social stability and financial security. It is true that Chaucer had attained advantageous status and connections at court, besides the annuities, through marrying Philippa.

18   Chapter I

After they married, perhaps in 1366, Chaucer made great progress in his own career. As mentioned above, he was engaged in diplomatic missions to France in 1368 and in 1370 and Italy during 1372–73. In 1374, he was granted a pitcher of wine daily by the King in April, he was provided a house in Aldgate rent-free by the King in May, he was appointed controller of customs and granted another £10 a year by the King in June 8th, and John of Gaunt gave both Chaucer and Philippa another life annuity of £10 on June 13th.

His prosperity in social life at court on this occasion might well be taken as compensation for Chaucer's marrying Philippa. If the conjecture that Philippa was John of Gaunt's mistress approaches the truth to some extent and Chaucer was forced to keep marital relations with Philippa, the experience in his marriage is not unimportant in viewing of Chaucer's treatment of women and marriage in his writing. He seemed to accept or was obliged to accept everything, both the merits and demerits, both the advantages and disadvantages of his marriage.

I-3   Cecily Champain and the Case of *raptus*

For most modern readers who admire Chaucer as the great father of English poetry, one of the most shocking, scandalous and unacceptable enigmas in his life records would be the Cecily Champain (or Cecilia Chaumpaigne) affair.

On May 4, 1380, Cecily Champain, a daughter of the London baker, William Champain and his wife Agnes signed a legal document at the King's Court of Chancery. The document released Geoffrey Chaucer of all manner of actions concerning her *raptus* or any other things or cause:

> Let all men know that I Cecily Champain, daughter of William
> Champain and Agnes his wife, have remitted, released and quit-
> claimed forever entirely for myself and my heirs to Geoffrey
> Chaucer, esquire, all manner of actions at law of whatever kind
> either concerning my *raptus* or any other lawsuit whatsoever I
> ever had, do have or shall have been able to have from the
> beginning of the world until the day of making this document. In
> testimony of which I have placed my seal on the document with
> these witnesses: Sir William Beauchamp, the chamberlain of the
> lord king, Sir John Clanvowe, Sir William Neville, knights, Sir
> John Philipot and Richard Morel. Given at London, the first day
> of May of the third year of the reign of Richard the Second after
> the Conquest.
>
> And be it remembered that the said Cecily came up to the
> king's Chancery near Westminster on May 4th of the same year
> and admitted the document mentioned above and all the contents
> as in the form written there.[7]

The definition of *raptus* has been repeatedly discussed. The argument has focused on whether it meant physical rape or merely abduction.

It is instructive to look over the comment on this matter of the compilers of the complete works of Geoffrey Chaucer. Skeat (1899, xxxiii) conjectures that Chaucer might have committed her "abduction" not as a ringleader but just as a fellow criminal, while he suggests a probable connection between Cecily and Chaucer's son, Lewis. He was ten years old when Chaucer wrote Treatise on the Astrolabe for him in

20   Chapter I

1391. He was therefore born in 1381, whence Skeat implies that his mother was Cicely Champain. Robinson (1986, xxiii) reluctantly admits that *raptus* would have meant an act of physical rape "after the passage of the Statue of Westminster in 1380." He concludes that the circumstances of this case and Chaucer's connection with the situation still remain unknown. Fisher (1977, 959) holds that the word *raptus* means literally just what it says; that is, Chaucer had been charged with rape and had to seek legal quittance. Fisher points out that this scandal must have occurred around the time when Chaucer's wife Philippa was away from London and living in Lincolnshire, where she was admitted to the fraternity of Lincoln Cathedral in a ceremony honoring the admission of Gaunt's eldest son, the future Henry IV. Larry D. Benson (1987, xxi–xxii) refers to the ambiguity of this word, *raptus* and mentions that what is made clear in this record is only the fact that Cecily Champain set Chaucer free from all responsibility. Other facts are ambiguous.

Derek Pearsall (1992, 137) claims that *raptus* in the legal terms of those days generally indicates the crime of *raptus* such as 'abduction.' Although he admits that the crime Chaucer may have committed would have been "indeed one of rape," there is no convincing proof of it and after all Pearsall concludes that this affair is an enigma which has no reliable evidence to define *raptus* as meaning 'rape.'

In Roman law, the noun *raptus* signified 'abduction' or 'forced coitus.' In the law in England from the middle of the 12th century to the late 13th century, *raptus* was defined by a narrower meaning than by *the Roman* law and suggested an act of physical rape. From the end of the 13th century to the 14th century, the meaning of *raptus* became obscure, expressing either 'abduction' or 'rape.' The reason for this ambiguity comes from the fact that most of the abduction cases accompanied sexual violence (Cannon 1993, 77–78).

According to Christopher Cannon (2000, 70), who examines numerous of cases of *raptus*, when the noun *raptus* is used in legal documents, the act of 'rape' is the issue itself in most of the cases. When 'abduction' without 'forced coitus' was at issue, the word *raptus* had never been seen in legal documents, as claimed by Cannon. If that is the case, Chaucer might possibly have committed a crime of rape and been sued, then been declared guilty. Afterwards Cannon, however, amended his opinion and insisted that the problem of Chaucer's case was not because of the definition of *raptus* itself but because of the dual meaning and ambiguity of the word in medieval legal diction. He suggested the possibility that *raptus* refers to 'abduction.'

Although many scholars have discussed the meaning of *raptus* in the document of the Cecily Champain release, no one can claim one exclusive definition of the word and thus it is almost impossible to know what actually happened between Cecily Champain and Chaucer. Some other documents suggest the more precise meaning of *raptus*. At the same time, they make the case more complicated and as a result all the more ambiguous.

Cecily Champain signed the document of release on May 4, 1380. Three days before, on May 1, the legal document was submitted to the Court of Chancery. This was witnessed by Chaucer's five friends and acquaintances. They were William Beauchamp, the chamberlain of the king's household; Sir John Clanvowe and Sir William Neville, knights of the king's chamber; Sir John Philipot, prominent merchant, then the collector of wool customs when Chaucer was controller; alderman, member of Parliament, Lord Mayor of London in 1378; and Richard Morel, Chaucer's neighbor and a member of Grocer's Company. They

22   Chapter I

were prestigious persons in London at that time. Their social rank, however, did not guarantee Chaucer's innocence. They merely ensured that Chaucer could escape prosecution. This leads easily to the suspicion that Chaucer eagerly tried to hush up the case with the help of those authorities as witnesses.

Moreover, there was a series of three enrollments in the court of the mayor and aldermen of London. The two other citizens of London, who were involved with this case—Robert Goodchild, a cutler, and John Grove, an armorer—submitted a document on June 28, 1380, which released Chaucer from "actions, complaints, and suits . . . by reason of any breach of contract or nonpayment of debt or any other matter real or personal" (Howard 1987, 319).

Chaucer.—On the last day of June in the second [an error for fourth] year of the reign of King Richard the Second, Richard Goodchild and John Grove, the armorer, admitted that the following document was made by them with their own words:

Let all men know that we Richard Goodchild, a cutler, and John Grove, an armorer, citizens of London, have remitted, released and quitclaimed forever for ourselves, our heirs and our executors to Geoffrey Chaucer, esquire, all manner of legal actions that, from the beginning of the world until the day of making this document, we ever had, do have or shall have been able to have towards the said Geoffrey caused by any transgressions, agreements, contracts and debts that either of us have in the future, or other legal actions concerning the real estate or personal property between either of us and the said Geoffrey. In testimony of this, we have placed our seals. Given at London on June 28th in the fourth year of the reign of King Richard the Second after the Conquest.[8]

Chaucer signed the document which mentioned nothing about Cecily Champain or *raptus*. More strangely, on the same day, Cecily Champain released the two men, Goodchild and Grove, from any actions. This was a document very similar to the one Chaucer enrolled:

Goodchild, Grove.—On the same day Cecily Champain appeared here and admitted the fact that the following document was made by them with their own words:

Let all men know that I Cecily Champain, daughter of William Champain and Agnes his wife, have remitted, released and quit-claimed forever entirely for myself, my heirs and my executors to Richard Goodchild, a cutler, and John Grove, an armorer, citizens of London, all manner of legal actions, arguments and demands concerning the real estate or personal property that, towards the said Richard and John or either of them, all manner of legal actions that I ever had, do have or shall have been able to have for some reason from the beginning of the world until the day of making this document. In testimony of this, I have placed our seals. Given at London on June 28th in the fourth year of the reign of King Richard the Second after the Conquest.[9]

Then a few days later, on July 2, Grove signed a recognizance to owe ten pounds to Cecily Champain and he promised to pay her the money by Michaelmas on September 29. He actually completed his promise to her:

24   Chapter I

> C. Champain. The entry was cancelled upon payment.
>
> On July second in the fourth year of the reign of King Richard the Second, John Grove, an armorer, came up to the mayor and aldermen and admitted his debt to Cecily Champain, daughter of William Champain and Agnes his wife, £10 to be paid by the next St. Michaelmas etc. If it is not done, he concedes etc.[10]

These three documents were signed with neither witnesses nor observers (Howard 1987, 319). In these records the word *raptus* was completely omitted and simply disappeared. The documents were not exchanged between the parties immediately concerned. It is naturally imagined that Goodchild and Grove may have stood between Chaucer and Cecily Champain as a third party and delivered ten pounds in compensation to Cecily for Chaucer. Here again, however, the truth of the matter is wrapped in a veil of mystery. Some simple queries arise from the facts in those documents: why this settlement was done by the two men even after two months from Cecily Champain's first release to Chaucer on May 4 and whether Goodchild and Grove acted on Chaucer's side or Champain's. Unfortunately, there is no persuasive evidence regarding these questions.

In search of a possible answer to the first question, some scholars have conjectured that it might have been the discovery of Cecily Champain's pregnancy. Skeat suggests a connection between Cecily and Lewis, Chaucer's son, as mentioned above. If Chaucer had had some relationship with Cecily Champain, it must have dated before May in 1380. Her pregnancy would possibly have been revealed after a few months. In fact, Lewis must have been born in 1381 because his father wrote *A Treatise on the Astrolabe* for him when he was ten years-old in

1391. As Pearsall (1992, 138) points out, all situations seem to cohere, according to calculations; nevertheless, this is nothing but deducing causes from effects and the evidence is only circumstantial and uncertain. Howard (1987, 320) gives a very interesting outlook on this matter: if her pregnancy was the result of *raptus* as sexual rape, Cecily's claim on Chaucer's *raptus* would have been reduced, "because by a maxim of medieval law it was delivered that a woman could not conceive if she had not consented!" Howard argues that even if that little Lewis was her son, or if so, all the more, *raptus* would not mean 'forced coitus.'

It is almost impossible to find an answer to the second question. No personal information remains about the two Londoners, Goodchild and Grove, by which to judge if they were Chaucer's agents or Cecily's. Haldeen Braddy's discovery, however, provides a sensational suggestion about the relationship of those involved. Braddy (1977, 906–08) finds evidence showing that Cecily Champain was a stepdaughter of Alice Perrers. Braddy read a note provided by the editor who produced an English translation of the contemporary Latin chronicle of Harley MS 6217 in the British Library. It showed that Alice Perrers's earlier surname was "Chawpeneys," an Anglicization of Chaumpaigne. As we have seen, in Cecily's release on May 4 it was clearly described that Cecily was the daughter of William Chaumpaigne and Agnes his wife. Braddy points out the salient fact that William Champain had two wives, Agnes and Alice. Moreover, he mentions that Alice Perrers had several surnames such as Chawmpeneys, Perrers, and Windsor. She was the wife of William of Winsor when she became a mistress of Edward III.

Alice Perrers was a notorious woman who came from the rich merchant class and an old acquaintance of Chaucer's. In his earlier article, Braddy (1946, 222–28) describes Chaucer as her "protege,"

26   Chapter I

because Chaucer received his Aldgate lease for free and his Customs office under the influence of Alice Perrers. In fact, his contemporary, French poet and chronicler Froissart, referred to Chaucer, the English poet, as 'le protégé de la favorite Alice Perrers' in 1377. Alice Perrers was of course known to Chaucer's friends including the witnesses of Cecily's release in May. She was so influential at the court and in the king's favor that the Good Parliament decided to forbid her to enter the court in 1376.

Alice was married to William Champain when very young and Cecily and Alice could have been almost the same age; or Cecily was perhaps older. This stepmother may have controlled her stepdaughter behind the scenes, trying to solve the affair with money. Goodchild and Grove were possibly her accomplices. They were more likely Chaucer's agents (Howard 1987, 319). Presumably Chaucer did not want further to disgrace his name in public and hoped to settle things with hush money. It is still uncertain that he raped her, abducted her or seduced her. The meaning of *raptus* in the document is ambiguous and obscure.

Pearsall (1992, 136) searched for Chaucer's financial situation after 1380. Chaucer received the half-yearly instalments on his two annuities and he was given £6. 13s. 4d. on each. He also obtained £14 in expenses for the Lombardy visit of 1378. On March 6, 1381, he was paid £22 as a gift in compensation for his expenses on journeys to France in 1377 and the following years. He also sold his father's house on June 19, 1381. Ten pounds was a large amount of money, but Chaucer's financial circumstances were not dire.

Finally, there is a newly discovered memorandum by Christopher— in 1993. To make matters even more complicated, the original Cecily Champain release on May 1 was copied on May 4 and the copy was brought to the Court of King's Bench and recopied into the form of a memorandum on May 7. Cannon's comment on the series of documents is worth citing:

> Although I have generally discussed the Chaumpaigne release throughout this essay, as if it were the very words copied onto the close rolls, the original release itself was presumably written—and certainly signed and sealed—on May 1, 1380, when it probably passed for good in Chaucer's possession and then ultimately into oblivion. Before it disappeared, however, the release was recopied three days later (on May 4, 1380) onto the membranes of the close rolls (to form the record I have been discussing throughout this essay.) The release was then brought into the Court of King's Bench and recopied in the form of a memorandum three days later (on May 7, 1380). (90)

According to Cannon (1993, 92–93), the original release was sealed but was lost. It was copied into both forms of the close rolls and the memorandum. There are two major differences between these documents. First, the number of witnesses was reduced from five in the close rolls on May 4 to three in the memorandum. Only Sir William Beauchamp, Sir John Clanovowe and Sir William Neville were named while others were omitted as "others." Second, more importantly, the phrase *de raptu meo*, "relating to my rape" is completely eliminated in the memorandum. This is not simply a scribal error caused by carelessness but clearly a deliberate revision. In this memorandum a hidden intention to conceal the inconvenient information of the original release can be seen. Cannon surmises that it is Chaucer himself who would have

28   Chapter I

wished to omit the phrase and gained a profit from such an omission. His personal connections in the court would make it easily possible for him to have opportunities to this manipulation either by himself or by taking advantage of his personal relationship.

As many scholars conclude that the truth of the Cecily Champain case is after all obscure and mysterious, it is difficult or almost impossible to give a clear picture of the whole matter unless new historical evidence is discovered. Even if we had new findings, it would be hard to bring an explicit meaning to *raptus*. Whether the meaning of *raptus* is 'rape' or 'abduction,' is not a crucial point. It is not our purpose to pursue and reveal whether Chaucer was a rapist or not. What matters is that Chaucer probably committed or was somehow involved in a dishonorable case. As the cited documents show, he was released by a young lady from all manner of actions concerning her *raptus* on May 1, 1380. Before the original release was sealed, it had been copied twice at the Chancery on May 4 and the King's Bench on May 7. When it was recopied, the phrase, *de raptu meo*, was eliminated. This shows how keenly and deeply the word annoyed Chaucer. Borrowing from Cannon (1993):

> the memorandum does tell us a great deal more about the language of the release than we have known, and it speaks directly to the implications of the phrase d*e raptu meo* that have troubled Chaucerians for so long. The memorandum makes clear that this phrase seemed just as inflammatory to Chaucer's contemporaries as it has seemed to its more modern readers.   (93–94)

The Cecily Champain case is surely one of the most mysterious and dishonorable enigmas in Chaucer's life records. Judging from the legal documents and newly discovered facts, Chaucer seemed to have somewhat or considerably guilty feelings regarding the woman. By taking advantage of his personal contacts in his social network, Chaucer seemed to conceal the inconvenient facts and settle things down with money through the agents. Not knowing exactly who was in the wrong and what happened between Chaucer and Cecily Champain, between Alice Perrers and Chaucer, or among the three, this case shows a part of Chaucer's unhappy experience with women. It may be true that Chaucer actually tried to exercise his masculine power and social authority over those ladies. Apparently, this case did not directly have a great influence on Chaucer's social life. These historical facts, however, may cast light on Chaucer's view of women.

Chapter II

Chaucer's Portrayals of Women

II-1 The Portrayal of the Wife of Bath

The portrait of the Wife of Bath in *The General Prologue* (henceforth *GP*) to *CT* tells much about her character. Chaucer offers 31 lines to describe this woman, starting with "A good Wif was ther of biside Bathe," (*GP*, 445).[6] The first and most individualized trait is the fact that the Wife is somewhat deaf, "somdel deef, and that was scathe" (446). Later she reveals by herself the reason in the prologue of her tale, when she talks about the strife against her fifth husband over his anti-feministic books. The fifth husband, named Jankin, a clerk of Oxford, always reads aloud the books on "wykked wyves" in the presence of Alison, the Wife. Finally she tears a few pages out of the book and strikes him on his cheek, which makes the husband so upset that he gives her a return blow:

> And whan I saugh he wolde nevere fyne
> To reden on this cursed book al nyght,
> Al sodeynly thre leves have I plyght
> Out of his book, right as he radde, and eke
> I with my fest so took hym on the cheke

[31]

32 Chapter II

> That in oure fyr he fil bakward adoun.
>
> And he up stirte as dooth a wood leoun,
>
> And with his fest he smoot me on the heed
>
> That in the floor I lay as I were deed.
>
> (*The Wife of Bath's Prologue* (henceforth *WBP*), 788–96)

In this way, the Wife of Bath has become partially physically deaf; she might be also psychologically deaf for the most part. She neither listens to her husbands when they stand against her desire nor shows her obedience to the anti-feminist tradition in ecclesiastical doctrine. She has no ear for anyone who speaks ill of her: "I hate hym that my vices telleth me," (662).

The Narrator of *GP*, who is the Pilgrim Chaucer, notes that the Wife has the skill of weaving and that she surpasses the experts of Ypres and Ghent, which were famous cloth-making centers in Flanders (modern Belgium). Some scholars pay special attention to the place where the Wife is from. As Chaucer tells us, she is not actually from Bath proper, but close by Bath. Manly (1959, 231–33) insisted that the Wife probably lived in St. Michael's parish, a small community just outside of the north gate of the walls of Bath, in which weaving was the chief occupation.[11] Weaving and spinning were the occupations traditionally assigned to women in the Middle Ages and not a few women were engaged in the trade of weaving there. Although nothing more is mentioned of the Wife's profession, Chaucer suggests that the Wife is a socially or economically independent employed woman. This must be one of the reasons why the Wife did not need to obey her husbands, especially when she was young. It is seen that women can be strong if they do not economically depend on their husbands and are socially accepted because of their profession.

Some scholars suggest that Chaucer's praise of her weaving skill is exaggerated, or rather ironical, because the textile industry in a suburb of Bath was not the very best in quality.[12] The following description of her portrait shows, at any rate, that the Wife had such a strong bent for competition that she always wanted to be 'number one':

In al the parisshe wif ne was ther noon
That to the offrynge bifore hire sholde goon;
And if ther dide, certeyn so wrooth was she
That she was out of alle charitee.
Hir coverchiefs ful fyne weren of ground;
I dorste swere they weyeden ten pound
That on a Sonday weren upon hir heed.
Hir hosen weren of fyn scarlet reed,
Ful streite yteyd, and shoes ful moyste and newe.   (*GP*, 449–57)

At the Mass, people went to the altar in person and gave their offerings according to rank. The Wife does not allow any other women to precede her at the offerings, and if another woman dares so, she loses her temper.

Her consciousness of fashion also shows her highly developed competitive character. Her Sunday headdress is more valuable and elaborate than all other women's in the parish. Her scarlet red stockings are tightly arranged and look brilliant. A pair of shoes made of soft leather in high quality are outstanding. No other women could surpass her. As the Wife is an extremely competitively spirited woman, it is easy for us to imagine that she makes a great effort to develop her weaving skills and successfully produce a fabric which is equivalent to the finest quality made by the professional weavers in Ypres and Ghent. It is not ironical for

34   Chapter II

Chaucer to choose the place of Bath as the Wife's residence. Her weaving skill defines her character, always as that of one who desires to be first.

Hope Phyllis Weissman (1980, 11) points out another interesting reason as to why Chaucer chose a suburb of Bath for the Wife's residence. Weissman insists that if Chaucer had intended to identify the Wife devotedly with the West-country cloth-making, "the city of Bristol would have been a more obvious choice" and that Chaucer must have had a further purpose in choosing Bath, the city of the baths because of which it was so named. As Weissman (1980, 12) supposes, there is only one simple and immediate interpretation of the baths and "the bath is a sign of sexual indulgence, indeed, of lust." In Ovid, Juvenal, Jerome and Jean de Meung, whom Chaucer often made reference to, the topos of the hot springs is love's house, the bathhouse of Venus; further, the baths function as a combination of sweat houses and massage parlors, where the association of bathing and sexual activity is established (Weissman: 13–17).

The motif of the bathhouse was wide-spread in later medieval culture. The vernacular of 'brothel' is in fact 'hot bath,' in Middle English, "stewe." Chaucer used this word meaning 'a small (heated) room or closet' in Book III of *TC* (601, 698). He also referred to this word in the plural form, "stewes/stywes/styves" at the beginning of the Friar's and the Pardoner's tales to be straightforwardly interpreted as 'whorehouses':

"Peter! so been wommen of the styves,"
Quod the Somonour, "yput out of oure cure!"

(*The Friar's Tale*, 1332–33)

> In Flaundres whilom was a compaignye
> Of yonge folk that haunteden folye,
> As riot, hasard, stywes, and tavernes,
> Where as with harpes, lutes, and gyternes,
> They daunce and pleyen at dees bothe day and nyght,
> And eten also and drynken over hir myght,
>
> (*The Pardoner's Tale*, 463–68)

The term "stewe" appears as a metaphor for whorehouses. A historical survey of Chaucer's time shows that there were taverns and stews in the suburb of Southwark, just outside of the city of London, where the Canterbury pilgrimage begins. Some of these stewhouses in Southwark actually disguised themselves as public baths (Weissman, 22–23).

From those associations Weissman (1980, 25–26) concludes that Chaucer represented the Wife of Bath as the theme of the bathhouse madam and Chaucer's Wife would indeed be the Wife "of biside Bathe." It is true that Weissman shed new light on Chaucer's Alison. The other reason why Chaucer chose a suburb of Bath for her residence than that it was famous for cloth-making is quite interesting and stimulating: Chaucer might have a meaningful connotation in mind and his audience might enjoy the allusion between the characters and her habitation; yet it would not be Chaucer's main purpose to set the domicile of the good wife, Alison, close to Bath.

The Narrator of the *GP* turns his eyes on the Wife's features to describe her character in brief: "Boold was hir face, and fair, and reed of hewe" (*GP*, 458). Her countenance is well-defined and her complexion of fair-skin with rosy cheek is clearly striking; that is to say, her face is eye-catching and attractive to men. She has no doubt a strong desire to

36   Chapter II

draw the attention of males, as the Narrator Chaucer tells us:

> She was a worthy womman al hir lyve:
> Housbondes at chirche dore she hadde fyve,
> Withouten oother compaignye in youthe—   (*GP*, 459–61)

When the poet uses the term "worthy," it sounds connotative and sometimes ironical. He says the Wife is "worthy" all her life because she had five husbands and numerous boyfriends when she was young. She herself mentions, "sith I twelve yeer was of age, / . . . Housbondes at chirche dore I have had fyve" (*WBP*, 4–6). It is a great wonder, however, to think when there would be time for her to have "oother compaignye" in youth. Since her first wedding was held when she was twelve years old, she must have had boyfriends along with her other marriges or dallied with them during the first three marriages. According to the autobiographical prologue to her tale, her fifth husband is dead: "My fifthe housbonde—God his soule blesse!—" (525), "I prey to God, that sit in magestee, / So blesse his soule for his mercy deere" (826–27). She says she is willing to have the next husband; "Welcome the sixte, whan that evere he shal" (45). Actually she had always been together with a certain man all her life. In other words, she cannot do without men. As the Wife herself admits, she is an amorous and lecherous woman who is familiar with "olde daunce" (*GP*, 476), a game of love.

Chaucer adds a keen and realistic detail to the Wife's face: "Gattothed was she, soothly for to seye" (*GP*, 468). Her teeth set wide apart signify that she is envious, irrelevant, luxurious by nature, bold, deceitful, faithless, suspicious and of a lecherous nature, according to medieval physiognomy (Curry 1960, 109). In the *WBP*, she mentions her teeth,

"Gat-tothed I was, and that bicam me weel" (603), and explains this nature of hers by making great use of the horoscope:

> For certes, I am al Venerien
> In feelynge, and myn herte is Marcien.
> Venus me yaf my lust, my likerousnesse,
> And Mars yaf me my sturdy hardynesse;
> Myn ascendent was Taur, and Mars therinne.   (*WBP*, 609–13)

The Wife justifies her personality and conduct according to astrological determinism. In the medieval period, it was believed that a horoscope, showing the position of the zodiac signs and the aspects of the planets at one's birth determined one's personal characters. Her ascendant, a rising sign of the zodiac from the horizon in the east when the Wife was born, was Taurus, which is a house of the planet Venus, and at that time it happened that the planet Mars was in it. The Wife defends her lecherousness as coming from the domination of Venus, Goddess of Love, in her horoscope when she was born. Also her bold and stubborn nature results from Mars, the God of war:

> Whenever they are in ascendance unfortunately one will bear an unseemly mark upon her face. At the nativities of women when a sign is ascending from one of the houses of Venus while Mars is in it, or vice versa, the woman will be unchaste.

> (Benson 1987, 870)

According to celestial physiognomists, every human being has printed upon his or her body, at the hour of conception or at birth, the 'marks' of

38   Chapter II

the ascendant sign and of the dominant star which are supposed to rue his or her fortune (Curry 1960, 104). In her prologue, the Wife notes, "Yet have I Martes mark upon my face" (*WBP*, 619). It is not certain how this mark appears upon her face, but, as we have seen, her face is described as 'fair, and reed of hewe' (*GP*, 458). The color combination of 'fair' and 'reed' signifies the images of Venus and Mars.

Iconographically, Chaucer places the image of Mars on her attire. She wears a hat like a buckler or shield: "As brood as is a bokeler or a targe" (471), and a pair of sharp spurs, "spores sharpe" (474), on her feet. The Ellesmere illustration shows the Wife riding astride, while the Prioress and the Second Nun are shown sidesaddle, which was used only by a limited court circle (Benson 1987, 819). The Wife is associated with a knight or warrior who mounts a horse with a broad shield and sharp spurs.

Chaucer gives the astrological, physiognomical and iconographical traits to her characters, which are skillfully developed and made great use of in her own prologue to describe and justify her ideas and behavior.

In the end of the description of the Wife's portrait in *GP*, Chaucer tells of her rich experience with pilgrimages. This is shown by a list of sacred places in the Christian world in the Middle Ages,

> And thries hadde she been at Jerusalem;
> She hadde passed many a straunge strem;
> At Rome she hadde been, and at Boloigne,
> In Galice at Seint-Jame, and at Coloigne.
> She koude muchel of wandrynge by the weye.   (*GP*, 463–67)

The Wife has been to the most famous and the most distant place of pilgrimage, Jerusalem, which is associated with the passion and resurrection of Jesus Christ. It would have taken almost a year to visit Jerusalem and return to England in those days. And she has been there three times, which is surprising. Her fourth husband passed away when she returned from Jerusalem: "He deyde whan I cam fro Jerusalem" (*WBP*, 495). Rome is the city which commemorates the martyrdom of St. Peter and St. Paul. Boulogne is a city on the northeast coast of France, where people worship a wooden image of the Virgin Mary. At Santiago di Compostella in Galicia, in northwest Spain, the Wife might well have visited the shrine of St. James, a martyr, killed by Herod Agrippa I. At Cologne there are the shrines of the three wise men and St. Ursula who, a princess of the Britons, is a legendary British saint and martyr, and who is said to have been to put to death with 11,000 virgins after being captured by the Huns near Cologne while on a pilgrimage.

In the Middle Ages, it would have been exceptional for a woman to go on pilgrimages to holy places, sailing across the ocean so many times in her life and with regard to safety and the expenses of a trip. The Wife of Bath is a wealthy enough weaver to be able to go on costly pilgrimages. In the autobiographical prologue to her tale, she refers to her first three husbands, who were "goode men," "riche" and "olde." They gave all their lands and property to her, "They had me yeven hir lond and hir tresoor" (*WBP*, 204). She blames them for keeping the key of their safes away from her:

> But tel me this: why hydestow, with sorwe,
> The keyes of thy cheste awey fro me?
> It is my good as wel as thyn, pardee!   (*WBP*, 308–10)

40   Chapter II

The Wife says that she retained all property after her husbands died. She gave everything to the fifth husband, Jankin, when she married him:

> And to hym yaf I al the lond and fee
> That evere was me yeven therbifoore.   (*WBP*, 630–31)

She seems to have come into a large amount of money after inheriting her fortune from her good, old and rich husbands. The Wife, over forty years old, ransomed the twenty year-old "joly clerk," Jankin, for a large amount of property. But in the end, following the strife over the anti-feminist books of Jankin's, as we have seen, the Wife recovered the fortune:

> He yaf me al the bridel in myn hond,
> To han the governance of hous and lond,
> And of his tonge, and of his hond also;   (*WBP*, 813–15)

During her life with the fourth husband, there are references to neither land nor money. She went, however, on one of her costly pilgrimages to Jerusalem, so that she must have had the right to spend cash. Under the common law, all a wife's holdings both in land and personal property, including cash, were vested to her husband, and she could not act against her husband. A husband could not alienate his wife's land without her consent, but he could deal with personal property at his pleasure. But the Wife of Bath must not have been subject to this rule because she could apparently spend the "tresoor" of her ex-husbands without too much difficulty, to make extravagantly expensive pilgrimages. As she tells us, she governs her husbands after her own law: "I governed hem so wel, after my lawe" (*WBP*, 219).

In *GP*, Chaucer describes one of the unique characters in his women. She is assumed to be a skillful professional weaver, not from the best place for cloth-making, Bristol, but from near Bath, the city of the baths, the bathhouse of Venus, which has a connotation of a whorehouse. The Wife of Bath is an expert on marriage life with five husbands in her life to date and is ready to take on the next one. She married the first one when she was twelve years old; after that, until she became forty, she had married four more times, except that she also seemed to have had a number of paramours when she was young. Chaucer tells us that her teeth are set wide apart, which alludes to her lecherousness, according to medieval physiognomy. The astrological influences upon her characters are also shown, such as her amorousness and hardiness, because Venus and Mars are set together in the sign of Taurus in her horoscope. Her first three marriages with old and rich husbands probably made her wealthier and wealthier so as to enable to make pilgrimages to some holy places in Europe across the ocean on several occasions. Although she does not have pious thoughts regarding those places, she likes to go abroad and she knows how to entertain herself along the way: "she koude muchel of wanderynge by the weye" (*GP*, 467).

When Chaucer describes the portrait of the pilgrims, he tells us how they are, what they do and how they look with their attire and features. The poet like an eminent journalist makes a report of the fascinating and unique facts respecting each pilgrim. They are not merely descriptions from the outside, but they detail their personal characteristics with outstanding realism. In the case of the Wife of Bath, her most distinctive inner qualities are lecherousness and hardiness, as pointed to in her horoscope. They are, furthermore, developed with her own words in the

42   Chapter II

prologue to her tale. As stated in *GP*, Alison, the Wife, is a cheerful, talkative person: "In felaweshipe wel koude she laughe and carpe" (*GP*, 474). She is loquacious in her prologue and constantly asserts herself to justify her position and her way of life. She is not just eloquent but sometimes persuasive, or rather she is a master of sophistry. It is true that this makes the Wife the most remarkable and extraordinary woman whom Chaucer created in his works.

II-2   The Portrayal of Criseyde

There is a long inheritance of literary works treating the Trojan War. Homer's *Iliad*, Virgil's *Aeneid*, *De excidio Toroiae historia* of Dares the Phrygian, and *Ephemeridos belli Troiani libri* of Dictys of Crete are ancient Greek and Latin epics and chronicles. In the late 12th century, the French poet Benoît de Saint-Maure, in his *Roman de Troie*, treated the tragic love story of Troilus and Briseïda for the first time. Guido delle Colenne wrote *Historia Trojana*, by translating Benoît into Latin prose at the close of the 13th century. Chaucer certainly knew Benoît and Guido. He also used the *Frigii Daretis Ylias* by Joseph of Exeter, dated 1188–90. Its editor, Ludwig Gomph, demonstrates that Joseph's reduction of Dares' *De excido* was often known as "Dares" in the Middle Ages. In 1338, Giovanni Boccaccio completed *Fil*. Chaucer of course indisputably owes a great deal to Boccaccio, because he emphasizes the lovers' tragedy and establishes three main characters: Troilo, Criseida, and Pandaro. As Chaucer indicates in his work, it is not his purpose to tell of the destruction of Troy as a historical story:

But how this town com to destruccion
Ne falleth naught to purpos me to telle,
For it were a long digression
Fro my matere, and yow to long to dwelle.
But the Troian gestes, as they felle,
In Omer, or in Dares, or in Dite,
Whoso that kan may rede hem as they write.   (*TC* I, 141–47)

To learn what happened to Troy, Chaucer recommends the reading of Homer, Dares, and Dictys, who were historians of the Trojan War. It is his purpose to tell "the double sorrowe" of Troilus in love: how he falls in love with Criseyde and how he is betrayed by her.

Nevertheless, the tragic love story of Troilus and Criseyde is based on the Greek myth. The whole plot of the story and its background are fundamentally fixed and cannot be easily changed. How a Trojan prince, Troilus, falls in love with Criseyde, how they are forcibly separated, and how she breaks her vow of love to Troilus are established as historical facts. Criseyde's reputation as a fickle and unfaithful woman had already been settled in the 14th century (Kellogg 1995, 1). What she has done to Troilus cannot be altered. Yet the manner of an author's treatment of her infidelity offers various possibilities.

It is instructive to take a look at the portrayal of Criseyde in the works of Chaucer's predecessors. Benoît makes his heroine, Briseïda, a very fickle and inconsistent woman. He emphasizes her unsettled mind and presents a misogynistic warning to men. Benoît mentions that a woman's sorrow is by nature short-lived. If she is sorrowful one day, she will be made happy soon again; while one eye weeps the other smiles. Her heart changes very quickly. Even having loved for seven years, she will

44   Chapter II

forget it within three days. He applies the condemnation of his heroine to women in general. In Guido, Cressida's reputation only gets worse. Laura D. Kellogg points out that Cressida has little to recommend her except her good looks. Cressida is famous for great eloquence of speech and attracts many lovers while failing to preserve consistency of heart to her lovers.[13]

Boccaccio depicts his Criseida as a beautiful widow as well as a prudent, noble and well-mannered lady:

> . . . in tanto male,
> sanza niente farlene sapere,
> una sua figlia vedova, la quale
> si bella e si angelica a vedere
> era, che non parea cosa mortale:
> Criseida nomata, al mio parere,
> acoorta, onesta, savia e costumata
> quant'altra che in Troia fosse nata.   (*Fil* I. 11)

> [. . . in this bad situation a daughter, without making known to her any of his plans, a widow, who was so beautiful and so angelic to see that she did not seem mortal: Criseida she was named, and in my judgemet she was as prudent, noble, wise and well-mannered as any other lady who had ever been born in Troy.]
>
> (Kellogg 1995, 38–39)

Boccaccio's Criseida is a beautiful widow and her beauty is compared to an angel's. She is also praised for her prudence, nobility and her good-manners. It will be examined later how Chaucer evidently borrows these features of his heroine from Boccaccio's first portrait of Criseida. Benoît adds Briseïda's inconsistency to her portrait. Boccaccio curiously does not mention her fickleness here. Kellogg points out, however, that the last two lines of the stanza cited above "link Criseida to her literary origins as the woman who betrays Troilus," because those lines recall the description from Benoît's *Roman de Troie* (1995, 39). Benoît's portrait of Briseïda shows her as being not only well-mannered and beautiful but also fickle and inconsistent (1995, 36). After all, Boccaccio places his Criseida in the middle of her literary heritage. Kellogg concludes:

> In the vein of Benoît and Guido, he [Boccaccio] explains that his poem, if read correctly, proves that women never should be trusted. Women are as unstable as a leaf in the wind, . . . It would seem that the perfect woman, "perfetta donna" ([*Fil*. VIII.]32.1), as Filostrato describes her, cannot exist.   (1995, 54)

Boccaccio's perspective on his Criseida follows the convention of Benoît and Guido. He introduces Criseida as "l'amorosa Criseida" [the amorous Criseida] (*Fil* I.3.4–5). When she is brought to the Greek side, escorted by Diomede, it is mentioned that her heart will change very soon (*Fil* V.14) Thus Boccaccio upholds the literary tradition and preserves her reputation in fact.

Before turning to the portrayal of Chaucer's Criseyde, two other literary successors treating this Trojan love story are worth considering: they are the 15th century Scottish poet Robert Henryson and William Shakespeare. Henryson writes a narrative poem of 616 lines, telling of the tragic fate that befalls to Cresseid after her betrayal of Troilus and acceptance of Diomede's seduction. She is deserted by Diomede and

46   Chapter II

turns into a whore. Moreover, she suffers from horrible illnesses such as leprosy. She is lonely and helpless, without the protection or assistance of her father or any Greek soldiers. She is forced to beg for a living. Lamenting her fate and repenting her behavior, in the end she dies. This is the extremity of her ill repute. Henryson describes what is untold by the previous authors of this story. She is punished for breaking her vow of love to Troilus. Henryson, who represents people or men in general, would never be able to forgive her for her betrayal but would rather hate women unfaithful in love. Nevertheless, the author in part sympathizes with her as a victim of fate.

Shakespeare describes his Cressida as more wanton than all other authors do. She is called "a Troyan drab" [a Trojan whore] (V.i.96)[14] by Thersities who is a servant to Diomedes, a Greek commander. She is also disdained by another Greek commander, Ulysses, for her seductive wantonness with respect to the Greek soldiers:

> *Uly.*   Fie, fie upon her!
> There's language in her eye, her cheek, her lip,
> Nay, her foot speaks; her wanton stpirits look out,
> At every joint and motive of her body.
> O, these encounterers, so glib of tongue,
> That give a coasting welome ere it comes,
> And wide unclasp the tables of their thoughts
> To every ticklish reader! set them down
> For sluttish spoils of opportunity,
> And daughters of the game.
>   (*Troilus and Cressida* (henceforth *Troilus*), IV. v. 54–63)

When Cressida is brought to the Greeks attended by Diomedes, the Greek general Agamemnon welcomes her with a kiss. Then Cressida exchanges kisses of greetings with the Greek soldiers who are present: the Greek commanders, Achilles and Patroclus, and Agamemnon's brother, Menelaus. Ulysses sees through to her lecherous nature and criticizes her for amorous attitudes: her eloquent eyes, cheeks, lips and every joint of her body would tempt men to seduce her. Shakespeare creates a scene in which Troilus witnesses the very moment of Cressida's treachery. At the Greek camp, Diomedes visits Calchas to see his daughter, Cressida. Troilus, who comes to the Greeks, is guided by Ulysses, and takes a secret look at them from a distance and Thersities follows them:

> Cres. Now, my sweet guardian, hark, a word with you.
>
> [Whispers.]
>
> Tro. Yea, so familiar?
>
> Ulyss. She will sing any man at first sight.
>
> Ther. And any man may sing her, if he can take her cliff; she's noted.
>
> Dio. Will you remember?
>
> [Cres.] Remember? yes.
>
> Dio. Nay, but do then,
>
> And let your mind be coupled with your words.
>
> Tro. What shall she remember?
>
> Ulyss. List!
>
> Cres. Sweet honey Greek, tempt me no more to folly.
>
> Ther. Roguery!
>
> Dio. Nay then—
>
> Cres. I'll tell you. what—

48   Chapter II

Dio.	Fo, fo, come, tell a pin. You are forsworn.
Cres.	In faith, I cannot. What would you have me do?
Ther.	A juggling trick—to be secretly open.
Dio.	What did you swear you would bestow on me?
Cres.	I prithee do not hold me to mine oath,
	Bid me do any thing but that, sweet Greek.
Dio.	Good night.
Tro.	Hold, patience.
Ulyss.	How now, Troyan?
Cres.	Diomed—
Dio.	No, no, good night, I'll be your fool no more.
Tro.	Thy better must.
Cres.	Hark a word in your ear.
Tro.	O plague and madness! (*Troilus*, V. ii. 7–35)

Shakespeare's Cressida playfully exchanges words with Diomedes quite soon after she is brought to her father. She does not seem to feel guilty for betraying Troilus. She has no hesitation in affecting insinuating attitudes towards Diomedes. In the following scene, Troilus watches her stroke the cheek of Diomedes. Before they part, Diomedes asks a love token of her and she gives him a sleeve which Troilus handed to her as a proof of his love. Shakespeare describes his Cressida as young and frivolous. She does not have a reminder of a heroine in the medieval romance at all.

As time changes and authors vary, the treatment of Criseyde acquires various possibilities. She is a classic example of treacherous woman. Observe how Chaucer's Criseyde is developed and how he deals with her. Chaucer's apparent portrait of Criseyde largely follows his

Chaucer's Portrayals of Women   49

precursors in respect of her stature, good-manners, peerless beauty and inconsistency. When she appears for the first time in the beginning of Book I, her supreme beauty is highly exaggerated:

> Criseyde was this lady name al right.
> As to my doom, in al Troies cite
> Nas non so fair, forpassynge every wight,
> So aungelik was hir natif beaute,
> That lik a thing inmortal semed she,
> As doth an hevenyssh perfit creature,
> That down were sent in scornyge of nature.   (*TC* I, 99–105)

She is not merely the most beautiful woman in Troy but she is as beautiful as an angel. Her heavenly perfect beauty is beyond that of a mortal creature and seems to disregard Nature itself.

Her physical traits and facial expressions are introduced in both Book I and Book V:

> *She nas nat with the leste of hire stature,*
> But alle hire lymes so wel answerynge
> Weren to wommanhod, that creature
> Was nevere lasse mannyssh in semynge;
> And ek the pure wise of hire mevynge
> Shewed wel that men myght in hire gesse
> Honour, estat, and wommanly noblesse.
>
> (*TC* I, 281–87, italics mine)

> *Criseyde mene was of hire stature;*
> Therto of shap, of face, and ek of cheere,

50   Chapter II

Ther myghte ben no fairer creature.
And ofte tymes this was hire manere:
To gon ytressed with hire heres clere
Doun by hire coler at hire bak byhynde;
Which with a thred of gold she wolde bynde;

And, save hire browes joyneden yefeere,
Ther nas no lak, in aught I kan espien.
But for to speken of hire eyen cleere,
Lo, trewely, they writen that hire syen
That Paradis stood formed in hire yën.
And with hire riche beaute evere more
Strof love in hire ay, which of hem was more.

She sobre was, ek symple, and wys withal,
The best ynorisshed ek that myghte be,
And goodly of hire speche in general,
Charitable, estatlich, lusty, fre;
Ne nevere mo ne lakked hire pite;
Tender-herted, slydynge of corage;
But trewely, I kan nat telle hire age.

(*TC* V, 806–26, italics mine)

Her height is mentioned twice: "She nas nat with the leste of hire stature (I, 281)," "Criseyde mene was of hire stature" (V, 806). She is neither too tall nor too short. "Mene" means that she is moderate in height. Criseyde's feminine shape, beautiful face and graceful bearing are all impeccable. She looks identical with a heroine of a romance. The heavenly image in her beauty makes her an idealistic but unrealistic heroine of romance. In this respect, she is different from the Prioress, one of the cleric pilgrims, who is called Madam Eglentyne. Her appearance and manners imply a traditional courtly lady and almost an ideal heroine of romance:

> Hir nose tretys, hir eyen greye as glas,
> Hir mouth ful smal, and therto softe and reed.
> But sikerly she hadde a fair forheed;
> It was almoost a spanne brood, I trowe;
> For, hardily, she was nat undergrowe.　　　　(*GP*, 152–56)

She has a well-formed nose, eyes shining like glass and a small, red and soft mouth. These features are the same as the conventional characteristics of a heroine in romance. The following three lines (154–56), however, spoil the perfect image of the examplar. Her fair forehead can be counted as one of the standard beauties in courtly poetry. Yet a span-broad forehead is surely extravagant. Moreover, she is not "undergrowe," this is to say, she is not short. In this sense, Chaucer's Prioress deviates from the courtly romance convention. Her imitating courtly table manners and general portrayal are a parody of a heroine of courtly romance. What Chaucer bestows on her peculiar characteristics and makes her a flesh-and-blood person, realistic and dynamic. At the same time the descriptions of her height and her broad forehead produce sharp irony, which may reflect Chaucer's negative view of women.

Interestingly, in Chaucer's main source, *Fil*, Boccaccio describes his heroine as a tall lady: "Ella era grande" (she was tall—*Fil* I.27)[15] The corresponding line in Chaucer's *TC* is, as cited above, "She nas nat with

52   Chapter II

the leste of hire stature" (I, 281). His Criseyde here is depicted as not extremely short, but this does not mean that she is tall. He clearly does not follow Boccaccio but he agrees with other sources such as Dares, Joseph of Exeter, Benoît and Guido (Benson 1987, 1052). He intends to create his heroine as of medium height and medium build because he wants to preserve her within the range of the ideal lady that appeared in courtly romance. Her average stature with its appropriate shape and celestial beauty are identical with the description of Reason in *RR*:

> Resoun men clepe that lady,
> Which from hir tour delyverly
> Com doun to me, withouten mor.
> But she was neither yong ne hoor,
> *Ne high ne lowe, ne fat ne lene,*
> *But best as it were in a mene.*
> Hir eyen twoo were cleer and light
> As ony candell that brenneth bright;
> And on hir heed she haddde a crowne.
> Hir semede wel an high persoune,
> For round enviroun, hir crownet
> Was full of riche stonys frett.
> *Hir goodly semblaunt, by devys,*
> *I trowe were maad in paradys,*
> For Nature hadde nevere such a grace,
> To forge a werk of such compace.
> For certeyn, but if the letter ly,
> God hymself, that is so high,
> Made hir aftir his ymage,

And yaff hir sith sich avauntage

That she hath myght and seignorie

To kepe men from all folye.   (*RR*, 3192–214, italics mine)

RR is a translation of the French poem, *Roman* written by Guillaume de Lorris and Jean de Meun in the 13th century. Guillaume de Lorris begins the story in the framework of a 'dream allegory or vision' and praises *ars amatoria* in the context of courtly love. The dreamer wanders in the Garden of Love on a lovely May morning. When he comes to the well of Narcissus, he sees a beautiful rosebud which is a symbol of his lover. He tries to approach the rose, but he is disturbed by allegorical figures such as Jealousy, Daunger, Shame and Wicked Tongue. Jean de Meun takes over the story following the frame of a dream vision. The dreamer, the lover, finally succeeds in plucking the rosebud in the strong castle of Jealousy by an all-out attack on the God of Love's troops. The worldview of the latter part by Jean de Meun is very different from that of Guillaume de Lorris. The respect of women evident in the courtly romance disappears Lorris's slight touches of satire are developed into a radical misogynistic attack. Reason becomes a major character and tries to persuade the dreamer to avoid the God of love. In the quotation cited above, Reason is described as being similar to a lady in courtly romance. She is, like Criseyde, neither too tall nor too short and neither too fat nor too thin. Her beauty is so flawless as to have been created in Paradise. Even Nature would not be able to create such beauty. In the appearances of Reason and Criseyde, Chaucer utilizes the conventional standard of the perfect beauty of a courtly heroine. Yet Chaucer never contemplates creating his Criseyde as a stereotyped, colorless and faceless heroine of romance. As cited above, Chaucer imposes her only blemish—the

54   Chapter II

one on her face, that is, her joined eyebrows: "And, save hire browes joyneden yefeere, / Ther nas no lak, in aught I kan espien" (V, 813–14).

Criseyde's joined eyebrows are not original with Chaucer. Dares, Joseph, Benoît and Guido all mention that her eyebrows are joined. Some scholars show that in ancient Greece joined eyebrows were a sign of beauty and passion while other demonstrate that they were thought to signify sadness, sagacity, vanity, cruelty, and envy, in medieval physiognomy. Only Benoît and Guido refer to it as a defect. (Benson 1987, 1053). Joined eyebrows are not usually suitable for a conventional heroine, because the separation of eyebrows is a sign of beauty for a romance heroine. The point is that Chaucer follows his precursors and considers it as a "lack." By attributing a flaw to an almost perfect, beautiful and well-made heroine, Chaucer makes her come vividly to life, more human and all the more attracive. Chaucer's skill at realism is here observed.

Other detailed information about Criseyde draws the attention of his audience and readers. The narrator sometimes shows up in the first person and tells about deeply personal matters concerning Criseyde, mentioning her children and her age:

> And in hire hous she abood with swich meyne
> As til hire honour nede was to holde;
> And whil she was dwellynge in that cite,
> Kepte hir estat, and both of yonge and olde
> Ful wel biloved, and wel men of hir tolde.
> *But wheither that she children hadde or noon,*
> *I rede it naught, therfore I late it goon.*
>
> (*TC* I, 127–33, italics mine)

Criseyde's father, Calkas, predicts the fate of Troy and leaves to join the Greeks. Grieving over his betrayal, she visits Hector and asks his mercy on her life. Hector is so tenderhearted that he allows her to live in safety and in dignity as before. Criseyde lives in Troy humbly and modestly so as to be loved by the people. Then the narrator in the end of the stanza, appears and says that he has not discovered whether she has children or not. If Chaucer had had a chance to read *Fil*, he would have known that Criseyde had no children. Boccaccio plainly states that she had neither sons nor daughters because she had never been able to have any (*Fil* I.15). In Benoît, she is called "la Pucele" (the virgin).[16]

In the last Book of *TC*, Criseyde's portrait is introduced again and her age is mentioned here:

> She sobre was, ek symple, and wys withal,
> The best ynorisshed ek that myghte be,
> And goodly of hire speche in general,
> Charitable, estatlich, lusty, fre;
> Ne nevere mo ne lakked hire pite;
> Tender-herted, slydynge of corage;
> *But trewely, I kan nat telle hire age.*

(TC V, 820–26, italics mine)

The narrator deliberately appears and states that he does not know her age. According to Dictys and the Greek tradition, Helen was twenty-one when she was raped. The Latin tradition from Dares does not mention her age. (Benson 1987, 1053) What is Chaucer's intention in introducing these topics? Although the information is not crucial, the narrator in person questions himself and evades the point. Chaucer's Criseyde is

56   Chapter II

a widow. So it is possible that she has already had children. Chaucer, following his source, would find it difficult to mention the fact that she has no children. Avoiding a definite statement about her children, however, makes her character more mysterious and stirs the audience's imagination. As to her age there is a similar effect. It is not necessary to show her exact age. She could be "neither yong ne hoor" (*RR*, 3196) like Reason and other ladies of the courtly romance. To expose Criseye's age would appear to be too realistic and inappropriate for a lover of Troilus. As a heroine of a love story, the description of Criseyde's age and her children would be better left ambiguous. The skillful mixture of reality and convention is one of Chaucer's true achievements.

Criseyde's inner beauty is fully expressed: she is a wholly sensible, honorable and well-mannered lady, merciful and kind. As for even her famous "slydinge of corage" (V, 825), Chaucer does not accuse her but rather seems to protect her. She has "slydinge of corage" because she is tender-hearted, charitable and full of pity.

It is often said that Chaucer is friendly to Criseyde in most cases. He shows deep sympathy for her pitiable circumstances. When he talks about her betrayal, he becomes quite reluctant to speak against her and rather strikes a defensive posture:

> Ne me ne list this sely womman chyde
> Forther than the storye wol devyse.
> Hire name, allas, is publysshed so wide
> That for hire gilt it oughte ynough suffise.
> And if I myghte excuse hire any wise,
> For she so sory was for hire untrouthe,
> Iwis, I wolde excuse hire yet for routhe.   (*TC* V, 1093–99)

Clearly Chaucer hesitates to mention the crucial part of the story and tries to delay the inevitable tragedy. Kellogg (1995, 61) mentions that "He [Chaucer's narrator] resists the medieval characterization of Cressida as a legendary figure for the false and inconstant woman, and although unsuccessfully, he attempts to rescue his Criseyde from those dispassionate portraits which have already determined her biographical history." Priscilla Martin (1990, 183) points out that "the narrator seems to be bending over backwards to defend the indefensible because he likes the heroine." It is true that Chaucer creates his heroine as remarkably attractive. Different from those of Henryson's and Shakespear's, Chaucer's Criseyde is calm, mature and noble. She is as beautiful as the heroines of Benoît, Guido and Boccaccio but more pleasing and amiable than their female protagonists. Her ideal beauty is described with special adoration and her inner virtue and noble attitude are highly praised.

Chaucer's Criseyde is portrayed as a beautiful widow, abandoned by her father Calkas who has fled to the enemy, Greeks. She hears a term of reproach by the people of Troy over her father's betrayal. She is socially placed in a weak, unstable, or rather dangerous situation. What makes Chaucer's Criseyde more attractive than other heroines is that she is well aware of her beauty and her situation and that she knows what she is doing and how she should act. Always wearing mourning dress, she lives humbly with shame and dread, but she is highly conscious of her beauty and full of self-confidence. She goes to the Temple of Pallas to celebrate a feast, where she happens to meet Troilus:

> As was Criseyde, as folk seyde everichone
> That hir behelden in hir blake wede.
> And yet she stood ful lowe and stille allone

58   Chapter II

> Byhynden other folk, in litel brede,
>
> And neigh the dore, ay undre shames drede,
>
> Simple of atir and debonaire of chere,
>
> With ful assured lokyng and manere.   (*TC* I, 176–82)

Although many people who visit the temple are in full dress, Criseyde, as a widow, dresses in black, and humbly stands behind people. Yet she is full of self-confidence in her looks and attitude, for she knows that she is beautiful. Troilus recognizes her self-conceit and thinks it attractive:

> And ek the pure wise of hire mevynge
>
> Shewed wel that men myght in hire gesse
>
> Honour, estat, and wommanly noblesse.
>
> To Troilus right wonder wel with alle
>
> Gan for to like hire mevynge and hire chere,
>
> Which somdel deignous was, for she let falle
>
> Hire look a lite aside in swich manere,
>
> Ascaunces, "What, may I nat stonden here?"
>
> And after that hir lokynge gan she lighte,
>
> That nevere thoughte hym seen so good a syghte.
>
>   (*TC* I, 285–94)

In this scene, Troilus is captivated by Criseyde at first glance in the temple. He is attracted not only by her beauty and womanliness, but also by her noble and sophisticated attitude, which causes his "double sorwe" in the course of time.

Her self-consciousness and firm self-confidence overflow in her long monologue in Book II, in which her uncle, Pandarus, visits and tells her that Troilus is deeply in love with her and that she should accept his affection. After he leaves, Criseyde, alone, thinks over what she should do regarding Troilus. When he returns from the battle field triumphantly along with many soldiers, he looks brave and valiant. Criseyde appreciates "his gentilesse," "his worthynesse," and his birth as "a kynges sone" and admits that his love naturally deserves her beauty:

> I thenke ek how he able is for to have
> Of al this noble town the thriftieste
> To ben his love, so she hire honour save.
> For out and out he is the worthieste,
> Save only Ector, which that is the beste;
> And yet his lif al lith now in my cure.
> But swich is love, and ek myn aventure.
>
> Ne me to love, a wonder is it nought;
> For wel woot I myself, so God me spede—
> Al wolde I that noon wiste of this thought—
> I am oon the faireste, out of drede,
> And goodlieste, who that taketh hede,
> And so men seyn, in al the town of Troie.
> What wonder is though he of me have joye?   (*TC* II, 736–49)

She boldly insists that she is the most attractive and the mot beautiful woman in this city and it is natural for Troilus to fall in love with her. She also declares: "I am myn owene womman" (750). She is an independent woman standing on her own two feet, and freely directing her own life.

60   Chapter II

She is neither a wife nor a nun, after all. The self-consciousness of her beauty and reputation overcomes her obstinate thought and compromises her. She decides to accept his love: "kepe alwey myn honour and my name, / By alle right, it may do me no shame" (762–63). Her social position is so fragile and insecure that she needs to control her behavior to keep her honor and good name.

Chaucer's Criseyde is described generally and apparently as a good and attractive woman. She is not simply a conventional character, changeable and unfaithful, but is more complicated and profound. She is beautiful, noble, modest, well-mannered, and pleasing. She is also wise and mature enough to recognize herself objectively and to understand her status and social situation. She knows well how to behave herself in struggling with adversity. Although she seems powerless and helpless, she is tough enough to survive hardship by making good use of any situation and by taking advantage of any men in power around her on that occasion. What she consequently does to Troilus is to break a promise and betray his love. Yet she always tries to seek the best way in any situation, though she has an over-optimistic view of reality.

As compared with other authors who treat the Trojan War and the story of the lovers, Chaucer obviously takes a sympathetic view of his heroine. He never severely condemns or violently savages her. He seems so friendly to Criseyde that he might well like her, as Martin says. He is unable to deal only with the surface. He describes his heroine closely and in detail. He reveals the subtleties of the psychology in her eloquent speech and monologue, where she discloses her faults such as selfishness, shrewdness, and toughness, as well as fragility, and the limitations of her ability as a woman. The details will be examined in Chapter IV.

II-3 The Portrayal of Prudence

Compared with the Wife of Bath and Criseyde, who are given conspicuous characteristics and attractive features, Dame Prudence in *The Tale of Melibee* (henceforth *Mel*) has fewer distinguishing traits. The tale is one of the two stories which Chaucer himself tells as a storyteller among the members of the pilgrims in *CT*. There is almost no information about the physical distinctions and countenance of his Dame Prudence. We do not know how tall she is or whether she is fat or thin, nor how she looks, whether beautiful or not. Chaucer gives admirable descriptions of characteristics to the Wife of Bath and Criseyde, which make their striking personalities come to life. Althogh Dame Prudence is one of the main characters in this story, which the poet chooses to tell in his own person, he shows no interest in portraying her in any detail.

There are two reasons why Chaucer makes his heroine faceless. Firstly, *Mel* is said to be a close translation of French work, *Livre de Melibee et de Dame Prudence*, written by Renaud de Louens some time in late 1336. This French version is a translation from the Latin, *Liber consolationis et consilii*, written by Albertanus of Brescia in 1246. Albertanus treated the Latin text freely, reducing it to about two-thirds of its original length, and making several additions. There is no evidence that Chaucer knew the Latin version. He depended only on the French text, in which the Griselda story was also included, and closely followed his source (Benson 1987, 923). His faithful rendering of the original means that the portrait of Prudence is not described in his original source. His few additional modifications and eliminations are recorded in the explanatory notes by Benson. There is no description of Prudence's portrait. Chaucer neither omitted nor added a detailed

62   Chapter II

picture of his heroine.

When Pilgrim-Chaucer is appointed to tell a story, he is also requested by the Host to offer something merry, this because the pilgrims have been rendered downcast and feel sad after listening to the piteous martyrdom of a little boy as told by the Prioress. Pilgrim-Chaucer starts telling his tale with *Sir Thopas*, which is a typical romance of the adventureous knight in love, fighting with the giants. But in the middle of the story, the Host abruptly interrupts the poet, regarding the story as completely worthless, and asks him to tell another story in prose which is mirthful and instructive in. Pilgrim-Chaucer, obeying his request, then tells a story which is "a moral tale vertuous" (939). He asks the other pilgrims not to blame him if he does not tell the story in the same way as they had heard it previously:

> Al be it told somtyme in sondry wyse
> Of sondry folk, as I shal yow devyse.
>   "As thus: ye woot that every Evaungelist
> That telleth us the peyne of Jhesu Crist
> Ne seith nat alle thyng as his felawe dooth;
> But nathelees hir sentence is al sooth,
> And alle acorden as in hire sentence,
> Al be ther in hir tellyng difference.
> For somme of hem seyn moore, and somme seyn lesse,
> Whan they his pitous passioun express—
> I meene of Mark, Mathew, Luc, and John—
> But doutelees hir sentence is al oon.
> Therefore, lordynges alle, I yow biseche,
> If that yow thynke I varie as in my speche,

As thus, though that I telle somewhat moore
Of proverbes than ye han herd bifoore
Comprehended in this litel tretys heere,
To enforce with th'effect of my mateere;
And though I nat the same wordes seye
As ye han herd, yet to yow alle I preye
Blemeth me nat; for, as in my sentence,
Shul ye nowher fynden difference
Fro the sentence of this tretys lyte
After the which this murye tale I write.   (*Sir Thopas*, 941–64)

Chaucer explains that he is going to tell a story in different ways from the original as told by various people, adding more proverbs, and changing the words. Although Pilgrim-Chaucer as a storyteller excuses himself for re-telling the story freely rather than word for word, he follows his source almost slavishly. This is one reason why Prudence is not granted a rich description.

Secondly, if Chaucer presents his Dame Prudence with no distinctive traits in accordance with the French original, he must have done so deliberately. He provides one significant addition to his source; that is, he names the daughter of Melibeus and Dame Prudence, Sophie which means 'wisdom.' As Helen Cooper (1983, 174) points out, "the name suggests the possibility of an allegorical reading of the scanty narrative that serves to introduce the debate in the rest of the treaties."

Melibeus is a rich, mighty and powerful young man. He has a wife called Prudence and a daughter named Sophie. One day he happens to go on an outing into the field for fun, leaving his wife and daughter at home. While Melibeus is away from home, a terrible thing happens to

64   Chapter II

his family. No reason being given, three enemies break into his house and beat his wife severely and inflict with five mortal wounds on the daughter'sr feet, hands, eyes, nose and mouth. "Thre of his olde foes" (*Mel*, 970) stand for the three enemies of man: the world, the flesh, and the devil as explained in the line, "for certes, the three enemys of man-kynde—that is to seyn, the flessh, the feend, and the world—" (1421). The five wounds symbolize the wounds which Jesus Christ received on the Cross.

When Melibeus returns home and learns of all the mischief, he becomes enraged and weeps heavily. His anger is so fierce that he is about to take revenge on the enemies by starting a war against them. Dame Prudence with her prudent speech tries to calm down her husband, give him some advice, and persuade him not to be so angry but to reconcile and forgive his enemies. In the end, she leads her husband to understand the Christian teaching.

Mel is simply able to be read as an allegory. Melibeus, "a man that drynketh hony" (1410), who enjoys the worldly pleasure, achieves Sophie, 'wisdom' with the guidance of Prudence, 'caution, wisdom, or providence.' Prudence embodies an allegorical concept. She needs to have neither a specific face nor distinctive characteristics, because her name itself stands for her character and the meaning.

At the beginning of the story, Prudence is described as "this noble wyf Prudence" twice, in lines 976 and 979:

> *This noble wyf Prudence* remembred hire upon the sentence of Ovide, in his book that cleped is the Remedie of Love, where as he seith, / "He is a fool that destoubeth the mooder to wepen in the deeth of hire child til she have wept hir fille as for a certein tyme, /

and thanne shal man doon his diligence with amyable wordes hire to reconforte, and preyen hire of hir wepyng for to stynte." / For which resoun *this noble wyf Prudence* suffred hir housbonde for to wepe and crie as for a certein space, / and whan she saugh hir tyme, she seyde hym in this wise: "Allas, my lord," quod she, "why make ye yourself for to be lyk a fool? / For sothe it aperteneth nat to a wys man to maken swith a sorwe. / Youre doghter, with the grace of God, shal warisshe and escape. / And, al were it so that she right now were deed, ye ne oughte nat, as for hir deeth, yourself to destroye. / Senek seith: 'The wise man shal nat take to greet disconfort for the deeth of his children, / but, certes, he sholde suffren it in pacience as wel as he abideth the deeth of his owene propre persone.'"   (*Mel*, 976–85, italics mine)

When Melibeus comes home and finds that his daughter has been seriously injured by the three enemies, he is nearly crazed with grief and is furious against them. He cries like a mad man, tearing his clothes. What this noble wife, Prudence, does to him is to let him cry till he feels better and calms down. She remembers the sentence from Ovid's *Remedie of Love*: it is foolish to disturb the mother crying over the death of her child until she cries enough to settle down. Then the noble Prudence observes the timing and advises him that a wise man should not cry over his child's death but, borrowing the words of Seneca, should suffer it with patience as if he accepted his own death. As long as their daughter is not dead, she insists that he should not feel overly depressed. When the enemies break into their house, Prudence is beaten badly. Although she is one of the victims along with her daughter, she is neither upset nor frightened at this mischief. Instead, she sounds perfectly calm and self-possessed,

66   Chapter II

so much so as to soothe her husband. Melibeus's reaction appears more natural and humane than Prudence's. It is a matter of course for him to lose his temper and become emotionally excited over the enemies after he finds out what had happened. Compared with his reaction, Prudence's tranquil attitude seems somewhat odd and unnatural.

So depressed is Melibeus that he loses his judgement and asks Prudence for advice. Prudence recommends that he should ask his true friends and some wise people in his family for their advice and follow their opinion. Believing that he follows her suggestion, he makes the mistake of inviting many different people to listen to their opinion, which is pointed out by Prudence later. He accepts the majority opinion, that he should take revenge on his enemies. When Prudence sees that he has decided to attack, she begins to give her opinion to her husband "in ful humble wise" (1051),

> "My lord," quod she, "I yow biseche, as hertely as I dar and kan, ne haste yow nat to faste and, for alle gerdons, as yeveth me audience. / For Piers Alfonce seith, 'Whoso that dooth to thee oother good or harm, haste thee nat to quiten it, for in this wise thy freend wole abyde and thyn enemy shal the lenger lyve in drede.' / The proverbe seith, 'He hasteth wel that wisely kan abyde,' and 'in wikked haste is no profit.' "   (*Mel*, 1052–54)

Prudence beseeches her husband not to make a hasty decision. She asks him in a very humble way, yet clearly insists on her opinion, citing an authority and a proverb. This is not effective, however. Melibeus refuses her advice with baseless, unfair reasons (1055–63). The reasons why he rejects her counsel are based on the anti-feministic thoughts which prevailed widely in the middle ages. First, he should have known better than to change his decision, which had been supported and approved by many people, by following his wife's opinion. Second, as Solomon believed, all women are wicked, and third, because he would retain dominance over his wife, her advice cannot be accepted. Fourth, women are talkative and cannot keep things secret. Last, as Aristotle says, women's evil counsel conquers men.

Prudence listens to her husband "ful debonairly and with greet pacience" (1064) then asks his permission to speak and argues back against each reason at full length. Her humble attitude to her husband is gradually changing into the strong will of an advisor and a leader. She is very patient and persistent, as well. She never gives up trying to persuade her husband to abandon the idea of taking vengeance on his enemies and to reconcile with them.

Chaucer does not take the same great pains to create a portrayal of Prudence that he does with the Wife of Bath and Criseyde. There is no concrete information about her stature, her features, or countenance. We do not know how old she is, if she is beautiful, or what color her hair is. Her appearance cannot be clearly visualized. Why does Chaucer not offer such a description? That can only have been intentional. He does not give Prudence a particular individuality, because she is a personified character. She does not have to bear the traits of a living creature such as the Wife of Bath with her teeth set apart or Criseyde with her joined eyebrows. *Mel* is to be read merely as an allegory. Prudence is an allegorical figure who stands for the concept of "prudence": she is sensible, careful, and cautious. She is, moreover, patient, persistent, reasonable, and logical. These traits come clear in her speech. Although Prudence is not depicted as a flesh-and-blood person, the fact that

68   Chapter II

Chaucer does not lose interest in her is shown in her long speech and earnest conversation with her husband, which may strike the modern reader as too tedious and dull. The tactic of her eloquent speech and its effects will be discussed in Chapter V.

Chapter III

The Wife of Bath's Eloquence in Her Prologue and Tale

III-1 Eloquence in Her Excuses for Remarriage

In *GP*, the Wife of Bath is introduced as a person who is well-spoken. She is one of the most talkative of all of Chaucer's female characters. Her prologue takes the form of a long tri-part monologue: first, her self-justification as to why she has been married five times; second, an autobiographical confession about her married life with three good and old husbands; and third, with two bad husbands. When she develops her arguments on marriage and shows off her method for taming her husbands, scolding and chiding them, she talks ceaselessly with an eloquent tongue. In this chapter, how the Wife's eloquence and talkativeness affect her assertions will be examined.

When the Wife talks about marital woes, she says that her own experience is enough and needs no support of written authority:

> Experience, though noon auctoritee
> Were in this world, is right ynogh for me
> To speke of wo that is in mariage;   (*WBP*, 1–3)

In her attempt to justify the fact that she had five husbands at the church

[69]

70   Chapter III

door, she is even prepared to dispense with "auctoritee" (the Bible). She complains that she was accused of being married several times. The reason behind the accusation is that Jesus Christ went to a wedding only once, at Cana, and that therefore she should not marry more than once:

> But me was toold, certeyn, nat longe agoon is,
> That sith that Crist ne wente nevere but onis
> To weddyng, in the Cane of Galiee,
> That by the same ensample taughte he me
> That I ne sholde wedded be but ones.   (*WBP*, 9–13)

The "He" whom she mentions is St. Jerome. This is a familiar argument in his *Adversus Jovinianum*. Chaucer borrows from St. Jerome here and there in her Prologue. In this sense, the Wife takes a similar position as Jovinian whom St. Jerome called an "Epicurus among Christians." But it is also true that Chaucer does not simply paraphrase the source; but his arrangement is purposeful (Robertson 1962, 318).

Dame Alison dismisses this accusation and defends herself by quoting the Bible, which gives no indication of the number of acceptable remarriages:

> Herkne eek, lo, which a sharp word for the nones,
> Biside a welle, Jhesus, God and man,
> Spak in repreeve of the Samaritan:
> 'Thou hast yhad fyve housbondes,' quod he,
> 'And that ilke man that now hath thee
> Is noght thyn housbonde,' thus seyde he certeyn.
> What that he mente therby, I kan nat seyn;

But that I axe, why that the fifthe man
Was noon housbonde to the Samaritan?
How manye myghte she have in mariage?
Yet herde I nevere tellen in myn age
Upon this nombre diffinicioun.   (*WBP*, 14–25)

The Wife quotes the biblical episode of the Samaritan woman with five
husbands (John 4.18). But she does not understand the import of the
whole story. When Jesus Christ sat down and rested beside the well in
Samaria, a woman happened to come to the well to draw water. He asked
her for water and gave her instruction. He asked her to call her husband
to the well. She answered that she had no husband. Then he told her
that she was right in saying that, because she had had five husbands and
the man she currently had was not her husband. It was those words of
Jesus Christ which made the woman believe in him. She perceived him
as a prophet. She then went to the city to persuade people to come and
see a man who told her all that she ever did. Many Samaritans coming
from the city believed in him because of the testimony of the woman,
namely, that he had told her all that she ever did. After that they believed
his words and knew that this was the Savior of the world (John 4.1–42).

Jesus Christ knew that she had had married five times and saw through
to the fact that she was living with a man out of wedlock; that she was
a woman of loose morals and yet he did not blame her or reproach her,
but guided her by his teaching. This is the point of the anecdote. He was
completely silent on the question of remarriage.

Robertson observes that her marital condition may be iconographically based on the story of the Good Samaritan, who listens to Jesus
Christ, whereas the Wife is somewhat deaf so that she has no ear for him

72   Chapter III

(1962, 320). She never tries to think about the reason why Jesus Christ talked to the Samaritan woman and spoke of her several acts of bigamy. The Wife of Bath has no intention to learn a lesson from the story.

She just tries to defend herself from being blamed for her multiple marriages, because she was told that Jesus Christ teaches monogamy. She, however, she rejects the idea of monogamy, applying a quote from the Old Testament: "to increase and multiply."

> Men may devyne and glosen, up and doun,
> But wel I woot, expres, withoute lye,
> God bad us for to wexe and multiplye;
> That gentil text kan I wel understonde.
> Eek wel I woot, he seyde myn housbonde
> Sholde lete fader and mooder and take to me.
> But of no nombre mencion made he,
> Of bigamye, or of octogamye;
> Why sholde men thanne speke of it vileynye?   (*WBP*, 26–34)

She utilizes the biblical statement concerning God's order to "increase and multiply;" however, the phrase is contradictory of her real interest in marriage. It is because she has no interest in procreation. Through her marital life with five husbands, there is no evidence that she has had a child. Dame Alison has been a wife but not a mother. As some scholars point out, her main purpose in marrying was not to produce offspring but to enjoy lust and, consequently, to gain property:

> For thanne th'apostle seith that I am free
> To wedde, a Goddes half, where it liketh me.

He seith that to be wedded is no synne;
Bet is to be wedded than to brynne.   (*WBP*, 49–52)

The Wife is a great proponent of marriage. She tries to justify herself
with her eloquent speech, though she takes advantage of the Bible
to evade accusation. Her statement is mostly based upon the biblical
background, as follows:

> A wife is bound to her husband as long as he lives. If the husband
> dies, she is free to be married to whom she wishes, only in the
> Lord.   (1 Corinthians, 7: 39)[17]

> But if they cannot exercise self-control, they should marry. For it
> is better to marry than to be aflame with passion.
>   (1 Corinthians, 7: 9)

Next the Wife proceeds to attack virginity and maidenhood by using
the apostle's words. The fundamental ideal in the Bible is, however,
based on the concept that "Virginitee is greet perfeccion" (105), as the
Wife admits. So she cannot be simply aggressive in assaulting virginity
and maidenhood:

> Wher can ye seye, in any manere age,
> That hye God defended mariage
> By expres word? I pray yow, telleth me.
> Or where comanded he virginitee?
> I woot as wel as ye, it is no drede,
> Th'apostel, whan he speketh of maydenhede,

74   Chapter III

> He seyde that precept therof hadde he noon.
> Men may conseille a womman to been oon,
> But conseillyng is no comandement.   (*WBP*, 59–67)

It is difficult for her to prove her position superior to that of the apostle. Because she cannot give a persuasive and convincing explanation, she is obliged to be emotional rather than logical, (not unlike 'sour grapes'): "I graunte it wel; I have noon envie, / Thogh maydenhede preferre bigamye" (95–96), "I nyl envye no virginitee" (142).

Her continuing attempt to protect marriage grows irrelevant to the original argument and turns toward the merely carnal aim and result of sexual activity. She points out that Jesus Christ did not order everyone to follow his steps. She is not such a perfectly moral person. But she wishes to give the flower of her youth in the act and in "fruyt" of marriage, although what she means by "fruyt" is not bearing a child but having pleasure:

> Glose whoso wole, and seye bothe up and doun
> That they were maked for purgacioun
> Of uryne, and oure bothe thynges smale
> Were eek to knowe a femele from a male,
> And for noon oother cause—say ye no?
> The experience woot wel it is noght so.
> So that the clerkes be nat with me wrothe,
> I sey this: that they maked ben for bothe;
> That is to seye, for office and for ese
> Of engendrure, ther we nat God displese.   (*WBP*, 119–28)

Her straightforward manner of speech makes her wary about offending God and the clerks. But she goes further and dares to declare that she uses her "thynges smale" to solve the problem of 'debt' between a husband and wife in marriage:

> In wyfhod I wol use myn instrument
> As frely as my Makere hath it sent.
> If I be daungerous, God yeve me sorwe!
> Myn housbonde shal it have bothe eve and morwe,
> Whan that hym list come forth and paye his dette.
> An housbonde I wol have—I wol nat lette—
> Which shal be bothe my dettour and my thral,
> And have his tribulacion withal
> Upon his flessh, whil that I am his wife.   (*WBP*, 149–57)

Chaucer also refers to the sexual duty in marital life in *The Shipman's Tale* and *The Merchant's Tale*. Here the Wife reveals that she is willing to use her instrument to make her husband pay his debt to her in bed. She takes advantage of St. Paul's notion of conjugal rights and completely abuses it to justify her lust:

> I have the power durynge al my lyf
> Upon his propre body, and noght he.
> Right thus the Apostel tolde it unto me,
> And bad oure housbondes for to love us weel.
> Al this sentence me liketh every deel—   (*WBP*, 158–62)

As for a husband's duty in marriage and a wife's subjection, the Bible

76   Chapter III

comments on its mutuality as follows:

> The husband should give to his wife her conjugal rights, and
> likewise the wife to her husband. For the wife does not rule over
> her own body, but the husband does; likewise the husband does
> not rule over his own body, but the wife does.
>
> (1 Corinthians, 7: 3–4)

> Wives, be subject to your husbands, as to the Lord. For the husband
> is the head of the wife as Christ is the head of the church, his body,
> and is himself its Savior. As the church is subject to Christ, so let
> wives also be subject in everything to their husbands. Husbands,
> love your wives, as Christ loved the church and gave himself up
> for her[.]   (Ephesians, 5: 22–25)

> Wives, be subject to your husbands, as is fitting in the Lord.
> Husbands, love your wives, and do not be harsh with them.
>
> (Colossians, 3: 18–19)

It is quite clear that the Wife misuses the Bible to suit herself and seizes
on only those ideas which are useful to her assertion.

In the first part of her Prologue, she tries to justify her five marriages.
It is clear, however, that she intentionally arranges the biblical statements
in her own way and twists them to support her assertion. She seems to
be a great defender of marriage, and is opposed to patriarchal society.
In defending marriage, she attacks virginity and maidenhood, and
accordingly her argument to defend marriage turns out to be nothing but
a reveling in carnal activity. She, moreover, inquires as to the purpose

of the genitals apart from gender discrimination. In the end, she utilizes her sexuality freely in order to make her husband pay his debt in bed. Her eloquent speech exposes her inner self, which women should not normally reveal so frankly in public. She shamelessly reveals her lecherousness with indecent words. This kind of speech of course may amuse a male audience, including the actual audience of her fellow-pilgrims. The Pardoner swiftly reacts to her speech with this ironic comment:

> "Now, dame," quod he, "by God and by Seint John!
> Ye been a noble prechour in this cas.
> I was aboute to wedde a wyf; allas!
> What sholde I bye it on my flessh so deere?
> Yet hadde I levere wedde no wyf to-yeere!"   (*WBP*, 164–68)

His interruption sounds sarcastic, as Lynne Dickinson (1990, 75) points out, the Pardoner addresses the very sort of ecclesiastical authorities, God and St. John, whom the Wife has been striving to reinterpret from a feminine or rather her own perspective. He also suggests that the Wife is 'a noble preacher,' which is inappropriate for a feminine speaker. What sounds more sarcastic is that he announces that he would soon have married if he had not heard her 'noble preaching.' In *GP*, the Pardoner is described as "a geldyng or a mare" (*GP*, 691), so that his interest in marriage appears to be ironic. It is true that his intervention reminds us of the presence of a masculine audience for her speech and also effectively functions to change the direction of her speech. She at last begins talking again about the main theme, which is her five husbands.

78   Chapter III

III-2   How to Control Three "goode" Husbands

In the second part of her Prologue, she describes the strategy of loquacity as a means of controlling and dominating her first three husbands. They are given no individual character, but are described simply as good, rich and old husbands. They are all so indulgent to their young wife, Alison, that they have given both their love and property to her. The Wife does not need to strive for their love. Instead, what she did to her husbands in order to control them was to give them a woe by lying, chiding and complaining. She dares to tell us: "For half so boldely kan ther no man / Swere and lyen, as a womman kan" (*WBP*, 227–28). In the next fifty plus lines, she exposes the way in which she accuses her husbands by quoting their words, with a repetition of "Thou seist . . . ":

> *Thou seist* to me it is a greet meschief
> To wedde a povre womman, for costage;
> And if that she be riche, of heigh parage,
> Thanne *seistow* that it is a tormentrie
> To soffre hire pride and hire malencolie.
> And if that she be fair, thou verray knave,
> *Thou seyst* that every holour wol hire have;
> She may no while in chastitee abyde,
> That is assailled upon ech a syde.   (*WBP*, 248–56, italics mine)

The Wife claims that those words are what she was actually told by her aging husbands; however, a refrain in calling them by the second person has the effect such that a masculine audience cannot but feel directly singled out and blamed (Dickinson 1990, 71).

She keeps on citing her husbands' words and juxtaposes their complaints about the Wife and women in general. Alison discloses herself by quoting her husbands. She as good as represents men's true feelings of misogyny:

> Thow seyst that droppyng houses, and eek smoke,
> And chidyng wyves maken to flee
> Out of hir owene houses; a, benedictee!
> What eyleth swich an old man for to chide?
> Thow seyst we wyves wol oure vices hide
> Til we be fast, and thanne we wol hem shewe—
> Wel may that be a proverbe of a shrewe!
> Thou seist that oxen, asses, hors, and houndes,
> They been assayed at diverse stoundes;
> …………………………………….
> But folk of wyves maken noon assay,
> Til they be wedded—olde dotard shrewe!—
> And thanne, seistow, we wol oure vices shewe.   (*WBP*, 278–92)

She continues to attack her husbands by blaming them, saying that they speak ill of her. She reproves them with cursing and swearing: "Sire olde lecchour, lat thy japes be!" (242), "With wilde thonder-dynt and firy levene / Moote thy welked nekke be tobroke!" (276–77), "olde dotard shrewe!" (291), "olde barel-ful of lyes!" (302). A feminine audience would be delighted with her sharp and eloquent speech. She utters one thing after another in rapid succession. This means that as a result, however, she exposes women's defects and faults.

80   Chapter III

Chaucer derived this anti-feministic idea from Theophrastus' *Aureolus liber Theophrastti de nupitiis*, Estache Deshamps' *Miroir de Mariage,* Jean de Meung's *Roman*, and St. Jerome's *Epistola adversus Jovinianum.* As Katharina M. Wilson and Elizabeth M. Makowaski (1990) claim:

> They include the envy of the neighbor's wife's clothes, the blind selection of a partner in marriage, a wife's insistence on praise for her beauty, the troublesomeness of her in-laws, the accusations of false suspicions by the wife.   (157)

This misogynistic idea was ubiquitous across the medieval patriarchal and clerical society. Women were traditionally spoken ill of by men. Chaucer creates a female narrator who talks about herself and women and wives in general from the viewpoint of women. Chaucer challenges misogynistic thoughts, that is, the anti-feministic tradition, through Alison, the Wife of Bath.

Why does Chaucer produce this kind of female character and through her challenge the misogynistic thoughts of the age? Under cover of the complexity of gender, the poet doubly protects himself from attack on every side. He can lay bare his views freely and frankly with no fear about reactions from either a masculine or a feminine audience. If men directly speak ill of women, a feminine audience would be displeased with the anti-feministic claims; or rather they would be very upset. But when a woman speaker exposes her own faults, they are obliged to be silent. On the other hand, a masculine audience would be amused, giggling and chuckling to hear a woman uncovering herself so openly. In addition to the audience of both sexes, Alison's speech elicits laughter even from a clerical audience, because she bears a striking resemblance to the "wykked wyves."

The Wife's tactics for attacking the husbands and strategies for dominating them, sound as though she is speaking ill of women:

> Deceite, wepyng, spynnyng God hath yive
> To wommen kyndely, whil that they may lyve.
> And thus of o thyng I avaunte me:
> Atte ende I hadde the bettre in ech degree,
> By sleighte, or force, or by som maner thyng,
> As by continueel murmur or grucchyng.   (*WBP*, 401–06)

Her unethical treatment of her husbands, however, ironically pleases them, especially when she accuses them of infidelity which they have never committed.

The good and aging husbands interpret her anger, complaints and chiding as deriving from her intense jealousy, which shows deep affection for them:

> They were ful glade to excuse hem blyve
> Of thyng of which they nevere agilte hir lyve.
> Of wenches wolde I beren hem on honde,
> Whan that for syk unnethes myghte they stonde.
>   Yet tikled I his herte, for that he
> Wende that I hadde of hym so greet chiertee!   (*WBP*, 391–96)

In this way, the Wife causes them pain and woe (384). It is her husbands who are suffering and tormented in their marital life. She actually talks about the woe in marriage not of herself but of her husbands. The Wife

82   Chapter III

treats them so harshly that she bites and whinnies like a horse and complains to them even if she is in the wrong (386–87). Although she is conscious of doing wrong to them, she tries to justify her behavior with two reasons: one is that: "Or elles often tyme hadde I been spilt" (388). She claims that anyone who comes to the mill first grinds first. She places the first stone of quarreling in order to stop their war. If not, she would have been ruined. The other reason is that she has endured their lust and pretended as if she has desire, though she has never been satisfied with them:

> For wynnyng wolde I al his lust endure,
> And make me a feyned appetit;
> And yet in bacon hadde I nevere delit.
> That made me that evere I wolde hem chide,   (*WBP*, 416–19)

Here, "bacon" means preserved old meat, indicating her old husbands. We can catch a glimpse of her marital woe when she was young. Alison has got married to three old men beginning at twelve years of age. The immature, naive bride must have had to put on a bold front to protect herself in facing up to old husbands. Unless she had begun to attack them first and had stood at an advantage over them, she would often have had a hard time. This way of living in the world she had learned from her experience in marriage. It is hard to imagine a twelve-year-old girl willingly marrying such an old man. She surely had to accept marriage against her will and endure connubial duty with patience. Yet her husbands are too old to carry out their duty satisfactorily: ". . . thogh he looked as a wood leon, / Yet sholde he faille of his conclusion" (429–30). By making good use of their inability she completely dominates them:

What eyleth yow to grucche thus and grone?
Is it for ye wolde have my queynte allone?
Wy, taak it al! Lo, have it every deel!
Peter! I shrewe yow, but ye love it weel;
For if I wolde selle my *bele chose*,
I koude walke as fressh as is a rose;
But I wol kepe it for youre owene tooth.
Ye be to blame, by God! I sey yow sooth.   (*WBP*, 443–50)

Married life with three "oolde and goode" husbands seems to suggest a victory. The Wife obtains their love, properties and domination over them. Yet she does not sound happy at all because she is always chiding, lying, grouching, and complaining. It is for the benefit of her own livelihood that Alison has developed these tactics with respect to her marriages with the old men.

Chaucer uses ventriloquial tricks through Alison. The Wife naturally and basically stands for women and represents their voices, telling the true feelings of women. Although she is profoundly pro-feminist, she shows how wicked women are by attacking her husbands' complaints about her.

III-3 Marital Conflicts with Two "badde" Husbands

The last part of *WBP* concerns the fourth and the fifth husbands. The description of the fourth husband is very brief. We have little information about him. Marital life with him is filled with furious jealousy, because

84   Chapter III

he is unfaithful to her: "My fourthe housbonde was a revelour— / This is to seyn, he hadde a paramour—" (453–54). As for the Wife, she is in the midst of the flower of womanhood:

> And I was yong and ful of ragerye,
> Stibourn and strong, and joly as a pye.
> How koude I daunce to an harpe smale,
> And synge, ywis, as any nyghtyngale,
> Whan I had dronke a draughte of sweete wyn!   (*WBP*, 455–59)

After the three marriages with the rich but aged husbands, the Wife has acquired considerable wealth from them and come to value herself. Although we do not know the age of the fourth one, he must have been a well-matched spouse. Alison might have decided to marry of her own free will, rather than having it arranged as before, possibly by her mother, who taught her how to deal with men. She may well have expected that this would be an ideal and happy marriage. But the fourth is not a good husband and she is betrayed so that her pride is torn to pieces and turned into furious anger for the sake of vengeance:

> I made hym of the same wode a croce;
> Nat of my body, in no foul manere,
> But certeinly, I made folk swich cheere
> That in his owene grece I made hym frye
> For angre, and for verray jalousye.
> By God, in erthe I was his purgatorie,
> For which I hope his soule be in glorie.   (*WBP*, 484–90)

She is now truly very jealous, whereas she had merely pretended jealousy with the former three husbands. Her revenge consists in making the husband jealous by seeming to be amiable to others. Then she carries on a flirtation with the young clerk Jankin. She uses metaphorical or proverbial expressions, such as, 'I made him a cross from the same wood', 'I made him fry in his own grease' and 'I was his purgatory in earth.' We do not know for sure what their real relationship was. She appears to have tortured him physically:

> For, God it woot, he sat ful ofte and song,
> Whan that his shoo ful bitterly hym wrong.
> Ther was no wight, save God and he, that wiste,
> In many wise, how soore I hym twiste.   (*WBP*, 491–94)

Though the Wife never stopped talking about the aged husbands very eloquently, she is mysteriously quiet about the fourth. If we interpret what she says to the letter, she seems to suggest that she kills her husband single-handedly. This leads to a conjecture of murder.

Some scholars suggest that the Wife might have murdered her fourth husband in a conspiracy with her fifth husband-to be, Jankin. Beryl Rowland (1972–73, 273–82) takes the conjured dream of a bed full of blood, with which she tries to woo Jankin, as a sign of an actual later occurrence: the murder of her fourth husband by her fifth, with her aid and consent. Dolores Palomo (1975, 303–19) gives her own version of a murder, stating that Alison first suggests murder on the day when she goes on a picnic in the field with Jankin and her friend. But she repents of the conspiracy and goes on pilgrimage to Jerusalem as her penance for the wicked idea. Yet after she returns home Jankin commits

86   Chapter III

the crime unaided. Alison betrays the terrible secret and then Jankin is proclaimed guilty of murder. Mary Hamel (1979, 132–39) does not believe that either Jankin or the Wife was a murderer; however, she suggests that some cases of contemporary murder in the report of the Westminster chronicler were on Chaucer's mind. They show a classic pattern in fourteenth-century crime: conspiracy between a wife and a chaplain or other clerk, or a servant, to murder husband and employer. Hamel claims that Jankin's preaching on "wykked wyves" who caused their husbands' death alludes to contemporary murder. It strengthens the anti-feminist case and reminds the audience that contemporary women were also capable of shocking extremes of behavior.

The presumption of murder is an imaginative fancy, although the Wife's transition from the fourth husband to the fifth is awkward. She promised to marry Jankin while her fourth husband was still alive. When the fourth husband is in London for Lent, the Wife goes out in a field with Jankin and her close friend. She tells Jankin: "If I were wydwe, sholde wedde me" (568). This is her way of preparing things, as she mentions, as taught by her mother:

> I holde a mouses herte nat worth a leek
> Thath hath but oon hole for to sterte to,
> And if that faille, thanne is al ydo.
>   I bar hym on honde he hadde enchanted me—
> My dame taughte me that soutilee—   (*WBP*, 572–76)

This shows her shrewdness. She is bent on finishing the marriage with the fourth husband and searching for the next one. Then she tells Jankin of her conjured dream in which she was slain by him in a bed full of blood. But she simply tells a complete lie, following her mother's instruction. The Wife interprets her dream as a convenience: "But yet I hope that ye shal do me good, / For blood bitokeneth gold, as me was taught" (580–81). There is surely an image of a murder in her dream.

At the funeral of the fourth husband, she pretends to mourn and cry with a few tears, as a widow, but she is fascinated with Jankin's white legs walking behind the bier:

> To chirche was myn housbonde born a-morwe
> With neighebores, that for hym maden sorwe;
> And Jankyn, oure clerk, was oon of tho.
> As help me God, whan that I saugh hym go
> After the beere, me thought he hadde a paire
> Of legges and of feet so clene and faire
> That al myn herte I yaf unto his hoold.   (*WBP*, 593–99)

This is a most sinful scene and it shows most strikingly who she is. Chaucer describes the woman with sharp insight and overwhelmingly detailed realism.

The last description of the fourth husband treats his tomb, which is not elaborately made, because: "It nys but wast to burye hym preciously" (500). Even so, at the end of the same month as the funeral, Alison gets married to the jolly clerk Jankin with great solemnity and gives him all the land and property that she has inherited from her ex-husbands (627–30). But she is soon enough going to repent that.

The Wife calls this fifth husband "the mooste shrewe" (505) but she loved him best (513). The reason is that he was not only "so fressh and gay" (508) in their bed but also he was so "daungerous" (514) to her,

88   Chapter III

that is, he did not give his love freely to her:

> We wommen han, if that I shal nat lye,
> In this matere a queynte fantasye;
> Wayte what thyng we may nat lightly have,
> Therafter wol we crie al day and crave.
> Forbede us thyng, and that desiren we;
> Preesse on us faste, and thanne wol we fle.   (*WBP*, 515–20)

Here is a reversal of gender in the rule of courtly love. In the courtly romances, a sovereign lady tends to take an indifferent attitude to her lover. She mentions that she has chosen him not for money but for love (526). This is the first of her marriages based on love. The clerk, who is twenty years younger than she, however, is the most difficult man for her to deal with. Even though she chooses her spouse of her own will and for the sake of love, Jankin, the husband leads her to hell as well as heaven.

Hell and Heaven coexist side by side in their marital life, keeping a subtle balance between physical violence and sensual pleasure:

> And yet was he to me the mooste shrewe;
> That feele I on my ribbes al by rewe;
> And evere shal unto myn endyng day.
> But in oure bed he was so fressh and gay,
> And therwithal so wel koude he me glose,
> Whan that he wolde han my *bele chose*;
> That thogh he hadde me bete on every bon,
> He koude wynne agayn my love anon.   (*WBP*, 505–12)

Finally her amorous desire seems to be satisfied with the last young husband. She exposes her lecherousness here again without hesitation, blaming her nature and behavior on astrological influences:

> I hadde the prente of seinte Venus seel.
> As help me God, I was a lusty oon,
> And faire, and riche, and yong, and wel bigon,
> And trewely, as myne housbondes tolde me,
> I hadde the beste *quoniam* myghte be.
> For certes, I am al Venerien
> In feelynge, and myn herte is Marcien.
> Venus me yaf my lust, my likerousnesse,
> And Mars yaf me my sturdy hardynesse;
> Myn ascendent was Taur, and Mars therinne.
> Allas, allas! That evere love was synne!
> I folwed ay myn inclinacioun
> By vertu of my constellacioun;
> That made me I koude noght withdrawe
> My chambre of Venus from a good felawe.   (*WBP*, 604–18)

She confesses that she has followed her carnal appetite and loved any man who loved her, regardless of his social status or physical characteristics. Her fluent speech comes to life again and discloses much more than women would ordinarily want to expose in public. Here again, a female audience would scowl at her while a male audience would hardly keep from chuckling or guffawing.

Even after marrying the husband of her own choosing, the Wife never changes her habit of wandering around, visiting from house to

90   Chapter III

house with her glib tongue. Her behavior makes Jankin so mad that
he often preaches to her, talking about "wykked wyves" from an old
Roman story and the Bible. He also owns books of anti-feminism such
as those by Valerius, Theophrastus, St. Jerome, Solomon and Ovid and
reads them night and day for pleasure (669–81). Different from the case
with the old husbands, Alison never argues the fifth husband into silence
by chiding and grouching. All she can do is to blame him, as a clerk,
from an astrological perspective:

> The children of Mercurie and of Venus
> Been in hir wirkyng ful contrarius;
> Mercurie loveth wysdam and science,
> And Venus loveth ryot and dispence.
> And, for hire diverse disposicioun,
> Ech falleth in otheres exaltacioun.
> ....
> Therfore no womman of no clerk is preysed.
> The clerk, whan he is oold, and may noght do
> Of Venus werkes worth his olde sho,
> Thanne sit he doun, and writ in his dotage
> That wommen kan nat kepe hir mariage!   (*WBP*, 697–710)

Her counterattack is less aggressive and energetic than before. This is
because she is aging. Even if she boasts of her youth and lecherousness,
she has to admit that she cannot stop the advancing years:

> But age, allas, that al wole envenyme,
> Hath me biraft my beautee and my pith.

Lat go. Farewel! The devel go therwith!
The flour is goon; ther is namoore to telle;
The bren, as I best kan, now moste I selle;
But yet to be right myrie wol I fonde.   (*WBP*, 474–79)

The Wife has become mature enough to evaluate herself, comparing past with present. She does not vent her anger without reason upon her husband. Otherwise, she has been patient in hearing many examples of "wykked wyves" and after all she seems to be half-resigned and complains: "For trusteth wel, it is an impossible / That any clerk wol speke good of wyves" (688–89) . . .

Who peyntede the leon, tel me who?
By God, if wommen hadde writen stories,
As clerkes han withinne hire oratories,
They wolde han writen of men moore wikkednesse
Than al the mark of Adam may redresse.   (*WBP*, 692–96)

This shows her small but significant resistance or Chaucer's challenge to the traditional patriarchal world. The books of "wikked wyves" are all written by males. Women have always been spoken ill of by men. They have been ruthlessly oppressed by patriarchal society. But if female authors had written stories, they would have written more and more stories than men did.

At the final battle of this couple, the frustration of the Wife explodes into a rage and causes violent behavior. Jankin reads the book aloud, as usual, by the fire. He starts with Eve, and continues with the tragedies of Samson, Hercules and Socrates, and the malicious queen of Crete,

92   Chapter III

Pasiphae and other shrewd women who put their husbands to death (715–70). Jankin defames women more than one can imagine and, furthermore, he knows numerous proverbs which insult women:

> He seyde, 'A womman cast hir shame away,
> Whan she cast of hir smok'; and forthermo,
> 'A fair womnan, but she be chaast also,
> Is lyk a gold ryng in a sowes nose.'
> Who wolde wene, or who wolde suppose,
> The wo that in myn herte was, and pyne?   (*WBP*, 782–87)

The last two lines are the Wife's outcry from the heart, a voiceless voice of women in general, and they are uttered by the poet.

Then the Wife suddenly plucks a few pages from his book and exchanges blows with her husband. Though one blow causes the loss of hearing in one ear, she achieves complete domination over his words and deeds and, as well, comes into possession of the house and land. The ideal husband for her is "meeke, yonge, and fressh abedde" (*WBT*, 1259). She has a contradictory wish, which is that she would like to control her husband during the daytime, while she wants to be dominated in bed at night. When Jankin hands over domination to her, her stubbornness turns into obedience and fidelity. The theme of the domination as between a husband and a wife is taken over in *WBT*.

III-4　The Sovereignty of Women in *The Wife of Bath's Tale*

The Wife's tale begins with a case of 'rape' by a young knight from King Arthur's court.

> And so bifel that this kyng Arthour
> Hadde in his hous a lusty bacheler,
> That on a day cam ridynge fro ryver,
> And happed that, allone as he was born,
> He saugh a mayde walkynge hym biforn,
> Of which mayde anon, *maugree hir heed,*
> *By verray force, he rafte hire maydenhed*;
>
> (*WBT*, 882–88, italics mine)

Chaucer does not use the word 'rape' but says "rafte hire maydenhed" (took her maidenhood). But it is "maugree hir heed" (against her will), "By verray force" (with the very force) that the young knight took her virginity. It is definitely a case of 'rape' in the modern sense.[18]

The source of this story is not exactly clear, but some relevant stories are known, such as *The Wedding of Sir Gawain and Dame Ragnell*, *The Marriage of Sir Gawain*. The Wedding is a prose romance. The Marriage is a short Ballad of 60 lines. In this story, it is King Arthur who takes up a challenge and an ugly old woman who divulges the right answer in exchange for marriage with Gawain. Similar stories can be found in the ballads and folklore of Scotland, Ireland and Iceland. These stories have a common motif of disenchantment: an ugly woman or monster turns into a peerless beauty after a spell or a curse is broken. None of them has 'rape' as a subject except *Sir Degare*. In this story a princess, lost in a

94   Chapter III

forest, is raped by a knight who comes from Fairy Land. It is not certain whether Chaucer used this story as a source. It is noticeable, however, that the plot in which a hero-knight wilfully commits a crime of rape, not by the power of magic, is original with Chaucer and the crime is deserving of capital punishment. (Saunders 2001b, 301–03)

The young knight is put on trial at the court and King Arthur himself sentences him to death. But the knight's life is saved by the long and earnest pleading of the queen and her ladies. His sentence is suspended until such time as he finds out the answer to the question which is posed for him by the queen:

> "Thou standest yet," quod she, "in swich array
> That of thy lyf yet hastow no suretee.
> I grante thee lyf, if thou kanst tellen me
> What thyng is it that wommen moost desiren.
> Be war, and keep thy nekke-boon from iren!
> And if thou kanst nat tellen it anon,
> Yet wol I yeve thee leve for to gon
> A twelf-month and a day, to seche and leere
> An answere suffisant in this mateere;   (*WBT*, 902–10)

After King Arthur agrees to turn over the knight's life into the queen's hands, the world is completely controlled by women. In public the queen holds sovereignty as a judge; in private the hag, who serves as the elf-queen, controls his fate.

King Arthur's queen is, naturally, Guinevere, although, her name is never mentioned in the story. Similarly, this knight, "lusty bachelor" is not identified with Sir Gawain. It would not be Chaucer's intention to give them the images and characteristics which are already widely known. They do not have to be Guinevere and Gawain; or rather they could be simply a lady who has sovereignty over him and a man who is subject to her. It matters more to the poet to build a female-dominant world.

After the knight has left the court, he begins to seek "every hous and every place" (919) for the answer. He merely finds out that no one has the same answer:

> Somme seyde wommen loven best richesse,
> Somme seyde honour, somme seyde jolynesse,
> Somme riche array, somme seyden lust abedde,
> And oftetyme to be wydwe and wedde.
> Somme seyde that oure hertes been moost esed
> Whan that we been yflatered and yplesed.   (*WBT*, 925–30)

The Wife, the narrator, has, unlike her prologue, rapidly developed her story; she interrupts at this point to give her opinion:

> He gooth ful ny the sothe, I wol nat lye.
> A man shal wynne us best with flaterye,
> And with attendance and with bisynesse
> Been we ylymed, bothe moore and lesse.
>   And somme seyen that we loven best
> For to be free and do right as us lest,
> And that no man repreve us of oure vice,
> But seye that we be wise and no thyng nyce.   (*WBT*, 931–38)

96   Chapter III

Being flattered, treated politely and being specially free to do anything she likes, not reproved but respected by men—all these are, in her prologue, what she has wished men to do and in fact she has hoped would happen, even though they are not perfectly ideal.

Chaucer here again does not forget to make her reveal women's fault: "Pardee, we wommen konne no thyng hele" (950). The Wife takes an example of King Midas and repeats once more: "Heere may ye se, thogh we a tyme abyde, / Yet out it moot; we kan no conseil hyde" (979–80).

When the young knight has realized that he could not find the right answer by the appointed day, he disappointedly decides to return. On his way back home, he happens to meet an ugly old woman who promises to teach him the answer. The knight is able to keep his promise with the queen and announce the answer to the question in front of all the women of the court, "With manly voys" (1036):

> "Wommen desiren to have sovereynetee
> As wel over hir housbond as hir love,
> And for to been in maistrie hym above.
> This is youre mooste desir, thogh ye me kille.
> Dooth as yow list; I am heer at youre wille."   (*WBT*, 1038–42)

They are all content with his answer and he saves his life with the help of the loathly lady. The rapist-knight who is a sinner and sentenced to death is twice saved by women, first by the queen and now by the hag. He must depend on women so much that he is helpless and becomes feminized like the heroine of a romance (Weisl 1995, 98).

When the ladies at court spare the knight's life, the old woman stands out and explains that she has taught him the answer and he has promised to fulfil her wish no matter what it is. After all, the knight is obliged to marry this loathly lady. He groans, anguishes and twists around when they get into the bridal bed, because she is old, ugly and of low birth. The old bride lying in the bed reproves his hesitation:

> . . . "O deere housbonde, benedictee!
> Fareth every knyght thus with his wyf as ye?
> Is this the lawe of kyng Arthures hous?
> Is every knyght of his so dangerous?
> I am youre owene love and youre wyf;
> I am she which that saved hath youre lyf,
> And, certes, yet ne dide I yow nevere unright;
> Why fare ye thus with me this firste nyght?   (*WBT*, 1087–94)

She urges him to consummate the marriage, which is very similar to the 'rape' of a male by a female in the female-dominant world. Yet the elderly woman tries to do so not by force, against his will, but by persuading him with a long sermon (1109–1216). This part is Chaucer's original addition.

The knight does not like to accept her because she is old, ugly and of low birth: "Thou art so loothly, and so oold also, / And therto comen of so lough a kynde" (1100–01). The old lady makes a long speech of over 70 lines and tries to make him understand that nobility has nothing to do with birth and ancestry but comes from God:

> For gentillesse nys but renomee
> Of thyne auncestres, for hire heigh bountee,
> Which is a strange thyng to thy persone.

98   Chapter III

> Thy gentillesse cometh fro God allone.
>
> Thanne comth oure verray gentillesse of grace;
>
> It was no thyng biquethe us with oure place.   (*WBT*, 1159–64)

To support the idea, she juxtaposes the authority's names, such as Dante, Valerius, Boethius and Seneca. The doctrine that gentility depends on character, not inheritance, is the commonly received opinion. Yet the hag's sermon on "gentillesse" is found only in Chaucer's version (Benson 1987, 873).

Then she mentions that poverty, a way of life Jesus Christ had chosen, contains a pathway to truth: "Poverte a spectacle is, as thynketh me, Thurgh which he may his verray freendes see" (1203–04). Finally concerning her age and ugliness, she asserts that he does not have to worry about being a cuckold because "filthe and eelde" must be guardians of chastity (1214–16). This is the old lady who is a woman of eloquence. Apart from a young maid who has been raped and then disappeared and a queen who has no face, the hag has a really strong presence with overwhelming dominance over the feminized hero.

The loathly lady seems to be successful in persuading the knight, yet she gives him an alternative question which he must answer in order to fulfill his worldly desire:

> "Chese now," quod she, "oon of thise thynges tweye:
>
> To han me foul and old til that I deye,
>
> And be to yow a trewe, humble wyf,
>
> And nevere yow displese in al my lyf,
>
> Or elles ye wol han me yong and fair,
>
> And take youre aventure of the repair

That shal be to youre hous by cause of me,
Or in som oother place, may wel be.   (*WBT*, 1219–26)

The choice offered to the hero, a wife ugly but faithful, or fair and possibly unfaithful, is Chaucer's original variation. In the usual version, a wife is fair by night and foul by day, or vice versa (Benson 1987, 873).

Faced with the ultimate choice, the knight thinks and sighs deeply, but cannot make a final decision and so leaves the matter entirely to his ugly wife:

"My lady ad my love, and wyf so deere,
I put me in youre wise governance;
Cheseth yourself which may be moost plesance
And moost honour to yow and me also.
I do no fors the wheither of the two,
For as yow liketh, it suffiseth me."   (*WBT*, 1230–35)

With his words the wife gets "maistrie" over her husband and she actually becomes most pleasant and honorable to him, that is, a wife both fair and faithful.

The metamorphosis of the loathly lady into a beautiful young wife is connected to the Wife of Bath's change from a "wykked wyfe" to a kind and true wife. This is a happy ending for the husband in every respect. Lee Patterson (1983) wisely notes:

The Tale tells us, first, that the husband who abandons maistrye will receive in return a wife who will fulfill his every wish, and second, that what women most desire is to be just this sort of

100   Chapter III

obedient wife. The feminine desire that is anatomized by a desire that is not only masculine but is beyond scrutiny. The Wife's 'queynte fantsye,' in short, is a masculine wish-fulfillment, and one in which she appears to be fully complicit.   (682–83)

With the disenchantment of the loathly lady, the female-dominant fantasy constituted by Alison has returned to the world of Arthurian romance, where a male-dominant society is restored and where there is no place for an old, ugly and smart heroine to live (Weisl 1995, 98).

Chapter IV

Criseyde's Eloquence

Chaucer creates his Criseyde as an attractive and beautiful widow and describes her with special adoration as if he is fascinated by her.[19] Yet she is very self-conscious of her beauty, reputation and her helpless situation in Troy. Although she appears humble, modest and fearful, she is by no means a weak and fragile woman and although her age is not discussed, she seems to be neither frivolous nor immature. She is self-possessed and knows how to behave properly and choose the best solution in order to survive.

She faces the serious dimensions of decision-making three times in the course of the story. The first is when she accepts Troilus' offer through Pandarus, and decides to go with him. The next is when she has to leave Troy to go to the Greeks for the exchange of Antenor, she persuades Troilus who wants to run away with her. The last is when she gives up returning to Troilus and decides to stay with Diomede and betrays Troilus after all. In each case, Criseyde makes eloquent speeches and tries to persuade Troilus or Pandarus, or even herself, and makes compromises in order to accept the reality that she confronts.

[101]

IV-1 Falling in Love with Troilus

As the heroine of the tragedy, Chaucer's Criseyde is placed in unfortunate circumstances. She has no husband to protect her. Her father predicts the fate of Troy and flees to the Greeks. As a daughter of the betrayer, she feels inhibited in living in Troy. Her uncle, Pandarus, seems to be the only relative to support her in Troy. He is fully aware that Criseyde is in a predicament and that it becomes extremely difficult to carry out his mission as a go-between. So when he comes to visit his niece on an important errand as a go-between, he demonstrates skillful a strategy in arousing her interest. He informs Criseyde that he brings wonderful news. She shows great interest in knowing what it is. Yet he does not easily let her know and cunningly changes the subject, keeping her in suspense. He intentionally avoids the point of his talk and has a chat with her about ordinary things. Then he pretends to leave without telling her the crucial point of his speech in order to make her urge him to tell. He knows that if he straightforwardly informs her of Troilus' love for her that she may harden her heart against him and turn a deaf ear to him. Pandarus is successful in preparing an advantageous occasion for making a confession to Criseyde on behalf of Troilus; for Criseyde is extremely eager to listen to his story:

> "Now, good em, for Goddes love, I preye,"
> Quod she, "come of, and telle me what it is!
> For both I am agast what ye wol seye,
> And ek me longeth it to wite, ywys;
> For whethir it be wel or be amys,
> Say on, lat me nat in this feere dwelle."

"So wol I doon; now herkeneth! I shal telle:

"Now, nece myn, the kynges deere sone,
The goode, wise, worthi, fresshe, and free,
Which alwey for to don wel is his wone,
The noble Troilus, so loveth the,
That, but ye helpe, it wol his bane be.
Lo, here is al! What sholde I moore seye?
Doth what yow lest to make hym lyve or deye. (*TC* II, 309–322)

Criseyde begs Pandarus to tell her his secret. Then he simply and clearly states that the noble prince Troilus loves her very much, and that without her help he is suffering life-threating distress and death. Pandarus' persuasive confession occupies the following nine stanzas, spending sixty three lines (323–85) without pausing. In his speech, he emphasizes the virtues and worthiness of Troilus, who wishes nothing but her "friendly cheere" (332) or "bettre chiere" (360). He warns her that if she should drive him to death, her beauty would prove cruel and merciless. He also understands that she worries about what other people would think of her if they see Troilus come and go. Yet Pandarus tries to remove all her anxieties with words: "every wight, but he be fool of kynde, / Wol dome it love of frendshipe in his mynde" (370–71). This is only a convenient excuse for him. What Pandarus emphasizes is that she should sweeten her standoffish attitude, "daunger" (384), and try to be nice and friendly to Troilus in order to please him and save his life.

After Criseyde listens to him, she is wisely aware of his roundabout way of speaking and asks what he really means and what he actually wants her to do. Criseyde cleverly and easily makes her uncle reveal

104   Chapter IV

his true intention. Pandarus does not really want her to be friendly and amiable to Troilus, but he wishes that she would accept his love and love him in return (390–92). With his words, Criseyde bursts into tears, curses her fortune, and condemns Pandarus who should have been the last person to ask of her such a favor:

> And she began to breste a-wepe anoon,
> And seyde, "Allas, for wo! Why nere I deed?
> For of this world the feyth is al agoon.
> Allas, what sholden straunge to me doon,
> Whan he that for my beste frend I wende
> Ret me to love, and sholde it me defende?
>
> "Allas! I wolde han trusted, douteles,
> That if that I, thorugh my dysaventure,
> Hadde loved outher hym or Achilles,
> Ector, or any mannes creature,
> Ye nolde han had no mercy ne mesure
> On me, but alwey had me in repreve.
> This false world—allas!—who may it leve?
>
> "What, is this al the joye and al the feste?
> Is this youre reed? Is this my blissful cas?
> Is this the verray mede of youre byheeste?
> Is al this paynted proces seyd—allas!—
> Right for this fyn? O lady myn, Pallas!
> Thow in this dredful cas for me purveye,
> For so astoned am I that I deye."   (*TC* II, 408–27)

What she declares is right: as a widow, and as the daughter of a betrayer, she wishes to live safely, humbly and quietly in Troy and she understands her position and knows how to behave herself very well. She expects Pandarus to be the protector and guardian who should supervise her behavior from a moral point of view. She never imagines that he would propose that she should love a Trojan prince. Criseyde keenly sees through his scheme which is presented in a decorous and superficially plausible discourse, "paynted proces seyd" (424). It is quite natural for her to blame him for that.

Without yielding to her conviction, Pandarus has another go at her. He cunningly threatens her by claiming that her rejection of Troilus will mean their death (429–46). Pandarus partially out of despair exaggerates the issue as a matter of life or death even of Troilus and himself. His inflated language sounds rather comical; nevertheless, Criseyde is "the ferfulleste wight" (450) so that she takes his words as they are and thinks that they might really kill themselves. His threat after all gives Criseyde second thoughts and leads her to change her mind:

> And thought thus: "Unhappes fallen thikke
> Alday for love, and in swych manere cas
> As men ben cruel in hemself and wikke;
> And if this man sle here himself—allas!—
> In my presence, it wol be no solas.
> What men wolde of hit deme I kan nat seye;
> It nedeth me ful sleighly for to pleie."　　　(*TC* II, 456–62)

She mostly fears that if Pandarus should kill himself in front of her, she would not know how to deal with the world. What she fears is whether

106   Chapter IV

she can keep her honor and appearance in fact; that is, what other people would think of her. She knows that she should behave cautiously in facing this jeopardy and then she proposes a solution to Pandarus:

> And with a sorrowful sik she sayde thrie,
> "A, Lord! What me is tid a sory chaunce!
> For myn estat lith in a jupartie,
> And ek myn emes lif is in balaunce;
> But natheles, with Goddes governaunce,
> I shal so doon, myn honour shal I kepe,
> And ek his lif"—and stynte for to wepe.   (*TC* II, 463–69)

Her first concern is to preserve her own honor rather than save the life of Pandarus and Troilus. Thus she decides to choose the less misfortunate of the two; that is, "have I levere maken hym good chere / In honour, than myn emes lyf to lese" (471–72). As long as she can protect her honor, trying to be amiable to Troilus is a lesser misfortune than losing her uncle. This is basically her point of view in making the better choice of the two harms. She is learning how to get on in life, bearing hardship.

Criseyde mentions that although she cannot love any man against her will and does not know how to love him, she tries to find a different way to please Troilus and still keep her honor. She compromises in accepting Pandarus' offer and treating Troilus amiably. In the end, however, in a sharp tone of voice, she warns her uncle that if he steps any further into this matter, she will be of no help to anyone:

> "And here I make a protestacioun
> That in this proces if ye depper go,

That certeynly, for no salvacioun
Of yow, though that ye sterven bothe two,
Though al the world on o day be my fo,
Ne shal I nevere of hym han other routhe." *(TC* II, 484–89)

What she promises to Pandarus here is that she will be friendly with Troilus and try to please him with an amiable face and maintain her honor. But if Pandarus should demand of her a closer relationship with Troilus, she would never be their salvation and never have pity on them whether they are dead or alive. Despite her concern, this warning has no effect on Pandarus. There is no need for Pandarus to take further steps because she falls in love with Troilus.

The process of her loving of Troilus is worth discussing. There are two important scenes concerned the matter: first, Criseyde sees Troilus return in triumph from battle and pass by her house; second, she soliloquizes at length after she sees him in order to make a compromise with herself about accepting Troilus' love.

After Pandarus takes his leave, Criseyde retreats to her bedroom, and sits down and, as still as stone, recalls every word of Pandarus. Then she sees Troilus himself ride and pass by under her window (610–86). He returns from the battle field after fierce fighting with the Greeks: his horse is wounded, his helm is chopped up in twenty places, and his shield has been bashed by numerous swords. His richly clad appearance and his prowess as a man of arms are highly praised (628–37). Troilus is so young, fresh, strong and brave that he comes off as a perfect knight. The townspeople in Troy hail him with applause: "Here cometh oure joye, / And, next his brother, holder up of Troye!" (643–44). When he hears the people cry for him, he blushes for shame and modestly casts down his

108   Chapter IV

eyes. Criseyde steals a glance at him and feels good will towards him:

> Criseÿda gan al his chere aspien,
> And leet it so softe in hire herte synke,
> That to hireself she seyde, "Who yaf me drynke?"
>
> For of hire owen thought she wex al reed,
> Remembryng hire right thus, "Lo, this is he
> Which that myn uncle swerith he moot be deed,
> But I on hym have mercy and pitee."
> And with that thought, for pure ashamed, she
> Gan in hire hed to pulle, and that as faste,
> Whil he and alle the peple forby paste,
>
> And gan to caste and rollen up and down
> Withinne hire thought his excellent prowesse,
> And his estat, and also his renown,
> His wit, his shap, and ek his gentilesse;
> But moost hire favour was, for his distresse
> Was al for hire, and thoughte it was a routhe
> To sleen swich oon, if that he mente trouthe.   (*TC* II, 649–65)

Looking at Troilus, who fought bravely on the battlefield and never boasts of his achievement but is self-effacing at the praise he receives, and upon listening to the people's praise of his courage, Criseyde falls in love with him. Even if she is not deeply in love at this moment, she has begun to favor him. That is why she asks herself, "Who yaf me drynke?" She becomes red in the face to remember her uncle telling her that he will die if she has no mercy and pity on him. Former editors such as Skeat and Robinson, in annotating, state that Criseyde refers to a love-potion as used in the story of Tristan and Isolde. Yet recent scholors take "drynk" more simply and clearly as any intoxicating beverage, that is to say, alcoholic drinks.[20] Amorous engagements are often accompanied by the imbibing of liquor which excites and enflames.

C. David Benson (1990, 134) compares how these two lovers fall in love and declares that in contrast to "the passion of Troilus, which we are allowed to see clearly, Criseyde's falling in love is deliberately kept hidden from the reader." He constantly observes that just how much Criseyde surrenders to love is not certain and that Chaucer's characterization of Criseyde is so opaque that readers are distanced from her heart and mind while she is falling in love with Troilus. It is true that Troilus is very passionate at being in love, while Criseyde is more passive and more careful than Troilus. But it is a matter of course because the process and motivation of their falling in love are different one from another. In the scene where Troilus sees Criseyde for the first time in the temple of Pallace, his eyes are glued on her: "His eye percede, and so depe it wente, / Til on Criseyde it smot, and ther it stente" (*TC* I, 272–73) and then his passion starts overflowing:

And of hire look in him ther gan to quyken
So gret desir and such affeccioun,
That in his herte botme gan to stiken
Of hir his fixe and depe impressioun.
And though he erst hadde poured up and down,
He was tho glad his hornes in to shrinke:
Unnethes wiste he how to loke or wynke.

110   Chapter IV

> Lo, he that leet hymselven so konnynge,
>
> And scorned hem that Loves peynes dryen,
>
> Was ful unwar that Love hadde his dwellynge
>
> Withinne the subtile stremes of hire yen;
>
> That sodeynly hym thoughte he felte dyen,
>
> Right with hire look, the spirit in his herte:
>
> Blissed be Love, that kan thus folk converte!   (*TC* I, 295–308)

Troilus is very enthusiastic and emotional when he falls in love at first sight. This is because he was stuck by an arrow of the God of love. Troilus scorns people who are in love and calls them fools. His arrogant attitude towards love invites the God of Love's anger, who shoots an arrow at Troilus. This is why Troilus is passionate in love and expresses his feelings openly.

Criseyde, on the other hand, thinks that she should behave cautiously and lead an inconspicuous life in acceptance of her situation. As C. David Benson declares, Chaucer deliberately keeps Criseyde's falling in love hidden. It is clearly his intention to create Criseyde as humble, modest, and passive in love. When she sees Troilus, a valiant figure, passing bravely by the window of her house, she is deeply stirred by him. Her words, "Who yaf me drynke?" (651) testifies to the moment when she is motivated to be in love with Troilus or at least she feels affetion for him. She thinks over his excellent prowess, his status, his renown, his intelligence, his appearance, and his nobility and, the most of all, she feels favorably toward him (659–63).

She is scrupulously supported by the narrator, who excuses her love of Troilus:

For I sey nought that she so sodeynly
Yaf hym hire love, but that she gan enclyne
To like hym first, and I have told yow whi;
And after that, his manhod and his pyne
Made love withinne hire for to myne,
For which by proces and by good servyse
He gat hire love, and in no sodeyn wyse.   (*TC* II, 673–79)

The narrator tries to protect his heroine from being blamed by some envious people, who criticize her for flippantly falling in love with Troilus at first sight. Instead of making Criseyde less passionate and less emotional than Troilus, Chaucer sometimes has the narrator appear and advocate for his heroine and also gives her a long monologue, which exposes her thoughts and her character.

Criseyde, sitting alone in her room, thinks over what the best way for her to do is and what she should most avoid. She seems somewhat upset and a little confused: "Now was hire herte warm, now was it cold" (698). Yet, it is not because she loses control of herself due to love of Troilus. She calculates the advantages and disadvantages of being loved by a son of the Trojan king:

She thoughte wel that Troilus persone
She knew by syghte, and ek his gentilesse,
And thus she seyde, "Al were it nat to doone
To graunte hym love, yet for his worthynesse
It were honour with pley and with gladnesse
In honestee with swich a lord to deele,
For myn estat, and also for his heele.

112   Chapter IV

> "Ek wel woot I my kynges sone is he,
> And sith he hath to se me swich delit,
> If I wolde outreliche his sighte flee,
> Peraunter he myghte have me in dispit,
> Thorugh whicch I myghte stonde in worse plit.
> Now were I wis, me hate to purchace,
> Withouten need, ther I may stonde in grace?   (*TC* II, 701–14)

Criseyde first proclaims that she ought not to accept his love and next considers that it is honorable for her to keep a friendly relationship with the king's son. If she invited his displeasure, she would possibly put herself in a worse condition. She realizes that it is not wise of her to make him angry. Her calculation is fundamentally based on self-interest. She knows what is beneficial to herself. She counts up the prince's virtues: he is a moral man, neither boastful nor foolish so that he never commits evil acts (722–25). What is disadvantageous to her is other people's eyes and the general risk of a love-affair (729–35). Criseyde worries about what people would think to know that Troilus loves her, not that she loves him. She considers that it would be dishonorable if that fact were disclosed. She also fears that men love women one-sidedly without their leave and once they lose interest in their love, women are deserted. Later, in her monologue, she repeats the same concern:

> "Also thise wikked tonges ben so prest
> To speke us harm; ek men ben so untrewe,
> That right anon as cessed is hire lest,
> So cesseth love, and forth to love a newe.
> But harm ydoon is doon, whoso it rewe:

For though thise men for love hem first torende,
Ful sharp bygynnyng breketh ofte at ende.

"How ofte tyme hath it yknowen be
The tresoun that to wommen hath ben do!
To what fyn is swich love I kan nat see,
Or wher bycometh it, whan that it is ago.   (*TC* II, 785–95)

She worries about what other people would think and say about her and also she is concerned that men tend to change their minds and find a new love and easily betray women. Here she feels uneasy and hesitates to step any further in accepting his love. Since her treachery is commonly known, her anxiety has ironical effects. Chaucer places these passages strategically to explain her hesitation here and to foretell her betrayal ironically in future.

Next Criseyde exposes her self-consciousness about her beauty. She thinks that the honor of having been chosen over all other women in Troy, is well-deserved:

"I thenke ek how he able is for to have
Of al this noble town the thriftieste
To ben his love, so she hire honour save.
For out and out he is the worthieste,
Save only Ector, which that is the beste;
And yet his lif al lith now in my cure.
But swich is love, and ek myn aventure.

"Ne me to love, a wonder is it nought;

114   Chapter IV

> For wel woot I myself, so God me spede—
> Al wolde I that noon wiste of this thought—
> I am oon the faireste, out of drede,
> And goodlieste, who that taketh hede,
> And so men seyn, in al the town of Troie.
> What wonder is though he of me have joye?   (*TC* II, 736–49)

She admits that Troilus is the worthiest warrior, second only to his brother, Hector, and that he has the privilege of having a lover who is the most attractive lady in this town. She does not feel bad that she is loved by him and that his life is in her own hands. She is convinced that she is the most beautiful lady in Troy and it is natural of Troilus to fall in love with her. This part is a good example of her self-confidence and self-consciousness. Chaucer describes his heroine as not only a humble, modest and self-effacing lady, but also as an independent, thoughtful, and self-possessed woman. She knows that she has the freedom to do what she likes regarding love:

> "I am myn owene womman, wel at ese—
> I thank it God—as after myn estat,
> Right yong, as stonde unteyd in lusty leese,
> Withouten jalousie or swich debat:
> Shal noon housbonde seyn to me 'Chek mat!'
> For either they ben ful of jalousie,
> Or maisterful, or loven novelrie.
>
> "What shal I doon? To what fyn lyve I thus?
> Shal I nat love, in cas if that me leste?

What, pardieux! I am naught religious.
And though that I myn herte sette at reste
Upon this knyght, that is the worthieste,
And kepe alwey myn honour and my name,
By alle right, it may do me no shame."   (*TC* II, 750–63)

She tries to persuade herself that she is free to be in love. There is
no jealous husband who exercises mastery over her. She asks herself
whether she should be in love if she wishes to be. Her answer is
affirmative, because she is not a nun. Then she reaches the conclusion
that it is not shameful for her to uphold her honor and good name, if she
feels favorably toward him.

Nevertheless, her mind is not settled but is unstable, like changeable
March weather (765). As dark clouds form and cover the brightly shining
sun, negative thoughts flow out and discourage positive feelings about
freedom to love and be loved:

That thought was this: "Allas! Syn I am free,
Sholde I now love, and put in jupartie
My sikernesse, and thrallen libertee?
Allas, how dorst I thenken that folie?
May I naught wel in other folk aspie
Hire dredfull joye, hire constreinte, and hire peyne?
Ther loveth noon, that she nath why to pleyne.

"For love is yet the mooste stormy lyf,
Right of hymself, that evere was bigonne;
For evere som mystrust or nice strif

116   Chapter IV

> Ther is in love, som cloude is over that sonne.
> Therto we wrecched wommen nothing konne,
> Whan us is wo, but wepe and sitte and thinke;
> Oure wrecche is this, oure owen wo to drynke.   (*TC* II, 771–84)

She hesitates as to whether she should expose her liberty to danger by falling in love with Troilus. She considers it a foolish act to fall in love because she knows that women are troubled by qualified joy, pain and woe. Love makes one's life stormy and produces feelings of mistrust and "nice," foolish conflict. This negative concept of love is developed in *RR*:

> This is the yvell that love they call,
> Wherynne ther is but foly al,
> For love is foly everydell.
> Who loveth in no wise may do well,
> Ne sette his thought on no good werk.
> His scole he lesith, if he be a clerk.
> Of other craft eke if he be,
> He shal not thryve therynne, for he
> In love shal have more passioun
> Than monk, hermyte, or chanoun.
> The peyne is hard, out [of] mesure;
> The joye may eke no while endure;
> And in the possessioun
> Is myche tribulacioun
> The joye it is so short lastyng,
> And but in hap is the getyng;

For I see there many in travaille,
That atte laste foule fayle.
I was nothyng thi counseler,
Whanne thou were maad the omager
Of God of Love to hastily;
Ther was no wisdom, but foly.
Thyn herte was joly but not sage,
Whanne thou were brought in sich a rage
To yelde thee so redily,
And to leve of is gret maistry.   (*RR*, 3269–94)

This is a speech of Lady Reason who advises the lover to avoid the God of Love. Here love is clearly defined as folly. Those who are in love are not wise and cannot be guided to right thinking. Because they are hindered in their work by love, scholars forget studying, for instance. Loving someone causes more severe suffering than clerics endure. Joyful moments do not last for long. Lady Reason knows that many people sacrifice their lives to love. She complains that the lover hastily devotes himself to the God of Love and she is sorry not to give him her advice not to be a servant of the God of Love. Lady Reason works to restrain people from falling in love.

Chaucer gives common characteristics and features to both Criseyde and Lady Reason. Both of them have the perfect beauty of celestial beings. They are not too tall, not too short, and neither too young, nor too old. They are similar to the idealized heroines of courtly romance, who are mostly involved with love-affairs. Chaucer also builds up Criseyde's character by presenting Lady Reason as one who opposes being in love. The contradictory concept of worshiping and despising

118   Chapter IV

love and the God of Love at the same time renders Criseyde a more complicated character. Her being of two minds as to whether she should be in love or not is founded on the love debate expanded in *RR*. Different from Lady Reason, Criseyde does not conlude her thought in a negative way. She realizes that she has freedom to fall in love and at the same time she wishes to preserve her liberty of independence without being involved with love. Coming and going between these two thoughts: hope and dread, Criseyde finally tries to make up her mind: "He which that nothing undertaketh, / Nothyng n'acheveth, be hym looth or deere" (807–08). Her decision reduces to, "Nothing ventured, nothing gained." After all, she does not take the position of rejecting the God of Love, because Troilus has already slipped into her heart: "The die is cast!"

When Pandarus returns to Troilus, he tells him that he had won "Hire love of frendshipe" (962), and that Troilus should write her a letter. He schemes to make them meet accidentally. Pandarus visits his niece to hand her Troilus' letter and tells her to reply to him. At that time Troilus riding by and passes by her house with nodding in greeting Pandarus:

> And right as they declamed this matere,
> Lo, Troilus, right at the stretes ende,
> Come rydyng with his tenthe som yfere,
> Al softely, and thiderward gan bende
> Ther as they sete, as was his way to wende
> To paleis-ward; and Pandare hym aspide,
> And seyde, "Nece, ysee who comth here ride!
>
> "O fle naught in (he seeth us, I suppose),
> Lest he may thynken that ye hym eschuwe."

> "Nay, nay," quod she, and wex as red as rose.
> With that he gan hire humbly to saluwe
> With dredful chere, and oft his hewes muwe;
> And up his look debonairly he caste,
> And bekked on Pandare, and forth he paste.   (*TC* II, 1247–60)

This is the second time for Troilus to pass nearby Criseyde's residence. Yet this is the first time for them to recognize each other with humble, innocent, and shy looks. Their reactions toward each other seem to be pure and simple: Criseyde becomes red as a rose, while Troilus' timidity changes the color of his face. Then she is clearly aware of her feelings toward him:

> God woot if he sat on his hors aright,
> Or goodly was biseyn, that ilke day!
> Good woot wher he was lik a manly knyght!
> What sholde I drecche, or telle of his aray?
> Criseyde, which that alle thise thynges say,
> To telle in short, hire liked al in-fere,
> His person, his aray, his look, his chere,
>
> His goodly manere, and his gentilesse,
> So wel that nevere, sith that she was born,
> Ne hadde she swych routh of his destresse;
> And how so she hath hard ben here-byforn,
> To God hope I, she hath now kaught a thorn,
> She shal nat pulle it out this nexte wyke.
> God sende mo swich thornes on to pike!   (*TC* II, 1261–74)

120   Chapter IV

In the last scene when Criseyde sees him, she feels attracted by his excellent prowess, his status, his renown, his wit, his physique, his nobility and, above all, she feels pity for the distress she has caused him (660–64). Here, she likes his person, his clothing, his expression, his behavior, and his nobility. Moreover, she has never felt such pity for his distress. Chaucer repeats the same pattern of movement in Criseyde. At first, she only feels somewhat attracted; then she moves towards "liking" him. In addition, she has been pricked by a thorn which she cannot pull out. It means that her feeling for Troilus has struck deeply into her heart; that is to say, she has already fallen in love with him.

IV-2 Leaving Troilus

Troilus and Criseyde overcome some difficulties, achieve true love and share great pleasure and happy moments with each other. Yet, as Lady Reason declares and Criseyde has previously warned herself, the joy of love does not last for long. The fated moment of their parting awaits them. The Greeks demand that the Trojans offer Criseyde in exchange for Antenor, the Trojan warrior who is taken prisoner by the Greeks. Chaucer describes how the details of the terms of exchange for the release of the hostage are brought up and resolved by the Greeks and how the offer is treated in Troy.

One day, the Trojan prince, Hector, leading many a brave warrior to battle, fights gallantly against their enemies, and yet they take the wrong strategy in the final attack and are disastrously defeated. As a result, Antenor is captured, which makes the Trojans fear they will lose a great part of their joy on that day: "So that, for harm, that day the folk of Troie/ Dredden to lese a gret part of hire joie" (*TC* IV, 55–56). At the request of the Greeks, the Trojan king, Priam, sues for a truce and they start to negotiate on a prisoner exchange.

When Calkas learns of the treaty, he butts into the council and appeals desperately the return of his daughter from Troy (71–119). Calkas dares to address the council and tell the people present at the meeting his purpose for fleeing Troy. He had taught them what the Greeks did when they destroyed Troy and burned the city down. Because he ran away with nothing but the clothes he was wearing, he had left all his property and fortune in Troy. He is willing to give up his money and land, but he feels deep regret about leaving his daughter behind. He wants to rescue his daughter from Troy by all means and humbly beseeches them to exchange her with one of the Trojan prisoners. By his long and pitiful pleading, his request is granted at last.

When the special messenger from the Greeks comes to Troy in order to present the Greek demand, Priam summons the parliament to discuss the matter. Hector strongly objects to the Greeks' request, but the majority of the parliament bitterly disagree with him and sharply rebuke him:

> The noyse of peple up stirte thanne at ones,
> As breme as blase of strawe iset on-fire;
> For infortune it wolde, for the nones,
> They sholden hire confusioun desire.
> "Ector," quod they, "what goost may yow enspyre
> This womman thus to shilde and don us leese
> Daun Antenor—a wrong wey now yow chese—

122   Chapter IV

"That is so wys and ek so bold baroun?
And we han nede to folk, as men may se.
He is ek oon the grettest of this town.
O Ector, lat tho fantasies be!
O kyng Priam," quod they, "thus sygge we,
That al oure vois is to forgon Criseyde."
And to deliveren Antenor they preyde.   (*TC* IV, 183–96)

People claim with one accord that they should recover Antenor and give up Criseyde instead. Some scholars indicate that "the noyse of peple" alludes to the Peasant Revolt of 1381 and that the phrase "blaste of straw" implies Jack Straw who is one of the three leaders together with Wat Tyler and John Ball (Benson 1987, 1045). Here, however, people are just found to be wrong in their wish to release Antenor for Criseyde who is no harm to them, because it is Antenor himself who is later called a betrayer and who causes the destruction of Troy after all (197–210). Those who make noise and insist on releasing Antenor are blamed for their shallow thinking. They do not know what the best way for Troy is. The reason why Antenor is called a betrayer is that he contrives to remove an image of the goddess Pallas (Athena), on which the safety of Troy was believed to depend, which causes its destruction.

Those scenes discussing the exchange of Antenor for Criseyde on both the Greek and the Trojan sides are not completely Chaucer's original idea. He just follows his precursors, mostly Boccaccio and others such as Benoît and Guido, in the details. The descriptions of this political strategy by each party prove successful in giving the story the tense atmosphere of war. Troilus and Criseyde are engaged in an overwhelming reality and an inevitable fate.

When Criseyde is informed of the news, she abandons herself to grief and bursts into a flood of tears. She feels herself fall from heaven into hell because she loses sight of Troilus: "Rememberyng hir, fro heven into which helle / She fallen was, syn she forgoth the syghte / Of Troilus" (712–14). She rends her rich and wavy golden hair with her long and fine fingers and begs God for mercy (735–39). How her appearance changes is often mentioned. Her complexion, once so bright, is now pale, bearing witness to her woe and distress (740–41); her face with a heavenly image is changed completely (864–65); two purple rings encircle her eyes as a symbol of her pain (869–70). The reason for her extreme grief lies in her deepest love connection with Troilus (673–79). Different from her detached feeling before falling in love with Troilus, Criseyde's heart and mind are united so closely with him that nothing in the world could possibly separate them. She is very passionate and highly emotional in expressing her love for Troilus. Now she declares that she cannot live without him:

> To what fyn sholde I lyve and sorwen thus?
> How sholde a fissh withouten water dure?
> What is Criseyde worth, from Troilus?
> How sholde a plaunte or lyves creature
> Lyve withouten his kynde noriture?
> For which ful ofte a by-word here I seye,
> That 'rooteles moot grene soone deye.'   (*TC* IV, 764–70)

As a fish cannot live without water, plants and animals cannot live unless they have nourishment, and a tree with green leaves dies soon if there is no root on which it depends, Criseyde dares to say that life is not worth

124   Chapter IV

living if she should stay apart from Troilus. Both Troilus and Criseyde
are so deeply in love and so strongly connected with each other that
when they share the information of the exchanging of hostages, they are
just lost for words and lost in bitter tears (1128–41).

Their grief is so great that they cannot exchange greetings but
embrace and kiss in a flood of tears. They completely share their sorrow
and distress. They writhe with pain and give out deep sighs of grief as
typical lovers of romance do. Then Criseyde is overcome with emotion
after a long lamentation and she loses her senses in a scream as if she
were dead (1149–55). This is not just a swoon, but she is in a temporary
state of apparent death: "she lay as for ded— / Without answere, and
felte hire lymes colde" (1157–58). She has no sign of life: "For signe of
lif, for aught he kan or may, / Kan he non fynde in nothyng on Criseyde"
(1164–65). She stops breathing so that Troilus comes to think that she has
gone out of this world (1177–80). Convinced of her death, he decides
to follow his love and unsheathes his sword. When he is about to kill
himself, Criseyde comes to herself. After she revives, she is not like
what she used to be; it is as if she is a different woman. For she becomes
sensible and is resolved to effect a breakthrough in the crisis, uttering
this eloquent speech:

> "Lo, herte myn, wel woot ye this," quod she,
> "That if a wight alwey his wo compleyne
> And seketh nougt how holpen for to be,
> It nys but folie and encrees of peyne;
> And syn that here assembled be we tweyne
> To fynde boote of wo that we ben inne,
> It were al tyme soone to bygynne.

"I am a womman, as ful wel ye woot,
And as I am avysed sodeynly,
So wol I telle yow, whil it is hoot.
Me thynketh thus: that nouther ye nor I
Ought half this wo to maken, skillfully;
For ther is art ynough for to redresse
That yet is mys, and slen this hevynesse.

"Soth is, the wo, the which that we ben inne,
For aught I woot, for nothyng ellis is
But for the cause that we sholden twynne.
Considered al, ther nys namore amys.
But what is thanne a remede unto this,
But that we shape us soone for to meete?
This al and som, my deere herte sweete.   (*TC* IV, 1254–74)

First, Criseyde suggests to Troilus that it is not wise of them to do nothing but complain about their misfortune instead of searching for a way out. Giving notice that although she is only a woman, she simply decides to survive. Before swooning, she was so bewildered and confused that she did not know at all what she should do. Now she knows clearly what the best way for them to do is. She analyzes the reason for their sorrow. The most serious problem they have is that they must be separated. A solution to the problem is simply for them to meet again. She will go over to the Greeks and come back within one or two weeks.

She well knows that the decision for her going enacted by the parliament will possibly never be overturned. She is obliged to leave Troy, yet she intends to return soon. Then she tries to explain her happy plan:

126   Chapter IV

(1) Criseyde mentions the distance between Troy and the Greek camp. It is no more than a few hours riding, which renders their sorrow the less. (2) She presumes that she will not be imprisoned and that he will hear from her everyday. (3) Before the truce is ended, she will return within ten days, so that they can live happily together she dares to declare. Her scheme does not have a solid footing supported by hard facts, but is only wishful thinking. She cannot even imagine what will happen to her in fact on the Greek side. At this point, it does not really matter to her, because since the resolution of the parliament is absolute, she cannot resist their decision. She continues to tell him in a cautioning tone:

> "I se that oft-tyme, there as we ben now,
> That for the beste, oure counseyl for to hide,
> Ye speke nat with me, nor I with yow
> In foutenyght, ne se yow go ne ride.
> May ye naught ten dayes thanne abide,
> For myn honour, in swich an aventure?
> Iwys, ye mowen ellis lite endure!   (*TC* IV, 1324–30)

She thinks that keeping the relationship with Troilus secret is the best way for them to uphold her good name, She advises him gently to be patient whether fourteen nights or ten days, both being the same to her, inasmuch as she cannot predict what will happen.

Next, she tells him how to catch her father without a net, that is to say, to persuade him to let her return to Troy again. She knows that she is making a rash decision, that her father is so old that he must be as fully greedy as the elders are. Her scheme is to take advantage of his greed for money; she takes some of her personal property with her and showing it to him she falsely explains that this has been sent from his friend in Troy, and he wants to send more. While the city is in danger under the siege by the Greeks, she is appointed to deliver a large amount of property secretly and safely. Moreover, she intends to stimulate his avarice with her sweet speech (1394–1400). She is fully confident that she can persuade her father who is blinded by his love of money just as she wishes. If she should fail in converting her father's mind inside a few days, she swears she will kill herself: "but I make hym soone to converte/ And don my red withinne a day or tweye, / I wol to yow oblige me to deye" (1412–14). What is wrong with her, however, is that she does not consider the true reason why her father abandoned his country and his daughter, giving up all of his properties. It would be entirely impossible for her to change Calkas' mind, remembering his words at the Greek council when he beseeched them to return his daughter (85–91). He has no interests in his properties: the money, the house and the land. He gives precedence to the benefit of the Greeks and is ready to leave his treasure in Tory, all except his daughter. Criseyde must surely understand the situation and notice the difficulties that she faces now and she is obliged to deal them with later. Yet, she sounds confident about inducing her father to follow her words. Her speech does not strike at the heart of the matter because it is based on, so-called, women's superficial thinking. In spite of that, the defensive comment of the narrator is interposed here:

> And treweliche, as writen wel I fynde
> That al this thyng was seyd of good entente,
> And that hire herte trewe was and kynde
> Towardes hym, and spak right as she mente,

128   Chapter IV

And that she starf for wo neigh whan she wente,

And was in purpos evere to be trewe:

Thus writen they that of hire werkes knewe.   (*TC* IV, 1415–21)

Chaucer intentionally focuses on the sincerity of her words, insisting that they come from the bottom of her faithful and good-hearted intention to Troilus. She intends to remain loyal to him throughout. As her plan is not fully formed and her view is too optimistic and thoughtless, the narration is needed all the more in order to keep Criseyde from harm.

Troilus, on the other hand, listening carefully to her, tries to consent to her plan. Nevertheless, he cannot agree to parting with her and begs her to stay, because he is sure that her scheme is likely to be a complete failure: "Tho sleghtes yit that I have herd yow stere / Ful shaply ben to faylen alle yfeere" (1451–52). He declares that Criseyde underestimates her father. He is so old and wise, experienced, and cunning that it is impossible for her to deceive him into returning to Troy:

"I not if pees shal evere mo bitide;

But pees or no, for ernest ne for game,

I woot, syn Calkas on the Grekis syde

Hath ones ben and lost so foule his name,

He dar nomore come here ayeyn for shame;

For which that wey, for aught I kan espie,

To trusten on nys but a fantasie.   (*TC* IV, 1464–70)

Troilus is definitely correct when he judges that Calkas would never come back to Troy again once his name was lost and disgraced, and that her facile expectation is just a fantasy. Then he presumes what will happen between father and daughter: Calkas is a good rhetorician in that he may praise a Greek and try to force her to marry him, and Troilus, who does not receive her compassion, will die, and Calkas cleverly makes her believe that the siege by the Greeks will never be finished until the city is completely burnt down. Criseyde may be attracted by many a worthy Greek knight, and if she finally decides to stay, he is as good as dead. Troilus is a man with a clear head here; he is not blind in love but wide-awake. What he presumes will become real.

As for Troilus, he has his own idea of how to break this deadlock. He asks her to run away with him instead of parting, because they still have an opportunity to choose a happy future. Yet, if she should go to her father, there is no guarantee that she can come back. He turns down Criseyde's idea which he thinks a great folly that would endanger her security (1506–12). Then he explains how they can elope. Financially, he has enough money for them to live in honor and joy in their lifetime. As for habitation, he has many friends and relatives who would provide refuge for them. Troilus searches for the best solution in his opinion. It is natural for him to think that there is no possibility for Criseyde to return. He calmly faces reality and judges the situation. He is very sober in planning their runaway trip. This is not an impulsive act but rather a carefully prepared plan, taking their future into consideration.

Criseyde, on the other hand, takes his proposal completely in a different way. When Criseyde learns Troilus' thinking, she expels a heavy sigh and resolutely refuses his offer and replies persuasively at great length. Her lengthy speech runs to as many as 160 lines (1527–1687) with two interruptios of Troilus (1597–03, 1653–59). The main purpose of her eloquence is to persuade him to drop the idea that she thinks has shamed her name. His plan sounds merely egoistic and the

130   Chapter IV

thoughtless talk of a spoiled child, and it is of course unacceptable to
Criseyde.

She gently admonishes him that they may well steal away from
Troy but find the new way profitless and sooner or later they will sorely
repent it: "We may wel stele awey, as ye devyse, / And fynden swich
unthrifty weyes newe, / But afterward ful soore it wol us rewe" (1529–
31). She says that his dread is baseless because she never lies and would
never be faithless to him so that Troilus simply must believe her. More
importantly, she wants him to take notice that if their secret runaway is
revealed, both her life and his name would be in great danger: "If this
were wist, my lif lay in balaunce, / And youre honour; God shilde us fro
meschaunce" (1560–61). Here again her keenest concern is what other
people may think of her and keeping her good name:

> "What trowe ye the peple ek al aboute
> Wolde of it seye? It is ful light t'arede.
> They wolden seye, and swere it out of doute,
> That love ne drof yow naught to don this dede,
> But lust voluptuous and coward drede.
> Thus were al lost, ywys, myn herte deere,
> Youre honour, which that now shyneth so clere.

> "And also thynketh on myn honeste,
> That floureth yet, how foule I sholde it shende,
> And with what filthe it spotted sholde be,
> If in this forme I sholde with you wende.
> Ne though I lyved unto the werldes ende,
> My name sholde I nevere ayeynward wynne;

Thus were I lost, and that were routhe and synne.

(*TC* IV, 1569–82)

She strongly suggests that he should not act rashly by thinking in haste, which would also endanger his name. That is because he would never be able to return to Troy again for shame, after the war is over. What she fears more than anything else is the spoilation of her reputation and honor, as well as his, now shining so brightly: that is, people may think that she is escaping from Troy because of sensual lust and cowardly dread, such that her good name would be defiled forever and she could never restore it. Criseyde entirely rejects his plan, claiming that it would lead ultimately to their ruin. In her mind, there is not the slightest idea of running away with Troilus. This is the last choice that she would make. As she said to herself previously, if there are two misfortunes, she always chooses the least harmful one. This time, however, she has only a firm resolution to obey the parliament in order to survive the adversity regarding her good reputation.

She tries to pacify Troilus who is acting up like a peevish child. She promises him that she will return on the tenth day: "Er Phebus suster, Lucina the sheene, / The Leoun passe out of this Ariete, / I wol ben here, withouten any wene" (1591–93). The astronomical description here is Chaucer's addition to his original (Benson 1987, 1050). The moon passes to the zodiacal sign Aries and moves through Taurus, Gemini, and Cancer, then goes beyond Leo, which would take about ten days. She declares: "The tenthe day, but if that deth m'assaile, / I wol yow sen withouten any faille" (1595–96). Chaucer intentionally mentions Luchina, the moon, which constantly changes its shape, as a sign of her treachery.

132   Chapter IV

Troilus reasonably understands what they need to do so that he reluctantly accepts her plan and agrees to wait for her for ten days:

> "And now, so this be soth," quod Troilus,
> "I shal wel suffre unto the tenthe day,
> Syn that I se that nede it mot be thus.
> But for the love of God, if it be may,
> So late us stelen priveliche away;
> For evere in oon, as for to lyve in reste,
> Myn herte seyth that it wol be the beste."   (*TC* IV, 1597–1603)

He declares that if her speech proves true, he will manage to wait for her patiently. Otherwise, he strongly desires to steal secretly away. He still clings to his own idea of escape from Troy. Living at rest and in peace with her is the best solution for him. He can calmly predict what will happen after she goes over to the Greeks. He believes that she will never be able to come back to him, judging from the situation. That is simply why he does not want to let her go. Criseyde is now, before his very eyes, within his reach. Love of Criseyde is the highest priority for Troilus.

As concerns Criseyde, however, love is not the first priority. She is so disappointed at his reply that she chides him for his obstinacy and laments that he does not trust her:

> "O mercy, God, what lif is this?" quod she.
> "Allas, ye sle me thus for verray tene!
> I se wel now that ye mystrusten me,
> For by youre wordes it is wel yseene.

Now for the love of Cinthia the sheene,

Mistrust me nought thus causeles, for routhe,

Syn to be trewe I have yow plight my trouthe.

"And thynketh wel that somtyme it is wit

To spende a tyme, a tyme for to wynne;

Ne, parde, lorn am I naught fro yow yit,

Though that we ben a day or two atwynne.

Drif out the fantasies yow withinne,

And trusteth me, and leveth ek youre sorwe,

Or here my trouthe: I wol naught lyve tyl morwe.

(TC IV, 1604–17)*

In the first stanza cited above, Criseyde appeals desperately to him to trust her and pledges to be faithful to him, "for the love of Cinthia the sheene" (1608). Once again she refers to the moon. Chaucer makes his heroine swear by the moon, which is a symbol of flippancy. The movement of the moon has already been connected to her return date. While Chaucer interposes in the narration to defend his heroine's sincerity, he builds up her image of infidelity. He says that all her words come from her good intentions and true heart toward Troilus (1415–21) and at the same time, he makes her swear by the moon which would guarantee that she would change her mind. Chaucer gives her seemingly contradictory characteristics, but they show her personality very well and explain how she makes her final decision in the end. She always tries to be true to everyone, but this contradiction causes her infidelity after all. In the second stanza, she urges him to trust her and to drop his fantasy about their escaping from Troy. If he does not, she says she

134   Chapter IV

would die before the next day comes (1616–17). She threatens Troilus
with her death. This is the same rhetorical device that her uncle used in
persuading her to accept Troilus' love.

After that she says one thing after another in rapid succession to
convince Troilus: how much she grieves over his suffering. If she does
not know a good means of comeback, she will die right now in this very
place, she says, and she continues:

> "But certes, I am naught so nyce a wight
> That I ne kan ymaginen a wey
> To come ayeyn that day that I have hight.
> For who may holde a thing that wol awey?
> My fader naught, for al his queynte pley!
> And by my thrift, my wendyng out of Troie
> Another day shal torne us alle to joie.   (*TC* IV, 1625–31)

Apparently she is confident that she can wisely arrange how and when
she will return so that even her father would be unable to stop her from
leaving for Troy. Then she warns him not to betray her while she is
absent. Unintentionally she seems to attack him to conceal her inner
self. She knows that it is not sure what will really happen when she
meets her father, even if she strongly intends to come back. If there is
no choice but her going over to the Greeks, it is Troilus whom she needs
to persuade to let her go at this very moment. She finally begs him to be
faithful for her sake:

> "For in this world ther lyveth lady non,
> If that ye were untrewe—as God defende!—

That so bitraised were or wo-bigon

As I, that alle trouthe in yow entende.

And doubteles, if that ich other wende,

I ner but ded; and er ye cause fynde,

For Goddes love, so beth me naught unkynde!"

(*TC* IV, 1646–52)

She reminds him that if he should be untrue to her, she would be the most miserably betrayed lover in the world, since she completely trusts him. If not, she cannot live. She asks him by no means to be unkind to her unless he finds a reason. Ironically, all her words apply exactly to Troilus later. She says "er ye cause fynde," which words also ironically apply to Criseyde herself: if she finds a reason, would she betray him?

At last Criseyde is successful in persuading Troilus and promises to come back to Troy in ten days. She is overly-optimistic about the state of warfare between the Greeks and Trojans. She also underestimates her ability to persuade her father to return her to Troy, although she knows the reason why he has fled Troy.

Her fantastic strategy is supported by her self-consciousness and self-confidence. What is important for her is to search for the best way to keep her reputation intact and to survive the hardships she faces.

IV-3 Remaining with the Greeks

In the last book, the story is mostly described from Troilus' side. His lamentation over the loss of Criseyde is exaggerated in the beginning.

136   Chapter IV

He spends the first few days moping in bed, writhing in agony, and suffering from pain. He remembers her words and behavior in the past days and rereads her letters hundreds of times, visualizing her figure and her womanliness. On the fifth day, he goes out and visits Criseyde's residence and rides about the places which remind him of his lover, such as the palace where they met for the first time and the gate where he saw her off. In this way, he spends a day or two. Moreover, he patiently waits for her until the tenth day, looking forward to her return.

While Criseyde, going over to the Greeks accompanied by Diomede, keeps silent, even when she meets her father, she only replies to him that she is glad to see him and then she stands silent: "stood forth muwet, milde, and mansuete" (194). In Book V, she actually appears in only three scenes. Her speech amounts to 130 lines out of the total of 1870. Her first speech is a soliloquy in which she complains about her circumstances:

> Upon that other syde ek was Criseyde,
> With wommen fewe, among the Grekis stronge,
> For which ful ofte a day "Allas," she seyde,
> "That I was born! Wel may myn herte longe
> After my deth, for now lyve I to longe.
> Allas, and I ne may it nat amende,
> For now is wors than evere yet I wende!
>
> "Myn fader nyl for nothyng do me grace
> To gon ayeyn, for naught I kan hym queme;
> And if so be that I my terme pace,
> My Troilus shal in his herte deme

That I am fals, and so it may wel seme:
Thus shal ich have unthonk on every side—
That I was born so weilaway the tide!

"And if that I me putte in jupartie
To stele awey by nyght, and it bifalle
That I be kaught, I shal be holde a spie;
Or elles—lo, this drede I moost of alle—
If in the hondes, of som wrecche I falle,
I nam but lost, al be myn herte trewe.
Now, mighty God, thow on my sorwe rewe!"   (*TC* V, 687–707)

She at last must admit that the situation is much worse than she had expected, and her father will absolutely not allow her to go back to Troy. This is what Troilus had predicted before they parted. He appropriately grasped the situation and made the right decision. Criseyde understands that she had been overly-optimistic. Now that she is aware of the harsh reality, she thinks if she runs away under cover of darkness, she would be found and caught or she might fall into some rogues' hands and lose her name. She deeply regrets what she has done and that she did not obey his advice.

Casting a glance at Troy, she remembers her joyful moments there with Troilus and repents that she did not run away with him. Yet she knows it is too late, like medicine after death. She says that nobody would have blamed her for doing wrong if she had fled with such a person as Troilus. Her words sound hollow, because to run away was the last means she wanted to take. She refers to Prudence who has three eyes, looking to past, present, and future, and she notices that she lacks

138   Chapter IV

the one looking to the future and that this is the cause of her sorrow
(729–49). What she says is completely controverted by reality. She
finally decides to return to Troilus at all costs:

> "But natheles, bityde what bityde,
> I shal to-morwe at nyght, by est or west,
> Out of this oost stele in som manere syde,
> And gon with Troilus where as hym lest.
> This purpos wol ich holde, and this is best.
> No fors of wikked tonges janglerie,
> For evere on love han wreches had envye.
>
> "For whoso wol of every word take hede,
> Or reulen hym by every wightes wit,
> Ne shal he nevere thryven, out of drede;
> For that that som men blamen evere yit,
> Lo, other manere folk comenden it.
> And as for me, for al swich variaunce,
> Felicite clepe I my suffisaunce.
>
> "For which, withouten any wordes mo,
> To Troie I wole, as for conclusioun."   (*TC* V, 750–65)

She says that she will escape and go back to Troilus and go anywhere
he desires. She no longer cares what wicked people would think of her.
She rejects anyone who takes notice of other people's words and who
is controlled by their opinions. It must be satisfying for her not to heed
the different thoughts of other people but to pursue her own happiness.

If she had set her mind free when she was with Troilus, they could have made a different choice. Yet, she dares to talk big, because she is aware that it is impossible for her to carry out her plan. She actually does not act:

> But God it wot, er fully monthes two,
> She was ful fer fro that entencioun!
> For bothe Troilus and Troie town
> Shal knotteles thorughout hire herte slide;
> For she wol take a purpos for t'abide.   (*TC* V, 766–70)

Her concerns about both Troilus and Troy and her intention of returning there completely disappear from her mind within two months. What does this time span mean? Is it too long or too short? Chaucer alone specifies the period of time during which Criseyde changes her mind. Other versions are silent. Suggesting the term of her change of mind succeeds in giving the story a touch of reality.

Comparing this scene with Boccaccio's, there are some differences. In *Fil*, Criseida's escape by night is not found. Chaucer omits any mention of his Criseyde's death from sorrow, even though he has her refer to several occasions when she tries to persuade Troilus to let her go over to the Greeks. Chaucer expands on Criseyde's disregard of public opinion. *Fil* does not include her resolution to return to Troy. In Boccaccio, Diomede visits Criseida here. Chaucer, on the other hand, before Diomede actually visits Criseyde, closely observes Diomede and exposes how he cunningly tries to lure her: "With al the sleghte and al that evere he kan, / How he may best, with shortest taryinge, / Into his net Criseydes herte brynge" (773–75). Chaucer's Diomede is

140   Chapter IV

more calculating than Boccaccio's. Chaucer omits that Diomede defects her from her purpose in *Fil*.[21] Those differences reflect the author's intentions. Chaucer clearly tries to describe his heroine in the real world. In spite of her father's rejection, Criseyde resolutely decides to go back to Troilus under the screen of night. This means that she honestly intends to keep her word with Troilus. In harsh reality, she no longer refers to death from sorrow. Her resolution cannot help to change the situation. Diomede's characteristics endanger her position. If there is no way to change the situation around her, it would be natural for her to think that she has to survive in the real world.

The next speech is made when Diomede comes to visit Criseyde on the tenth day and she welcomes him to her tent, lets him sit biside her, and has a long chat over wine. Diomede cunningly explains how Troy and the Trojan people are destined to be destroyed, and that is why her wise father offers to exchange her for Antenore, so that she would forget about Troy and the Trojans. He continues to ask her for her favor and tells her he will keep serving her as long as he lives. Criseyde replies to him putting on a distant air:

> As she that hadde hire herte on Troilus
> So faste that ther may it non arace;
> And strangely she spak, and seyde thus:
> "O Diomede, I love that ilke place
> Ther I was born; and Joves, for his grace,
> Delyvere it soone of al that doth it care!
> God, for thy myght, so leve it wel to fare!
> ....
> "But as to speke of love, ywis," she seyde,

"I hadde a lord, to whom I wedded was,

The whos myn herte al was, til that he deyde;

And other love, as help me now Pallas,

Ther in myn herte nys, ne nevere was.

And that ye ben of noble and heigh kynrede,

I have wel herd it tellen, out of drede.   (*TC* V, 953–80)

Although she gives the cold shoulder to Diomede, when she tells him that she was once married and is not interested in being in love, she obviously hides her lover, Troilus, from Diomede and rather praises his nobility. She has already decided not to return to Troy at all, because she allows him to visit her again the next day and expresses a sympathetic attitude toward him:

"To-morwe ek wol I speken with yow fayn,

So that ye touchen naught of this matere.

And whan yow list, ye may come here ayayn;

And er ye gon, thus muche I sey yow here:

As help me Pallas with hire heres clere,

If that I sholde of any Grek han routhe,

It sholde be youreselven, by my trouthe!

"I say nat therfore that I wol yow love,

N'y say nat nay; but in conclusioun,

I mene wel, by God that sit above!"

And therwithal she caste hire eyen down,

And gan to sike, and seyde, "O Troie town,

Yet bidde I God in quiete and in reste

I may yow sen, or do myn herte breste."   (*TC* V, 995–1008)

She confesses that if she should show her pity to any Greek soldier, it must be Diomede and that even now she fancies him. This actually acts on Diomede as a confession of her love to him. She obviously shows him some hope which he can take advantage of. That is why this Greek soldier persistently asks her mercy and finally receives her glove with great pleasure. Under cover of darkness, Diomede takes his leave, and then the bright star Venus appears and the moon, "Cynthea," (1018) urges her carriage horse to pass the sign of Leo. The planet Venus is also a goddess of love. Criseyde swore her return to the moon with Troilus before it would pass through Leo. The moon suggests her betrayal in fact:

> Retornyng in hire soule ay up and down
> The wordes of this sodeyn Diomede,
> His grete estat, and perel of the town,
> And that she was allone and hadde nede
> Of frendes help; and thus bygan to brede
> The cause whi, the sothe for to telle,
> That she took fully purpos for to dwelle.   (*TC* V, 1023–29)

It does not take two months but only ten days until she comes to think of staying with the Greeks. Diomede's skillful seduction, his high status, a critical situation for Troy, her solitatry and helpless position cause her to break the promise to Troilus. Her feeling for Troilus and her agony of breaking the promise are not mentioned. Just as when she is in Troy, she is obliged to choose the less harmful of the two situations in the real world. Naturally she needs someone to protect her. The return to Troy is accompanied by great trouble and danger. The next day, that is, the eleventh day, Diomede comes to visit her and with his wily speech he manages to free her of most of her pain.

The last speech is made when Criseyde finally gives up keeping her promise to return to Troy. Before her final words, some evidence of her betrayal is shown: she gives her broach to Diomede, which once Troilus had presented to Criseyde; she also makes him wear her sleeve as a pennon; she cries a great deal when Diomede is injured in the battle with Troilus, devotedly nurses him and in order to heal his sorrow she gives him her heart:

> And *after this the storie telleth us*
> That she hym yaf the faire baye stede
> The which he ones wan of Troilus;
> And ek a broche—*and that was litel nede*—
> That Troilus was, she yaf this Diomede.
> And ek, the bet from sorwe hym to releve,
> She made hym were a pencel of hire sleve.
>
> *I fynde ek in stories elleswhere,*
> Whan thorugh the body hurt was Diomede
> Of Troilus, tho wep she many a teere
> Whan that she saugh his wyde wowndes blede,
> And that she took, to kepen hym, good hede;
> And for to helen hym of his sorwes smerte,
> Men seyn—*I not*—that she yaf hym hire herte.

(TC V, 1037–50, italics mine)

144   Chapter IV

Her faithless behavior is intentionally written in the first person of
the poet as narrator, who hesitates to express Criseyde's treachery. By
emphasizing that he takes those episodes from his sources, Chaucer shifts
the responsibility onto the previous authors. He is merely following his
sources and he avoids blaming Criseyde. Yet there occurs only a half-line
in which Chaucer criticizes her: when Criseyde gives Diomede a broach
which was given her by Troilus, a narration is inserted, "and that was
litel nede" (1040). This broach delivers proof of her betrayal to Troilus.
He finds it inside the surcoat worn over his armor, which Deiphebus tore
away from Diomede as a sign of victory on the battlefield. Troilus' heart
freezes when he finds the broach that he gave his love as a token on the
day she left Troy. She swore to keep it always. Now that he realizes that
he cannot trust her any longer, he complains about her change of mind,
his true love and penance, to Pandarus and after that he strongly longs
for death (1653–73).

His over-scrupulous honesty shows a sharp contrast with Criseyde's
last speech expressing her lamentation and her suffering:

> But trewely, the storie telleth us,
> Ther made nevere womman moore wo
> Than she, whan that she falsed Troilus.
> She seyde, "Allas, for now is clene ago
> My name of trouthe in love, for everemo!
> For I have falsed oon the gentileste
> That evere was, and oon the worthieste!
>
> "Allas, of me, unto the worldes ende,
> Shal neyther ben ywriten nor ysonge

Criseyde's Eloquence 145

No good word, for thise bokes wol me shende.
O, rolled shal I ben on many a tonge!
Thorughout the world my belle shal be ronge!
And wommen moost wol haten me of alle.
Allas, that swich a cas me sholde falle!

"Thei wol seyn, in as muhe as in me is,
I have hem don deshonour, weylaway!
Al be I nat the first that dide amys,
What helpeth that to don my blame awey?
But syn I se ther is no bettre way,
And that to late is now for me to rewe,
To Diomede algate I wol be trewe.   (*TC* V, 1051–71)

She laments that her reputation for being faithful in love is lost forever and that she will be labeled as a betrayer, which is what she has feared most. It is emphasized that what she worries about is only her name after all and not about poor Troilus. The last three lines expose her true feelings and her survival technique. Since there is no better way and it is too late for her to repent, she decides to be faithful to Diomede. She, as usual, chooses the better way, or less harmful way in the situation she is facing. That is her best tactic to survive.

In the end of her last speech, she at last refers to Troilus and proffers him:

"But, Troilus, syn I no bettre may,
And syn that thus departen ye and I,
Yet prey I God, so yeve yow right good day,

146   Chapter IV

> As for the gentileste, trewely,
> That evere I say, to serven feythfully,
> And best kan ay his lady honour kepe"
> And with that word she brast anon to wepe.
>
> "And certes yow ne haten shal I nevere;
> And frendes love, that shal ye han of me,
> And my good word, al sholde I lyven evere.
> And trewely I wolde sory be
> For to seen yow in adversitee;
> And gilteles, I woot wel, I yow leve.
> But al shal passe; and thus take I my leve."   (*TC* V, 1072–85)

She says that she cannot do anything better, for they are separated and she praises him as the kindest of men, who serves faithfully and best keeps his lady's honor. She declares that she will never hate him and that she will love him as a friend and speak well of him as long as she lives. She would be sorry to see him suffer in adversity. She knows very well that she is leaving him even though he is guiltless. Her words sound very simple and rather curt to Troilus. Passionate affection for her lover is absent, as are a sense of the bitter sorrow of being helplessly apart, and wholehearted apology for betraying him. It is no wonder, however, that Criseyde should conduct herself and treat Troilus in this way, because she constantly regards things from a practical point of view and her thought and behavior are always based on the real world. She knows how to deal with reality in the way best for herself. Although she would be regarded as self-centered and blamed for faithlessness, her betrayal of Troilus is a consequence of the best choice in each case.

Troilus, on the other hand, is out of touch with reality. He eagerly and patiently waits for her return. On the ninth night, he can hardly sleep and on the tenth day, he stands on the wall of the town with Pandarus and they wait at length for her in vain. Since he cannot doubt her sincerity he tries to think of the reasons why she does not come back: she does not want to leave her father so easily, she will creep back at night so as not to be seen by any one, and she might have mistaken the date. Even after the tenth day, he still trusts her, though uneasily, and waits for her. When he judges that she has broken her promise, his hope is completely lost and his suffering is so great that he feels as if his heart is bleeding: "But for the peyne hym thoughte his herte bledde, / So were his trowes sharpe and wonder stronge" (1200–01). He refuses food and drink, avoids the company of anyone, and longs for nothing but death (1219–32).

Troilus looks so sick that one can hardly recognize him as the brave Trojan prince. Now he is a hopeless fellow, facing harsh reality. He is very weak and lacks the power and means to stand against adversity. As a man in love, he looks like he is afloat in a fanciful world of love. It is ironical, however, that he notices her betrayal in a symbolic dream in which he walks in the woods, where he sees a huge wild boar with great tusks sleeping with his beautiful Criseyde and they are embracing, constantly kissing (1235–41). As soon as he wakes up from the sinister dream, he calls Pandarus and tells him about the dream, suspicious that Criseyde would betray him. Pandarus patiently calms Troilus down and skillfully interprets his dream in a different way; he takes the boar for her father at the moment of death and Criseyde was kissing her father as she cries in being overwhelmed with grief.

Then Pandarus urges him to write a letter to her. Troilus writes her a long letter in which he points to his sorrorw and pain, with tears,

148   Chapter IV

eagerly awaiting her return and stating that he keenly wishes to know
how she has been getting along and why she tarried so long, for over
two months. Criseyde replies with a brief and cold letter, in which she
shows understanding and pity for his grief and suffering, yet she firmly
declares that they can no longer be together. Although she cannot tell
him the reason why she tarries, she complains about Troilus and makes
up a plausible excuse:

> "Grevous to me, God woot, is your unreste,
> Youre haste, and that the goddes ordinaunce
> It semeth nat ye take it for the beste.
> Nor other thyng nys in youre remembraunce,
> As thynketh me, but only youre plesaunce.
> But beth nat wroth, and that I yow biseche;
> For that I tarie is al for wikked speche.
>
> "For I have herd wel moore than I wende,
> Touchyng us two, how thynges han ystonde,
> Which I shal with dissymelyng amende.
> And beth nat wroth, I have ek understonde
> How ye ne do but holden me in honde.
> But now no force. I kan nat in yow gesse
> But alle troute an alle gentilesse.
>
> "Come I wole; but yet in swich disjoynte
> I stonde as now that what yer or what day
> That this shal be, that kan I naught apoynte.
> But in effect I pray yow, as I may,

Of youre good word and of youre frendship ay;
For trewely, while that my lif may dure,
As for a frend ye may in me assure.   (*TC* V, 1604–24)

Criseyde criticizes Troilus for not accepting the situation as the best possible destiny. He seems to have nothing but his desire in mind. She complains about his not accepting reality and for clinging obstinately to a desperate hope. To her, Troilus is a stubborn, inflexible and willful child. Then she fabricates a reason for her stay: she has heard a gossip about them, in which Troilus is said to be leading her on and deceiving her. This is a malicious and unreasonable lie.

Troilus feels that her reply is cold and off-putting and takes it as a sign of her inner change. At last Troilus realizes very well that Criseyde is not as kind as she ought to be and finally he is assured that all that he has done for her is in vain (1642–45). It is worth noticing that Chaucer has Troilus mention that Criseyde is not so kind after all, because that would spoil the celestial image that Chaucer creates for his heroine.

From this moment when he reads her letter, his love-blinded eyes are wide open on the real world. After that he faces harsh realities one after another. His sister Cassandra analyzes his dream and tells him that it is Diomede who is staying with Criseyde. Troilus recovers himself as a brave warrior and finds her broach on the surcoat of Diomede. On the battle field, he wanders about in search of a battle with Diomede. They fight at the risk of their lives, yet in the end, Troilus is killed by Achilles. Then his soul ascends to the eighth sphere of the heavens. As he blissfully rises, he looks down on the earth where he was slain, at despising people who are crying over his death and he laughs. He sees that "blynde lust" cannot last. Eyes open wide, he finally realizes that

150   Chapter IV

all human activities are meaningless. In the earthly world he failed to see reality, suffering from "blynde lust," (1854) and after death he takes a philosophical view of worldly things and stands aloof from it. His laughter means that he has transcended all human knowledge and has achieved the salvation of his soul.

Although Criseyde's letter delivers her last words to Troilus which awakes him to the fact that she is no longer trustworthy, Chaucer narrates, here and there, his hesitation in calling her betrayal of Troilus a historical fact. At the beginning of the Book IV, in writing about the deterioration of this romance, the poet bleeds from his heart: "myn herte right now gynneth blede," (12) and he shakes his pen: "myn penne . . . / Quaketh for drede of that I moste endite" (13–14), because he must refer to how Criseyde forsakes Troilus and how she treats him cruelly. Still Chaucer tries to protect his heroine and deplores that the authors of this story had ever found fault with her. Even after describing her farewell address to Troilus and her decision to be faithful to Diomede, Chaucer confesses his compassion for Criseyde and states that he wants to protect her:

> Ne me ne list this sely womman chyde
> Forther than the storye wol devyse.
> Hire name, allas, is publysshed so wide
> That for hire gilt it oughte ynough suffise.
> And if I myghte excuse hire any wise,
> For she so sory was for hire untrouthe,
> Iwis, I wolde excuse hire yet for routhe.   (*TC* V, 1093–99)

The poet no longer wants to blame this lady because she had been widely known as a notorious woman already and he thinks that she has been punished enough for her guilt. Although he wishes out of pity to excuse her for her falsity, his protection is only in word and does not work to redeem her. Chaucer describes the inner feelings of Criseyde quite well in eloquent monologues or long persuasive speeches to Troilus. Her eloquence shows her self-consciousness regarding her appearance and reputation and reveals, moreover, her shrewdness in surviving an adverse situation in the real world. Criseyde, as a weak, powerless woman, is obliged to calculate things for her own interests in order to live on. She flexibly and forthrightly deals with reality and tries her best. This is the point at which the poet should protect her, yet he only feels pity that her name has been disgraced. In fact, he mostly puts the focus on Troilus and expresses fully not only his honesty and sincerity, but also his distress and deep sorrow. Here again underneath Chaucer's gentle smile, his hidden unfriendliness to women is in part disclosed.

Priscilla Martin (1990, 184) tries to defend Criseyde in a different way from the narrator. Martin's defence of Criseyde sounds completely agreeable because her defense is based on her own ideas. In Troy, she manages to live safely and humbly without Troilus who actually cannot openly serve as a protector. Yet in the Greek camp, Diomede's help is vital for her survival because Criseyde is a helpless outsider. It is no wonder that she changes her mind in order to find a way of surviving in such a world.

As Chaucer's justification of Criseyde is not convincing or even if he may try hard to protect her and people would find her betrayal excusable, he anticipates a reproach especially from a female audience for revealing Criseyde's unfaithfulness. He attributes the fault to the original story and suggests writing about women who never betrayed men (1772–78). This anticipates Chaucer's next work, *The Legend of Good Women*. The poet mentions that he would like to write such stories not only about the falsity of men but mostly on behalf of women who are betrayed. He appears to be sympathetic with females. But who can trust the poet when he says, "Beth war of men, and herkneth what I seye!" (1785)?

Chapter V

Prudence's Eloquence

The greater part of *Mel* consists of conversation between Dame Prudence and her husband Melibeus. Their dialogue takes the form of a debate. Prudence makes a long and eloquent speech in order to express her opinion, give him some advice and persuade him to agree with her.

The story starts with a shocking incident that happened to a rich, mighty and powerful young man called Melibeus. While he is away from home, three burglars break into his house and attack his wife, called Prudence, and a daughter named Sophie. They beat his wife severely and injure the daughter with five mortal wounds, in her feet, hands, eyes, nose and mouth. When Melibeus returns and finds out what has happened to his family, he becomes enraged and weeps heavily. He does not know what to do and asks the advice of his wife. Dame Prudence tells him to gather various opinions from his true friends and wise relatives on this matter and then make a decision. Following her advice, "by the conseil of his wyf Prudence" (1004), Melibeus invites numerous people to his house. He sends for surgeons and physicians, doctors of internal medicine, both old and young people, some of his old enemies reconciled and neighbors who hold respect and awe for him, and also many flatterers as well as wise lawyers. He tells them what happened to his family with sorrow and outrageous anger towards the men who attacked his daughter and wife. He is so furious that he is

[153]

154   Chapter V

ready to take revenge. Instead, he asks them for advice.

First, the surgeons state their opinion that they are on neutral ground as doctors who have to take care of the wounded of both parties from the viewpoint of medical care. The physicians answer in the same way, adding a few words: "that right as maladies been cured by hir contraries, right so shul men warisshe werre by vengeaunce" (1017). They show a preference for revenge, because 'Like cures like.'

After that the envious neighbors, false friends and flatterers pretend to feel tearful sympathy and proceed to praise him for his wealth, might and power, and then declare that he should launch a war at once. Next a wise lawyer rises up and expresses his opinion loud and clear to all the congregated people (1022–34). The wise lawyer opposes rashly waging a war for vengeance. He clearly states that first he should have someone protect himself and his family as well, and he should appoint some guardians to watch his house; he should take time to consider things well. The lawyer continues that even if slow-going makes people irritated and annoyed, a hasty judgment may not lead to true repentance, especially when he faces a hard decision as to whether he should seek revenge or not. The lawyer preaches the importance of deliberation.

At that time the young men stand up, ignoring the wise old man, grow rambunctious and shout, "Werre! Werre!" (1036). The wise old man rises again and tells them what actually happens once a war breaks out (1038–42). The wise man explains that it is easy for anyone to join war, but it is hard to realize how war will end up. War involves people, especially mothers and children, and gives them a miserable life and a wretched death. Therefore people must deliberately consider before deciding. When he tries to discuss the matter and make his case, the young men stand against him and interrupt his speech. The wise old lawyer drops the subject with the proverb, "good conseil wanteth when it is moost nede" (1048).

When Melibeus receives the copious advice of many people and observes that the majority of them advise him to start war on his enemies, he agrees and begins preparing to take his revenge. It is at this time that Dame Prudence with her prudent and eloquent speech persuades her husband not to be blinded by anger but to reconcile and forgive his enemies. In the end, she leads her husband to understand the Christian teaching. Her persuasive speech consists of three parts. Just what is debated between Melbius and Prudence and how she leads her husband to her own ideal solution are matters well worth discussing.

V-1 The First Part of Her Argument

At first, Dame Prudence "in ful humble wise" (1051) and earnestly asks her husband not to make a hasty decision:

> "My lord," quod she, "I yow biseche, as hertely as I dar and kan, ne haste yow nat to faste and, for alle gerdons, as yeveth me audience./For Piers Alfonce seith, 'Whoso that dooth to thee oother good or harm, haste thee nat to quiten it, for in this wise thy freend wole abyde and thyn enemy shal the lenger lyve in drede.' / The proverbe seith, 'He hasteth wel that wisely kan abyde,' and 'in wikked haste is no profit.'" (*Mel*, 1052–54)

She takes care to borrow the words of authorities and proverbs to support

156   Chapter V

her opinion and humbly begs him for consideration; nevertheless, Melibeus answers that he will not follow her advice "for many causes and resouns" (1055). He actually lists the five reasons why he will never obey his wife. The first is that if he changes his decision, which is supported and approved by many people, to his wife's opinion, he will be regarded as a fool. The second is that "alle wommen been wikke, and noon good of hem alle. For 'of a thousand men,' seith Salomon, 'I foond o good man, but certes, of alle wommen, good womman foond I nevere'" (1057). This is an anti-feminist thought which prevailed widely in the middle ages. Thirdly, he would have to be dominated by his wife. If he should accept her advice, he would give over mastery in marriage to his wife. This topic is treated and discussed in the several tales called the 'Marriage Group' in *CT*. The fourth reason is that talkative women cannot hold things in themselves so that it would be impossible for him to keep his plan secret if he told his wife his plan. Last, as the philosopher, Aristotle says, women's evil counsel conquers men.

Listening to her husband "ful debonairly and with greet pacience" (1064), Prudence asks his permission to speak and argues against each reason Melibeus gives for not following the wife's advice. To the first reason, Prudence retorts that it is not a fool, but rather a wise man who dares to change his determined resolution depending on circumstances (1065–67). She points out the importance of flexibility in a wise man from a general viewpoint, using proverbial wisdom, such as that the wise adapt themselves to changed circumstances, a wise man changes his mind, a fool never, and a wise man needs not blush for changing his purpose.

The second reason being concerned with the problem of gender as well as the misogynistic viewpoint in medieval Christian society, her speech is prolonged and sounds increasingly, ardently eloquent. She carefully counters his over-emotional belief that all women are evil, effectively using a conventional Christian idea. First, she moderately blames her husband for his despising all women. Borrowing from a book and from Seneca, she insists that a respectable person should not despise people. Next, she identifies the essential part of the misogyny, which is hard to refute. Misogynistic thought traces back to the story of Eve whose behavior resulted in the notion of original sin. She makes good use of the Blessed Mary in order to object to misogyny. This is a conventional controversy in medieval literature. Prudence points out that if all women are evil, Jesus Christ would never have been born of a woman (1073). She continues that if all women are evil, Jesus Christ, who was resurrected three days after his death, would, never have come to see the woman, Mary Magdalene, before he revealed himself to men, the Apostles. Last, she cites Solomon who has never seen "sovereyn bounte" (1078) in any women and argues again that no one has, is, and embodies the highest good except God alone.

The third reason is about mastery or sovereignty between a husband and a wife in marriage:

> Youre thridde reson is this: ye seyn that if ye governe yow by my conseil, it sholde seme that ye hadde yeve me the maistrie and the lordshipe over youre persone. / Sire, save youre grace, it is nat so. For if it so were that no man sholde be conseilled but oonly of hem that hadden lordshipe and maistrie of his persone, men wolden nat be conseilled so ofte. / For soothly thilke man that asketh conseil of a purpos, yet hath he free choys wheither he wole werke by that conseil or noon. (*Mel*, 1081–83)

158   Chapter V

Melibeus thinks that if he should take her advice, he would feel controlled by his wife and would yield up his sovereignty. He does not want to be dominated by his wife, yet Prudence shows no interest in holding mastery over her husband.

The fourth reason why Melibeus does not take Prudence's advice is that chatty women are said to be unable to hold their tongues and that they 'tell' everything they know. Prudence replies that his words are applicable only to those who are talkative and wicked:

> And as to youre fourthe resoun, ther ye seyn that the janglerie of wommen kan hyde thynges that they wot noght, as who seith that a womman kan nat hyde that she woot; / *sire, thise wordes been understonde of wommen that been jangleresses and wikked; / of whiche wommen men seyn that thre thynges dryven a man out of his hous—that is to seyn, smoke, droppyng of reyn, and wikked wyves;* / and of swiche wommen seith Salomon that 'it were bettre dwelle in desert than with a womman that is riotous.' / And sire, by youre leve, that am nat I, / for ye han ful ofte assayed my grete silence and my grete pacience, and eek how wel that I kan hyde and hele thynges that men oghte secreely to hyde.
>
> (Mel, 1084–89, italics mine)

Interestingly enough, Prudence's reply here about 'wicked woman' is identical to the reply which the Wife of Bath quotes from her husbands:

> Thow seyst that droppyng houses, and eek smoke,
> And chidyng wyves maken men to flee
> Out of hir owene houses; a, benedicitee!

What eyleth swich an old man for to chide? *(WBP*, 278–81)

'Bet is,' quod he, 'thyn habitacioun
Be with a leon or a foul dragoun,
Than with a womman usynge for to chyde. *(WBP*, 775–77)

Although both the Wife of Bath and Prudence cite similar references, the effects of their words are completely different. The Wife states that she is condemned by her husband as a wicked wife and she answers him with curses. Her words are strong and powerful because she herself is concerned about being called a wicked wife. That is why her passionate reaction to her husbands' words amuses an audience of both genders. The male audience enjoys hearing her call herself wicked. The female audience is pleased to hear her lively and delightful attack on her husbands. Prudence calmly dissociates herself from those "wykked wyves." She insists that she is not such a kind of woman and that her husband must be completely familiar with her silence and patience. Prudence's insistence is completely rational and reasonable but not particularly fascinating.

The fifth reason is that the wicked advice of women destroys men. Prucence retorts with the paradoxical statement. She says that Melibeus asks advice only to take revenge on his enemies, which means he is going to commit a wicked act. If his wife keeps him from achieving the wrong purpose and persuades him with reason and good advice, then she should be praised rather than blamed. She names helpful women who give good advice to men:

Loo, Jacob by good conseil of his mooder Rebekka wan the

160   Chapter V

benysoun of Ysaak his fader and the lordshipe over alle his bretheren. / Judith by hire good conseil delivered the citee of Bethulie, in which she dwelled, out of the handes of Olofernus, that hadde it biseged and wolde have al destroyed it. / Abygail delivered Nabal hir housbonde fro David the kyng, that wolde have slayn hym, and apaysed the ire of the kyng by hir wit and by hir good conseillyng. / Hester by hir good conseil enhaunced greetly the peple of God in the regne of Assuerus the kyng.

(*Mel*, 1098–1101)

These examples of women advisors appear in the same order in *The Merchant's Tale* (1362–74). By these examples from the Bible, Prudence tries to bring forward evidence to show that many women are good and that their suggestions are virtuous and profitable. She goes on to quote the two lines of verse written by a clerk in order to establish her claim firmly: "What is bettre than gold? Jaspre. What is bettre than jaspre? Wisedoom. / And what is better than wisedoom? Womman. And what is bettre than a good womman? Nothyng" (*Mel*, 1107–08). In the end, Prudence makes a rather practical and pragmatic promise to Melibeus: "And therfore, sire, if ye wol triste to my conseil, I shal restoore yow youre doghter hool and sound. / And eek I wol do to yow so muche that ye shul have honour in this cause" (*Mel*, 1110–11).

Prudence skillfully marshals counterarguments to Melibeus's five reasons why he does not want to accept her advice. She humbly and cleverly tries to persuade her husband, opposing his misogynistic discussion.

V-2 The Second Part of Her Argument

In the first part, Prudence is a humble confuter who proves her husband completely wrong as to the five reasons why he does not follow her advice. Her development of an argument is logically clear and authoritative, making use of a myriad of the words of accredited persons and books. After hearing Prudence's speech, Melibeus suddenly tones down his passionate language in a way that renders the husband flexible by softening his position:

> "I se wel that the word of Salomon is sooth. He seith that 'wordes that been spoken discreetly by ordinaunce been honycombes, for they yeven swetnesse to the soule and hoolsomnesse to the body.' / And, wyf, by cause of thy sweete wordes, and eek for I have assayed and preved thy grete sapience and thy grete trouthe, I wol governe me by thy conseil in alle thyng." (*Mel*, 1113–14)

Melibeus is simply and easily convinced by his wife, such that he obeys her in everything. She then instructs him how to choose advisers: "syn ye vouche sauf to been governed by my conseil, I wol enforme yow how ye shul governe yourself in chesynge of youre conseillours" (1115).

She also changes her attitude to Melibeus here. Although she has so far humbly asked and beseeched her husband, once she finds him being obedient, she henceforth uses stronger expressions such as "shul, or shalt," telling him what to do:

> Ye *shul* first in alle youre werkes mekely biseken to the heighe God that he wol be youre counseillour; / and shapeth yow to swich

162   Chapter V

> entente that he yeve yow conseil and confort, as taughte Thobie
> his sone: / 'At alle tymes thou *shalt* blesse God, and praye hym
> to dresse thy weyes, and looke that alle thy conseils been in hym
> for everemoore.' / Seint Jame eek seith: 'If any of yow have nede
> of sapience, axe it of God.' / And afterward thanne *shul* ye taken
> conseil in yourself, and examyne wel youre thoghtes of swich
> thyng as yow thynketh that is best for youre profit. / And thanne
> *shul* ye dryve fro youre herte thre thynges that been contraiouse to
> good conseil; / that is to seyn, ire, covetise, and hastifnesse.
>
> (*Mel*, 1116–22, italics mine)

Prudence tells him how to adjudicate the opinions of advisers. First
of all, he should humbly ask God to be his advisor and take in God's
advice, and try himself to consider what is best. He should drive three
things out of his mind, which are opposed to good advice: anger, greed
and haste. She gives reasons why he should avoid those three. Firstly
because a person who harbors great anger and wrath in himself always
thinks that he can do what he in fact cannot do; secondly because a
short-tempered man can neither consider things well nor accept good
advice; and thirdly because an irritable man can speak nothing but ill
of others, which generates anger and wrath in others. Next he should
drive greed away, because it causes widespread harm. A greedy man
cannot render a good judgement. He just tries to satisfy his covetousness
and can never be satisfied with himself. The more he gains, the more
he desires. Finally, hastiness should be avoided because a rash thought
cannot lead to the best judgement, as in the common proverb; "he that
soone deemeth, soone repenteth" (1135).

Thus Prudence extends advice to her husband not in a humble way but on a level equal with Melibeus and she puts some requests to him using imperative sentences and authoritative expressions:

> "Whan ye han taken conseil in youreself and han deemed by good deliberacion swich thyng as you semeth best, / thanne *rede I yow that ye kepe it secree*. / Biwrey nat youre conseil to no persone, but if so be that ye wenen sikerly that thurgh youre biwreyyng youre condicioun shal be to yow the moore probfitable.
>
> (Mel, 1138–40, italics mine)

> And therfore *yow is bettre to hyde your conseil* in youre herte than praye him to whom ye han biwreyed your conseil that he wole kepen it cloos and stille. (Mel, 1146, italics mine)

> But nathelees, if thou wene sikerly that the biwreiyng of thy conseil to a persone wol make thy condicion to stonden in the bettre plyt, thanne *shaltou tellen hym thy conseil* in this wise. / First *thou shalt make* no semblant wheither thee were levere pees or werre, or this or that, *ne shewe hym* nat thy wille and thyn entente. (Mel, 1148–49, italics mine)

> And after that thou *shalt considere* thy freendes and thyne enemys. / And as touchynge thy freendes, *thou shalt considere* which of hem been moost feithful and moost wise and eldest and most approved in conseillyng; / and of hem *shalt thou aske* thy conseil, as the caas requireth. / I seye that first *ye shul clepe* to youre conseil your freendes that been trewe.
>
> (Mel, 1154–57, italics mine)

164   Chapter V

Prudence tells Melibeus that when he has made the best decision after grave consideration for a sufficient time, he should secretly keep it to himself lest he be beguiled by others. She suggests that he should discern his true friends, who are the most faithful, trustworthy and wise. She also instructs him as to the kind of persons of whom he should ask advice. She lists true friends who are intelligent and thoughtful, wise old men who are authorized and adequately experienced, and many other advisors who are possessed of three such conditions as faithfulness, wisdom, and experience.

Then Prudence explains what kind of advice Melibeus should avoid accepting, showing here again, as she always does, examples of the words and maxims of the authorities such as Solomon, Cicero, Cato, Seneca, and Aesop. First of all, Prudence tells her husband to give no ear to a fool's advice because his counsel is based merely on his own lust and liking. Next she says that flatterers' advice is useless because they never tell the reason or the way things should be, but would merely offer sweet words to praise and please Melibeus. They never tell the truth but try to lead true friends into a trap. She also refers to the old enemies who are reconciled with each other. No matter how humble and friendly they seem to be, the old enemies should not be trusted. They may pretend to be agreeable only for their own profit. Then she mentions that the counseling of people who attend as servants and have a great respect for Melibeus should be avoided, because their words derive from fear, not from fidelity. She continues to attack the advice of drunkards, wicked people, and young men, for the reasons that drunkards cannot keep their words secret, wicked people's advice is always deceitful, and young men's counsel is premature.

Her opinions are always supported by authoritative texts and persons so that she can never be wrong but can only be completely right. In giving Melibeus her opinion, she gradually turns herself into a teacher or instructor, with words such as 'inform, teach, and, show':

> *I wol enforme yow* how ye shul governe yourself in chesynge of youre conseillours.   (*Mel*, 1115, italics mine)

> Now, sith that I have toold yow of which folk ye sholde been counseilled, now *wol I teche yow* which conseil ye oughte to eschewe.   (*Mel*, 1172)

> now *wol I teche yow* how ye shal examyne youre conseil, afer the doctrine of Tullius.   (*Mel*, 1201, italics mine)

> Now is it resoun and tyme that *I shewe yow* whanne and wherfore that ye may chaunge youre counsei withouten youre repreve.   (*Mel*, 1223, italics mine)

Prudence is a perfect teacher who leads her husband into giving up the idea of taking revenge on the enemies who had hurt their beloved daughter. Her flawless speech has changed Melibeus and persuaded him into following her advice. Now he expresses his gratitude for her instruction and, furthermore, he asks her opinion about the advisors whom he has chosen:

> This Melibeus, whanne he hadde herd the doctrine of his wyf dame Prudence, answerde in this wyse: / "Dame," quod he, "as yet into this tyme *ye han wel and covenably taught* me as in

166   Chapter V

general how I shal governe me in the chesynge and in the with-
holdynge of my conseillours. / But now wolde I fayn that ye wolde
condescende in especial / and *telle me how liketh yow, or what
semeth yow*, by oure conseillours that we han chosen in oure
present nede."   (*Mel*, 1232–35, italics mine)

Melibeus totally changed his attitude. At first he never followed
Prudence's advice because he considered it shameful to change, in
accordance with a woman's judgment, a decision made by himself
with the help of many advisors. After listening to Prudence's long and
eloquent speech, he amends his thought and accepts her advice, and
now he asks her opinion about the counselors he gathers. Before she
expresses her thoughts, she excuses herself in advance and asks him
not to grow angry if she displeases him in her reply. She swears that
she speaks for his best, for his honor and profit. She then dismisses his
counsel as folly, pointing out that Melibeus has made errors "in many a
sondry wise" (1240):

"First and forward, ye *han erred* in th'assemblynge of youre
conseillours. / For ye sholde first have cleped a fewe folk to youre
conseil, and after ye myghte han shewed it to mo folk, if it hadde
been nede. / But certes, ye han sodeynly cleped to youre conseil a
greet multitude of peple, ful chargeant and ful anoyous for to
heere. / *Also ye han erred*, for theras ye sholden oonly have cleped
to youre conseil youre trewe frendes olde and wise, / ye han
ycleped straunge folk, yonge folk, false flatereres, and enemys
reconsiled, and folk that doon yow reverence withouten love. /
And *eek also ye have erred*, for ye han broght with yow to youre

conseil ire, coveitise, and hastifness, / the whiche thre thinges been contrariouse to every conseil honest and profitable; / the whiche thre thinges ye han nat anientissed or destroyed hem, neither in yourself, ne in youre conseillours, as yow oghte. / *Ye han erred also*, for ye han shewed to youre conseillours youre talent and youre affeccioun to make werre anon and for to do vengeance. / They han espied by youre wordes to what thyng ye been enclyned; / and therfore han they rather conseilled yow to youre talent than to youre profit. / *Ye han erred also*, for it semeth that yow suffiseth to han been conseilled by thise conseillours oonly, and with litel avys, / whereas in so greet and so heigh a nede it hadde been necessarie mo conseillours and moore deliber-acion to parfourne youre emprise. / *Ye han erred also*, for ye ne han nat examyned youre conseil in the forseyde manere, ne in due manere, as the caas requireth. / *Ye han erred also*, for ye han maked no division bitwixe youre conseillours—this is to seyn, bitwixen youre trewe freendes and youre feyned conseillours— / ne ye han nat knowe the wil of youre trewe freendes olde and wise, / but ye han cast alle hire wordes in an hochepot, and enclyned youre herte to the moore part and to the gretter nombre, and there been ye conde-scended. / And sith ye woot wel that men shal alwey fynde a gretter nombre of fooles than of wise men, / and therfore the conseils that been at congregaciouns and multitudes of folk, there as men take moore reward to the nombre than to the sapience of persones, / ye se wel that in swiche conseillynges fooles han the maistrie."   (*Mel*, 1241–60, italics mine)

Prudence points out seven errors which Melibeus had made in choosing

168   Chapter V

the advisors. First, he had made a mistake in his choice of certain people for counselling. Although Melibeus invites many people to his house in order to ask their advice, at Prudence's suggestion, he is blamed for making a mistake in so doing. This is because he should have sent for only a few people. Second, he had been wrong in calling for strangers, young men, false flatterers, and reconciled enemies, instead of sending for cordial friends who are old but wise. Third, he had brought into the counsel the three matters which are opposed to any honest and profitable advice: anger, greed and hastiness. The fourth error is that Melibeus had revealed his hope and intention of attacking his enemies immediately, which had induced the counselors to follow his wish. Fifth, he had been satisfied with their answers only, while he should have inquired of a number of more deliberative advisers what to do in so great and high a case of need. Sixth, he had not examined the advice well or wisely enough. Lastly, he erred in not distinguishing between true and false friends among his advisors.

Prudence enumerates the mistakes which her husband had committed in choosing his advisors. This is a compilation of her preceeding speech concerning what kind of advisors to choose and what kind to avoid. The method of her juxtaposing the faults of her husband and criticizing him reminds us of that of the Wife of Bath. She lists the faults of women repeating the words of her husband who speaks ill of women:

> *Thou seist* to me it is a greet meschief
> To wedde a povre womman, for costage;
> And if that she be riche, of heigh parage,
> *Thanne seistow* that it is a tormentrie
> To soffre hire pride and hire malencolie.

And if that she be fair, thou verray knave,
Thou seyst that every holour wol hire have;
She may no while in chastitee abyde,
That is assailled upon ech a syde.   (*WBP*, 248–56, italics mine)

The Wife of Bath lists the faults of women quoting the words of her husband in order to retaliate for her own ends while Prudence admonishes her husband for the errors that he had committed in order to lead him to her own purpose. Although their causes and effects are different, they exhibit curious contrasts and similarities. The one becomes a parody of the other.

Melibeus's mistakes having been pointed out to him in the selection of his advisors, he immediately admits his errors and tells his wife to replace them:

"I graunte wel that I have erred; / but there as thou hast toold me heerbiforn that he nys nat to blame that chaungeth his counseillours in certein caas and for certeine juste causes, / I am al redy to chaunge my conseillous right as thow wolt devyse. / The proverbe seith that 'for to do synne is mannyssh, but certes for to persevere longe in synne is werk of the devel.'"

(*Mel*, 1261–64)

In the beginning of the story, Melibeus is so enraged by the enemies he had brought into his house and who had injured his daughter severely that he was confused and rejected Prudence's opinion, because it was a woman's. As a result of Prudence's reasonable speech, Melibeus drove away his misogynic thoughts, became obedient to her advice, and asked

170   Chapter V

her how to proceed. Here he honestly acknowledges his fault and meekly
obeys his wife. Prudence's persuasion seems to end in a victory over her
husband. She, however, continues to reason him into compliance. She
investigates what each advisor has told Melibeus by way of advising
him.

She starts with the advice of surgeons and physicians. They wisely
and discreetly mention that their responsibilities are to give everyone
honour and profit and the best treatment to their patients as doctors.
Prudence greatly admires their noble speech and proposes Melibeus that
he should give them a generous reward:

> And, sire, right as they han answered wisely and discreetly, / right
> so rede I that they been heighly and sovereynly gerdoned for hir
> noble speche, / and eek for they sholde do the moore ententif
> bisynesse in the curacion of youre doghter deere. / For al be it
> so that they been youre freendes, therfore shal ye nat suffren that
> they serve yow for noght, / but ye oughte the rather gerdone hem
> and shewe hem youre largesse.   (*Mel*, 1271–75)

Prudence gives the most practical reason for rewarding them. She
believes that the doctors would give their daughter better treatment if
they received a reward. Even if they are friends, Melibeus should not
have them work without compensation but should show them generosity.

She then asks Melibeus how he interprets the physicians' words.
Adding to the idea of the surgeons, they give advice such as that "right
as maladies been cured by hir contraries, right so shul men warisshe
werre by vengeaunce (1017)." Prudence paraphrases this such as, "in
maladies that oon contrarie is warisshed by another contrarie— (1277)."

Melibeus takes their words literally and replies:

> "Certes," quod Melibeus, "I understonde it in this wise: / that
> right as they han doon me a contrarie, right so sholde I doon hem
> another. / For right as they han venged hem on me and doon me
> wrong, right so shal I venge me upon hem and doon hem wrong; /
> and thanne have I cured oon contrarie by another."
>
> (*Mel*, 1279–82)

Melibeus takes the physicians' words to suit his own convenience. He
understands it as justifiable that if his enemies show him hostility and if
they commit evil for revenge, he would reply in kind. This is the idea of
'An eye for eye, a tooth for a tooth,' which is forbidden by Jesus Christ
in the Sermon on the Mount:

> "You have heard that it was said, 'An eye for eye and a tooth
> for tooth.' But I say to you, Do not resist one who is evil. But if
> any one strikes you on the right cheek, turn to him on the other
> also; and if any one would sue you and take your coat, let him
> have your cloak as well; and if any one forces you to go one mile,
> go with him two miles. Give to him who begs from you, and do
> not refuse him who would borrow from you.
>
> "You have heard that it was said, 'You shall love your neighbor
> and hate your enemy.' But I say to you, Love your enemies and
> pray for those who persecute you,
>
> (Mathew, 5: 38–45)

This is one of the essential teachings of Christian doctrine. Prudence

172   Chapter V

makes good use of it in order to amend Melibeus's thoughts by interpreting the physicians' advice correctly:

> But certes, the wordes of the phisiciens sholde been understonden
> in this wise: / for good and wikkednesse been two contraries, and
> pees and werre, vengeaunce and suffraunce, discord and accord,
> and manye othere thynges; / but certes, wikkednesse shal be
> warisshed by goodnesse, discord by accord, werre by pees, and
> so forth of othere thynges. / And heerto accordeth Seint Paul tha
> Apostle in manye places. / He seith, 'Ne yeldeth nat harm for
> harm, ne wikked speche for wikked speche, / but do wel to hym
> that dooth thee harm and blesse hym that seith to thee harm.' /
> And in manye othere places he amonesteth pees and accord.
>
> (*Mel*, 1288–94)

Prudence asks Melibeus's opinion and tells him that he is wrong, and
then tries to make him understand why he is wrong and reasonably
guide him to an ethically honorable position. She takes the "contrarie"
of the physicians' words in a different way from Melibeus. The word
"contrarie" does not mean, to her, that one's hostility is directed against
the enemy's hostility, in the same way that one's revenge is directed
against the enemy's. But it signifies such pairs of antonyms as war for
peace, good for evil, revenge for forgiveness. Although they are contrary
concepts, one is balanced out by the other. War is cured by peace, evil is
healed by goodness, and revenge is restored by forgiveness. She locates
its base in the Bible, citing the words of St. Paul.

Prudence next examines the advice offered by men of law and
wise people. They had made a special effort to tell Melibeus to protect

himself and his house with guardians: "And after that, we conseille that in thyn hous thou sette sufficeant garnisoun so that they may as wel thy body as thyn hous defende" (1027). She inquires of Melibeus how he understands their words and what his opinion is about their advice. Melibeus answers in this way:

> Melibeus answerde and seyde, "Certes, I undrestande it in this wise: That I shal warnestoore myn hous with toures, swiche as han castelles and othere manere edifices, and armure, and artelries, / by whiche thynges I may my persone and myn hous so kepen and deffenden that myne enemys shul been in drede myn hous for to approche." (*Mel*, 1333–34)

Here again Melibeus takes the advisors' words to the letter. He understands that he should build a house with high towers armed with a number of weapons to protect himself and his family. A well-defended house will keep his enemies away. Prudence replies to this:

> "Warnestooryng," quod she, "of heighe toures and of grete edifices apperteyneth somtyme to pryde. / And eek men make heighe toures, [and grete edifices] with grete costages and with greet travaille, and whan that they been accompliced, yet be they nat worth a stree, but if they be defended by trewe freendes that been olde and wise. (*Mel*, 1335–36)

Prudence explains that no matter how high the towers are, no matter how large the buildings are, no matter how strong the weapons are, and no matter how well-protected the fortress is, they are worthless and useless

174   Chapter V

by contrast with the protection of friends who are old but wise. The best and strongest protection for the rich man to defend not only himself but also his property is to hold the love and trust of his friends, neighbors and retainers. Prudence cites Cicero to prove her idea: "For thus seith Tullius, that 'ther is a manere garnysoun that no man may venquysse ne disconfite, and that is / a lord to be biloved of his citezeins and of his peple'" (1339–40). She warns him that protection by high towers and solid building is related to "pryde" (1335) and it is not always durable but is sometimes fragile, and he says moreover that a firm bond of his people united in fidelity and loyalty is necessary to make defense highly resistant to his enemies.

As the third point, Prudence completely agrees with the advice of the old and wise men:

> Now, sire, as to the thridde point, where as youre olde and wise conseillours seyden that yow ne oghte nat sodeynly ne hastily proceden in this nede, / but that yow oghte purveyen and apparaillen yow in this caas with greet diligence and greet deliberacioun; / trewely, I trowe that they seyden right wisely and right sooth.
>
> (*Mel*, 1341–43)

Their advice is very simple and clear. They urge him to avoid rough-and-ready thoughts and make a clear-cut resolution after long deliberation and careful preparations. This is exactly the same advice which Prudence first had already given to her husband. After consulting all the people whom Melibeus had invited to his house, and seeing the majority agreeable to making war, he finally decided, in rage, to take revenge on his enemies. Although Prudence asked him very humbly and sincerely not to make a hasty, rash decision but to take time for deliberation, Melibeus rejected her counsel because she was a woman. Prudence here could have expanded the wise men's advice to persuade her husband away from his desire for vengeance, but she proceeds to examine the next advisors.

They are such people as neighbors who are superficial friends, who pretended to respect him but lacked affection; reconciled enemies, flatterers who advised him something in private but completely reversed it in public; and young men, who hastily insisted that he begin a war of revenge. Prudence reveals a special hatred for them and again blames Melibeus for inviting them. Although Prudence admits that they had been sufficiently condemned in her previous speech, she moreover deeply investigates their advice in detail following the doctrine of Marcus Tullius Cicero, as expressed in his *De officiis*. It is a three-volume philosophy tome written in AD 44. The work is in the form of letters addressed to Cicero's son, Marcus. The first volume discusses the fundamental elements of moral goodness and duties generated by them. The second book explains what is expedient to one's advantage by applying moral elements to actual life and citing numerous practical examples in Greek and Roman history.

Chaucer chiefly quotes from Book II here. According to the Benson's note, Chaucer "departs from both the French and Latin, perhaps because his source was 'faulty or incomprehensible at this point'" (Benson 1987, 926). If this part is Chaucer's original, it is necessary to consider why the poet inserts this passage in Prudence's speech.

Prudence analyses this happening by using the five conditions of Cicero. The first condition is to know what kind of people and how many people had agreed and disagreed on Melibeus's revenge, which

176   Chapter V

is already known. The second condition is "consentynge." She explains how the advice of revenge is not reasonable and is hardly subject to consent. Her persuasive speech informing Melibeus why he should not take a revenge against his enemies is overwhelming (1366–76). Prudence addresses very practical matters. Even though Melibeus has might and wealth, he has no brothers and close relatives but only one daughter. He does not have anyone who would wreak vengeance for him if he should be killed; while his three enemies have numerous children, cousins, and relatives. Even if he should kill two or three of them, there would still be many kindred left to retaliate. They have such stronger relationships with their families than Melibeus that they are more advantaged at this point. It is crystal clear that he should not seek revenge. More effectively and eloquently than any other advisor, Prudence tries to prove that he had better give up the idea of revenge. Moreover, she examines what had happened and what would happen should he attempt vengeance, following Cicero's conditions: "consequent," "engendrynge," and "causes." She explains that the revenge which he is going to take will result in still an endless chain of acts of revenge, peril and war. She adds that this evil act is engendered by the hatred of his enemies and the vengeance engendered by vengeance which in turn engenders deep sadness and a waste of real property. Lastly, she traces the sufferings which he had experienced back to its causes. The primary cause is Almighty God who is the farthest removed cause of everything; and the near cause is his three enemies. The accidental cause is their hatred and the material cause is the five wounds of the daughter. The formal cause is such acts as their having broken into and entered the house with a ladder. The final cause is to slay the daughter. As for the farthest removed cause, which befalls the enemies, she ends this speech with the proverb: "'Seelden, or with greet peyne, been causes ybroght to good ende whanne they been baddely bigonne'" (1404).

If Chaucer originally had introduced this part of the speech into his source in this work, he would have had special intention to do so. It is true that the essence of her advice is the most practical and convincing in the real world. That is to say, even if he were to vent his present resentment, this would cause the future destruction of his family because his enemies would have more offspring and closely related relatives who could attack him. Nevertheless, her long analysis and explanation using the method of Cicero seem to be admirably rational and logical for persuading her husband, and the more perfectly reasonable her eloquent speech is the more formalistic it becomes in its deviation from the most essential part of the problem. Chaucer probably intended to make of his heroine a more reasonable and persuasive person than those in his source. Her righteousness and flawlessness as "prudence" render her speech unpleasant to hear.

V-3   The Third Part of Her Argument

In the previous two parts of her speech, Prudence almost monopolizes the argument. She gives dominant speeches one after another to persuade Melibeus to give up the idea of taking revenge on his three enemies. He never speaks against her but inserts short words of agreement between her eloquent speeches. She tries her best to give him the language which would be most effective in the real world. He understands the demerits of revenge, but he does not totally agree with her. Her final purpose is to

178   Chapter V

argue him into reconciling and forgiving his enemies. In the third part of
her speech, she approaches the subject from a different angle. She tries
to explain the basic cause of this misfortune, specifying its etymological
relation to his name:

> Thy name is Melibee; this is to seyn, 'a man that drynketh
> hony.' / Thou hast ydronke so muchel honey of sweete temporeel
> richesses, and delices and honours of this world / that thou art
> dronken and hast forgeten Jhesu Crist thy creatour.

(*Mel*, 1410–12)

She condemns him for always directing his attention to worldly
satisfaction and indulging himself in empty pleasure and vain wealth,
so that he forgets to pay honor and respect to Jesus Christ, in which case
God would despise him, turn his mercy away from him, and require him
to be punished. She declares that it is Melibeus himself who is the cause
of this. She then explains the meaning of allegory in the event given as
a punishment by God (1420–26). His three enemies embody the three
enemies of mankind: the flesh, the devil, and the world. Melibeus does
not protect himself from attack and temptation, and thus God inflicts
five wounds upon him and his soul and afflicts him with the deadly
through the five senses. Prudence explains that the root cause of this
tragic affair is Melibeus himself. His indulgence in worldly joy keeps
him separated from God. As a result, he had unknowingly committed a
sin against God. The misfortune that had befallen him is a punishment
for his neglecting God.

Prudence suggests that it is Melibeus who had caused the sorrow to
his family and tries to make him both admit his fault and give up repaying

his enemies. Melibeus at this point interjects words of objection:

> "Certes," quod Melibee, "I se wel that ye enforce yow muchel by wordes to overcome me in swich manere that I shal nat venge me of myne enemys, / shewynge me the perils and the yveles that myghten falle of this vengeance. / But whoso wolde considere in alle vengeances the perils and the yveles that myghte sewe of vengeances-takynge, / a man wolde nevere take vengeance, and that were harm; / for by the vengeance-takynge been the wikked men dissevered fro the goode men, / and they that han wyl to do wikkednesse restreyne hir wikked purpos, whan they seen the punyssynge and chastisynge of the trespassours."
>
> (*Mel*, 1427–32)

Although Melibeus understands that Prudence does not want him to seek avenge, he never agrees with her. He declares that if he does not avenge his enemies, thinking about the peril and harm generated by the retaliation would cause additional harm, because just as Melibeus says, taking revenge has a deterrent effect on crime or war. Admitting the disadvantage of repaying, he thinks revenge, in a sense, simply a necessary evil, repaying violence for violence and getting even with his enemies.

Prudence replies that he should sue his enemies in court and ask a judge to pass a fair judgement, if he wishes revenge. She believes that it is only a judge who is privileged to give punishment and that giving vent to personal resentment is the same thing as committing a sin. She repeatedly insists that a judge should treat the matter of revenge:

180   Chapter V

> For, as by right and resoun, ther may no man taken vengeance on
> no wight but the juge that hath the jurisdiccioun of it,
>
> (*Mel*, 1379)

> And yet seye I moore, that right as a singuler persone synneth in
> takynge vengeance of another man, / right so synneth the juge if
> he do no vengeance of hem that it han disserved.
>
> (*Mel*, 1435–36)

> If ye wol thanne take vengeance of youre enemys, ye shul retourne
> or have youre recours to the juge that hath the jurisdiccion upon
> hem,   (*Mel*, 1442)

> But yet ne folweth it nat therof that every persone to whom men
> doon vileynye take of it vengeance, / for that aperteneth and
> longeth al oonly to the juges, for they shul venge the vileynyes
> and injuries.   (*Mel*, 1468–69)

Melibeus opposes his wife and says that he does not like that kind of
vengeance at all: "this vengeance liketh me no thyng" (1444) and that
unless he by himself takes revenge on them who had done wrong to him,
he would as good as invite further harm:

> If I ne venge me nat of the vileynye that men han doon to me, /
> I sompne or warne hem that han doon to me that vileynye, and
> alle othere, to do me another vileynye. / For it is writen, 'If thou
> take no vengeance of an oold vileynye, thou sompnest thyne
> adversaries to do thee a newe vileynye.'   (*Mel*, 1461–23)

At this point, Melibeus stands against Prudence with his own strong will, not following the advisors' opinion. He is not easily persuaded by her. Seemingly somewhat accepting each other's opinion, they speak against each other and continue the discussion in the form of a debate.

Then Prudence teaches him how foolish it would be to fight against his enemies. She points out that they are in a better position than Melibeus, and thus it is not wise of him to start a war against them, because they are at an advantage in number and are more powerful. In her view he should not fight against his enemies whether they are stronger or not:

> Forthermoore, ye knowen wel that after the comune sawe, 'it is a woodnesse a man to stryve with a strenger or a moore myghty man than he is hymself, / and for to stryve with a man of evene strengthe—that is to seyn, with as strong a man as he is—it is peril, / and for to stryve with a weyker man, it is folie.'
>
> (*Mel*, 1481–83)

Prudence quotes the words of such authorities as Solomon, Seneca, and Cato. She preaches to him that it is an honorable deed for a man to keep himself out of troubles and away from problems, and that he should not place himself in great peril struggling with those who have greater power than he; also, she says he needs to be patient when someone who is in a better position and is of a higher rank than he causes him unreasonable suffering, for the man might well be of help to him on a different occasion.

She changes the direction of her criticism and aims the brunt of it directly at him. She reminds him that it is Melibeus himself who causes the suffering so that he should be patient and restrain his anger against

182   Chapter V

his enemies:

> if ye wole considere the defautes that been in youre owene
> persone, / for whiche defautes God hath suffred yow have this
> tribulacioun, as I have seyd yow heer-biforn.   (*Mel*, 1494–95)

She once more repeats that the cause of this misfortune is his own
personal fault. Melibeus enjoys worldly pleasure so much that he stays
away from God. He deserves this adversity because of his weakness
and sin, neglecting God. She suggests that he should accept suffering
with patience, admitting that he has many defects. Jesus Christ showed
an example of patience by his own act when he received the greatest
sufferings for the sake of human beings, although he had neither
committed sins nor displayed weaknesses.

Prudence keeps insisting that he should be a man of great patience:

> Also the grete *pacience* which the seintes that been in Paradys han
> had in tribulaciouns that they han ysuffred, withouten hir desert
> or gilt, / oghte muchel stiren yow to *pacience*. / Forthermoore
> ye sholde enforce yow to have *pacience*, / considerynge that
> the tribulaciouns of this world but litel while endure and soone
> passed been and goon, / and the joye that a man seketh to have by
> *pacience* in tribulaciouns is perdurable, after that the Apostle seith
> in his epistle. / 'The joye of God,' he seith, 'is perdurable'—that
> is to seyn, everlastynge. / Also troweth and bileveth stedefastly
> that he nys nat wel ynorissed, ne wel ytaught, that kan nat have
> *paciene* or wol nat receyve *pacience*. / For Salomon seith that
> 'the doctrine and the wit of a man is knowen by *pacience*.' / And

in another place he seith that 'he that is *pacient* governeth hym by greet prudence.' / And the same Salomon seith, 'The angry and wrathful man maketh noyses, and the *pacient* man atempreth hem and stilleth.' / He seith also, 'It is moore worth to be *pacient* than for to be right strong; / and he that may have the lordshipe of his owene herte is moore to preyse than he that by his force or strengthe taketh grete citees.' / And therfore seith Seint Jame in is Epistle that '*paciene*' is a greet vertu of perfeccioun.'"

(*Mel*, 1505–17, italics mine)

There are two points in her speech: one is that being patient in adversity is a virtue of great merit which leads to "the joy of God," this is to say, eternal joy; and the other is that one who is not able to put up with difficulties with patience is neither well-educated nor a man of learning, for it is patience or the lack of it which determines whether a man is intelligent and wise. Her reasoning about the importance of patience sounds fair-spoken and plausible. Yet her plethora of words neither touches the heart of Melibeus nor calms his anger. Although he can comprehend that patience is an ideal virtue, he knows that nobody can be perfect and he himself is conscious of his imperfection:

"Certes," quod Melibee, "I graunte yow, dame Prudence, that pacience is a greet vertu of perfeccioun; / but every man may nat have the perfeccioun that ye seken; / ne I nam nat of the nombre of right parfite men, / for myn herte may nevere been in pees unto the tyme it be venged. / And al be it so that it was greet peril to myne enemys to do me a vileynye in takynge vengeance upon me, / yet tooken they noon heede of the peril, but fulfilleden

184   Chapter V

> hir wikked wyl and hir corage. / And therfore me thynketh men
> oghten nat repreve me, though I putte me in a litel peril for to
> venge me, / and though I do a greet excesse; that is to seyn, that I
> venge oon outrage by another." (*Mel*, 1518–25)

His speech in opposition to Prudence is understandable. It is natural for him to think he is not a perfect person, as no one else is either, so that he would not be able to agree with his wife, who insists that he should be patient. He might well be opposed to his wife who tells him that it is his fault for having to face such hardship and that he should reflect on himself to amend his own faults and learn a lesson from the adversity which God gives him. His outrage might never be abated until he inflicts upon his enemies the same experience as he had been suffering. Compared with Prudence's excessively logical speech, his emotional argument is rooted in honest human feelings. Melibeus's words sound more sympathetic because they are based upon worldly affairs. Prudence, on the other hand, tries to persuade him by the use of Christian paradox. Based on different stances as they are, their conversation is not productive.

Melibeus mentions that as long as he is richer and stronger than his enemies, they would never be able to retaliate so well, even after he had taken revenge, for he thinks "that by moneye and by havynge grete possessions been alle the thynges of this world governed. / And Salomon seith that 'alle thynges obeyen to moneye'" (1549–50). Prudence replies with a considerably long sermon on how to get money and how to spend it from a Christian point of view; after all she indicates three things which he should bear in mind in treating of riches: God, a good conscience, and a good name:

First, ye shul have God in youre herte, / and for no richesse ye shullen do no thyng which may in any manere displese God, that is youre creatour and makere. (*Mel*, 1626–27)

And yet seye I ferthemoore, that ye sholde alwey doon youre bisynesse to gete yow richesses, / so that ye gete hem with good conscience. (*Mel*, 1632–33)

Afterward, in getynge of youre richesses and in usynge of hem, / yow moste have greet bisynesse and greet diligence that youre goode name be alwey kept and conserved. (*Mel*, 1636–37)

Prudence admonishes him that holding God always in mind and acquiring a little wealth are preferable to having abundant property and yet losing God's love. It is important not to displease God over the desire for wealth, only to gather riches greedily, and to respect his honor in the acquisition and use of his property. She advises that he should not start war against his enemies by placing confidence in his wealth. She provides some reasons and examples of biblical wise men to prove her point.

What Melibeus understands from her "faire wordes" and "resouns" in her long speech is only the fact that she does not at all approve of war. He neither comprehends what she really means nor is completely convinced by her words. Admiring her eloquent speech, he makes no objection this time but instead asks her own opinion of what he should do on this occasion. Here he changes his attitude a little and tries to lend an ear to her thoughts. Although she had continued telling him her opinion, he does not take care to listen to her. She consistently advises that he should reconcile and make peace with his enemies. Returning to

186   Chapter V

the starting point, Melibeus makes the last objection to his wife:

> "A," quod Melibee, "now se I wel that ye loven nat myn honour ne my worshipe. / Ye knowen wel that myne adversaries han bigonnen this debaat and bryge by hire outrage, / and ye se wel that they ne requeren ne preyen me nat of pees, ne they asken nat to be reconsiled. / Wol ye thanne that I go and meke me, and obeye me to hem, and crie hem mercy? / For sothe, that were nat my worshipe.
>
> (*Mel*, 1681–85)

It would be unreasonable for him to settle the problem by compromising. Although he is a victim, how can he make a humiliating concession? He condemns her for not loving his "honour" or "worshipe." After all, it is his pride which stands as the largest barrier for making peace with his enemies. Prudence does not take his sense of pride as one of the Deadly Sins; instead of blaming him, she assumes a defiant attitude in insisting on the legitimacy of her opinion:

> Thanne bigan dame Prudence *to maken semblant of wratthe and seyde*: / "Certes, sire, sauf youre grace, I love youre honour and youre profit as I do myn owene, and evere have doon; / ne ye, ne noon oother, seyn nevere the contrarie. / And yit if I hadde seyd that ye sholde han purchaced the pees and the reconsiliacioun, I ne hadde nat muchel mystaken me ne seyd amys.
>
> (*Mel*, 1687–90, italics mine)

It sounds contradictory for her to insist that she should love his dignity and profit as much as she loves her own if she admonishes him to hold

God uppermost. Yet she does not notice the inconsistency but claims that she had done nothing wrong in urging him to make peace and reconcile with his enemies. At this point she is emotionally aroused for the first time: "Thanne bigan dame Prudence to maken semblant of wratthe and seyde" (1687). Even though she only pretends to be angry, this is the point at which Melibeus turns obedient to her advice:

> Whanne Melibee hadde herd dame Prudence *maken semblant of wratthe*, he seyde in this wise: / "Dame, I prey yow that ye be nat displesed of thynges that I seye, / for ye knowe wel that I am angry and wrooth, and that is no wonder; / and they that been wrothe witen nat wel what they don ne what they seyn. / Therfore the prophete seith that 'troubled eyen han no cleer sight.' / But seyeth and conseileth me as yow liketh, for I am redy to do right as ye wol desire; / and if ye repreve me of my folye, I am the moore holden to love yow and to preyse yow.
>
> (*Mel*, 1697–703, italics mine)

It is her wrath which all of a sudden changes his attitude completely. He begs her not to be angry with his words and asks her to guide him carefully because his eyesight is not clear on account of his outrage at his enemies. He excuses himself by claiming that angry men do not understand their own words and behavior, so that they are not able to make a clear judgment. He also tells her that he does not know how to answer her "so manye faire resouns" which she had amassed so that "Seyeth shortly youre wyl and youre conseil, and I am al redy to fulfille and parfourne it" (1712).

Prudence advises him to reconcile with God and put himself in His

188   Chapter V

grace and then she asks for permission to speak with his enemies in order to establish peace. In his reply he is complicit: "dooth youre wil and youre likynge; / for I putte me hoolly in youre disposicioun and ordinaunce" (1724–25). This is a perfect surrender of Melibeus to his wise wife. This conclusion would be something to which the Wife of Bath would consent. The wife wins a complete victory over the husband in discussion. It is ironic, however, that Melibeus follows his wife because he does not want her to become angry at his words. Actually he neither wholly understands her long sermon nor is convinced of her advice in her fair and eloquent speech.

Helen Cooper (1983) is right when she points out:

> "If the Wife of Bath has little sympathy for the authorities she quotes, Dame Prudence's sole function is to cite authorities, sometimes to develop an argument of her own, sometimes to beat down an argument of her husband's by sheer weight of ammunition. *Melibee* substitutes *auctoritee* for *experience*. Words, however, are also shown to be notoriously slippery things, and Prudence has no difficulty in showing Melibee that he has totally misunderstood the sense of something said by accepting its surface meaning: . . . Melibee, more than any other of the *Canterbury Tales*, conists solidly of words, but words alone cannot be trusted."   (172–73)

Prudence relies on the authorities because they are indispensable to justify her insistence and make it logical and reasonable. She makes a deliberate effort to render her eloquent speech rhetorically effective. As a result, the mass of her words turn out to be a mere formality although they are seemingly apt. The harder she argues, the farther the nature of the argument becomes remote from the true argument. She is eager to persuade, but never becomes excited. Her greatest concern is to be logically legitimate and righteous; her argument is reasonable but not in the least touching. The Wife of Bath, on the other hand, deliberately twists the original meaning of the authorities she cites and promotes her own opinion. Her argument sometimes sounds incoherent and irrational, but her way of speaking is passionate and powerful because she has her own voice. That is why she is attractive as a woman as well as a human being and her insistence is energetic and moving even if it is not logical in general.

After Prudence had won her husband's ready obedience to her advice, she visits the enemies and persuades them to show their deep repentance to Melibeus so that they could establish a peaceful settlement. She suggests that they meet Melibeus, express their regret for felonious deeds, and beg forgiveness from him. Melibeus's final judgment is to banish them from his land forever with all their properties seized. Prudence remonstrates with him about his narrow-mindedness and advises him to show his magnanimity in order to keep his honor rather than to be blamed for covetousness. Then at last Melibeus completely agrees with her advice:

> Whenne Melibee hadde herd the grete skiles and resouns of dame Prudence, and hire wise informaciouns and techynges, / his herte gan enclyne to the wil of his wif, considerynge hir trewe entente, / and conformed hym anon and assented fully to werken after hir conseil, / and thonked God, of whom procedeth al vertu and alle goodnesse, that hym sente a wyf of so greet discrecioun.
>
> (*Mel*, 1870–73)

190   Chapter V

Melibeus praises Prudence's speech as remarkably skillful and reasonable, admits the woman's advice is wise, and completely agrees to follow her counsel. Here again is a perfect surrender of the husband to his wife.

Then the tale is terminated rather abruptly with his announcement of total forgiveness of their offenses. The purpose of Prudence's eloquent speeches is to persuade her husband to give up taking revenge against his enemies and forgive them. In this sense, her didactic speech is successful. Yet it is not her interminable speeches that make Melibeus obedient to her. It is simply that he does not want her to be displeased wih him. Although Melibeus and Prudence conduct one series of discussion after another, the final solution is not a result of their controversy. Their long debate with numerous citations and quotations from the authorities has nothing to do with the crucial moment of this tale. Their argument turns out to be something just barren and wasteful. As debate, their discussion was meaningless. Melibeus's intentions were otherwise. He merely wanted to please her and so reached a compromise with her.

Chaucer the Poet, who is extremely careful in his use of details, would never employ a lengthy and longwinded discussion with no particular intention. Why did Chaucer the Pilgrim choose to tell this story himself? As a 'moral tale vertous,' in the way he was asked to tell by the Host, this tale could be successful and should be meant and taken seriously, but as Helen Cooper notices "in Chaucer's mouth," it "indicates different qualities" (174). This tale is both comical and ironical. With all Prudence's persuasive and didactic speech, employing eloquence and rhetorical techniques, her words ultimately turn into a mere shell and do not reach Melibeus's heart. Otherwise, he is movtivated to act because of her pretended wrath over his disagreeing with her advice. The prudent words of Prudence do not work after all. Although she is ostensibly the most prominent person in this tale, the central focus is on Melibeus, as the very title indicates: not "The Tale of Prudence" but "The Tale of Melibee." He is a man who is able to learn from 'female counsel' and whose name means "a man who drinks honey," which suggests "sweet learning" or "sweet knowledge."[22]

Prudence's tedious, long speech, then, is divided into three parts. In the first part she advises that he should gather the opinions of others. As a result of counseling, when Melibeus had almost decided to take vengence on his enemies, she humbly asks him to abandon the idea. Yet he does not change the plan which had been agreed on by his advisors and also by his own wish. He does not intend to follow a woman's advice in any case. She opposes him and explains how wonderful women are and finally succeeds in making him reject such misogynistic thoughts. In the second part, she closely examines and criticizes each piece of the councellors advice and tries to make Melibeus give up the idea of taking vengeance. Here Dame Prudence stands on equal footing with her husband or rather on a higher level, inducing him not to do as he at first intended.

The third part of Prudence's speech is basically different from the previous parts. She changes the manner of persuading him. She points out that Melibeus himself is the cause of the mishap and tries to make him give up the idea of repaying his enemies and persuades him to reconcile himself to them and, in the end, to forgive them. Melibeus speaks against her and claims that an act of revenge would help to prevent another evil deed. He also believes that his might and wealth would protect him from attack by his enemies. Prudence condemns his weaknesses which had caused the adversity given by God and admonishes him to hold God uppermost and make peace with Him, and then be reconciled and forgive

192   Chapter V

his enemies. It is ironical, however, that Melibeus's motive to obey his wife is not the result of their long debate. He is not totally persuaded by her abundance of rational words. But he decides to do whatever she says because he does not want to displease her. If this is the only reason why Melibeus surrenders to his wife, the previous serious and long speech would seem to mean nothing.

Chaucer the Pilgrim begins telling the tale of Melibee, being asked by the Host to talk about something moral and virtuous in prose. Some scholars consider that Chaucer might have inserted this tale as a joke in order to take revenge on the Host who has interrupted the first tale of Sir Thopas and judged it worthless. If Chaucer had aimed to take vengeance on the Host, his intention would have turned out to be a failure, because the Host was pleased with the tale:

> Whan ended was my tale of Melibee,
> And of Prudence and hire benignytee,
> Oure Hooste seyde, "As I am feithful man,
> And by that precious corpus Madrian,
> I hadde levere than a barel ale
> That Goodelief, my wyf, hadde herd this tale!
> For she nys no thyng of swich pacience
> As was this Melibeus wyf Prudence.
>
> (*The Prologue of the Monk's Tale*, 1889–96)

The Host respects Prudence's patience and wants to tell his wife about her. After that he discloses how wicked his wife Goodelief is. She is similar to the Wife of Bath in many ways: she is displeased if she is not treated well at church, she is always complaining about her husband,

and she is so powerful and so brave of heart that her husband lacks the courage to stand against her. Even though he complains about his wicked wife, he does not desire to have such a wise wife as Prudence. Would husbands in general wish for such a wife, who is so prudent and patient, righteous and judicious, and reasonable and logical? Some would. Most would not, perhaps.

Chapter VI

Chaucer's Intention in Creating Female Eloquence

This chapter discusses why these three women are treated in this dissertation and clarifies how they relate to the theme of 'eloquence,' by comparing their individual similarities and differences, and examines what Chaucer's view of women and his intention in creating female eloquence are.

VI-1 The Wife of Bath and Criseyde

Although the Wife of Bath and Criseyde appear to be completely different types of women and are seemingly opposite types of person-alities, they have some similar elements in common: they are widows, keenly self-conscious, who assert themselves by employing eloquence. Yet how they differ is absolutely obvious.

Criseyde, as a widow, is humble and modest and she wishes to live quietly as if she is hiding from the world in her black dress. When she hears about Troilus' love for the first time from her uncle, Pandarus, who acts as a go-between, she grieves bitterly over her lot and wishes to keep her life peaceful. She is forsaken by her father and socially dispossessed,

[195]

196   Chapter VI

and is isolated from the patronage of men in power. She asks Hector to assure her safety in Troy. Her only wish is to live inconspicuously and calmly. The Wife of Bath, on the other hand, is an experienced widow, who had had five husbands. She is indifferent to the number of times she has been married, though she justifies her frequent remarriages with a biblical reading of her own. That is why she dares to declare that she is looking forward to having a sixth husband, if she has a chance. She becomes bolder and more energetic in character, and stronger and more powerful financially, every time she marries, either for better or for worse.

Both women are outstanding in their self-consciousness. The Wife of Bath's strong self-consciousness is reflected in the sense of her fashion: she wears fine hose of scaret red and a large round hat like a buckler or target, and a pair of new and supple shoes when going on pilgrimage. On Sunday, she puts on a headdress made of a cloth of high-quality, weighing ten pounds. She insists on being the first person to give offerings at church. Her face is fine-featured and full of confidence. The Wife's self-consciousness comes from her obstinate and selfish nature. She likes to make herself conspicuous and hates to lose; that is, she is always competitive and not content to be second best. Criseyde is quite conscious of her beauty, and knows herself to be the most beautiful woman in Troy, so that she thinks that she deserves to be loved by Troilus. Being humble as a widow, she behaves as if she thinks nothing at all amiss about her being in the temple of Pallas. She has the air of looking down on other people. She is a woman of great self-respect. The difference in their self-consciousness is clear: it is important for the Wife of Bath to do whatever she desires to do, while Criseyde cares about nothing but keeping up appearances and mostly worries as to what other people think of her.

Compared with their speech, similarly, they are not women who silently follow men, but they assert themselves and counter the men with their eloquent speech. The ways of their self-assertion are different. The Wife's is based on her egoistic way of self-justification. When she excuses her five-time marriages, she abuses the Bible as she wishes. To obtain domination over her husbands, she attacks them with a hostile tone of voice and keeps complaining about and chiding them. She also boldly expresses her lust by using shamelessly coarse language. Her assertion is so self-centered that she does not care about what others think of her. Criseyde, on the other hand, becomes eloquent only to protect herself. She asserts herself when her honor and good name are in danger. When she is pressed by Pandarus to accept Troilus' love, and when she persuades Troilus to let her go over to the Greek camp in exchange for Antenore, she is concerned about her reputation; what other people think about her.

Although the Wife of Bath and Criseyde share some important traits in common, they are totally opposite in their ways. What makes them different from each other? A key point of the difference of the two is the social class they belong to. The Wife of Bath represents a woman who is from the middle class. She lives in a realistic world. She is a rising and powerful bourgeois. She is free from any social restrains except those of the patriarchal and male-dominant society. That is why she dares to challenge them by speaking against them in a loud voice. Her desire is to live freely by instinct and to do what she wants to do.

Criseyde lives in a different world from the Wife. Chaucer creates *TC* as a well-established courtly romance. He makes his Criseyde an ideal heroine of romance. She is, in short, a noble lady. It is natural for her to be humble and modest and to keep her good name in order to preserve

198   Chapter VI

her own honor. Yet what Chaucer makes her unique in is that she is not an expressionless, emotionless, and mindless heroine of romance. She is realistic enough to face the difficulties and grasp the situation she is put to and find the best way out of it very skillfully. She can wisely calculate how to put herself in a better position. Even when she betrays Troilus, she worries about her name being disgraced forever, but compromises by saying that there is no better way than staying with the Greeks, so that then she should be faithful to her new love, Diomede. This is basically her policy in choosing the less misfortunate option of the two.

Flexibility toward reality is one kind of typical trait of women. This is the way of Criseyde's getting on in life. She is also blamed for her flexibility because it comes from her "slydyng of corage," and betrays Troilus after all. Yet she needs to be amenable to the changing situation as a powerless woman needing to survive in a harsh world. The Wife of Bath has stubbornly insisted on her will and struggled with her husbands in her marital life. She finally, however, turns into a most obedient and faithful wife after her fifth husband cedes complete domination to her. Her sudden and complete change might well embarrass audiences medieval and modern. Yet if the situation changes, she could change herself like a willow. She always holds a contradictory desire: she wants to be ruled over by men as well as to rule over men. Her ideal husband is obedient but "fressh and gay in bed."

Both the Wife of Bath and Criseyde are among the most attractive characters in Chaucer's works. The Wife of Bath is a woman of the common class. She lives a 'real' life, speaks her true feelings, and discloses her real desire and deep emotions sometimes aggressively in vulgar words. Criseyde, who is a noble lady like a heroine of romance, struggles to survive in a bitter world of war as a helpless widow. Their eloquence is a tactic for flesh-and-blood women to conduct themselves in real life. That is why their words are powerful and real, and render them as attractive speakers.

VI-2　Prudence vs Criseyde and the Wife of Bath

Different from the Wife of Bath and Criseyde, who are given rich descriptions of their characteristics and attractive features, Chaucer gives us no details for visualizing her features, her hairdo and her costume. It is impossible to imagine her age, her height, and her figure. Dame Prudence is not given any particular individuality. She is entirely faceless. Why does Chaucer, who is a master of portraiture, intentionally exclude any of the realistic traits of a living creature? This is because he draws her as a personified character. Dame Prudence is an allegorical figure who stands for the concept of "prudence": she is sensible, careful and cautious, and moreover, patient, persistent, reasonable and logical.

Prudence and Criseyde are similar in their nobility and decency. Their ways of eloquent speech are stylish and elegant. The purpose of Prudence's eloquence is to persuade her husband to follow her advice and to give up the idea of taking vengeance against his enemies and make peace with them. Dame Prudence uses numerous citations from the authorities of Greek, Latin and the Bible, such as Solomon, Cicero, Seneca, Ovid, St. Paul, and Augustine. Her speech consists of a long catalogue of proverbs and an abundance of metaphors and authoritarian advice. The words from a faceless woman do not have realistic substance; they do not carry practical meanings but they show merely abstract and idealistic concepts. Although her speech is logical and reasonable, it sounds too formalistic to touch her husband's heart. There is no bridge between her words and the realistic world. In the end, at last, what moves Melibeus is not her persuasive words but her anger. As soon as he perceives a glimpse of hysteria on her face, he suddenly changes his attitude and immediately obeys her advice. Ironically, all her efforts to persuade her husband with copious words come to nothing. What he as a husband fears most is to displease his wife.

The same method is applied in the case of Criseyde. When Troilus asks her to escape from Troy before she has to leave for the Greeks side, Criseyde tries hard to make him give up the idea by saying that she is sure to persuade her father and return to Troilus within ten days. He feels convinced that her plan will not succeed and refuses to agree with her. She urges him to trust her and to drop his fantasy about their escape from Troy. If he does not, she says she would die before the day is out. She threatens Troilus and this is the same rhetorical device that her uncle used in persuading her to accept Troilus' love. Her persuasive words are effectively menacing. The logic of her speech is not necessarily as righteous as Prudence's but it is sufficiently acceptable to her ego in its own way to protect her reputation.

Prudence and the Wife look different at first glance; however, their speech techniques share the same style. Melibeus thinks that all women are wicked and that it would be shameful to change his decision about warring against his enemy. Prudence refutes her husband's anti-feministic thoughts using proverbs and authoritative citations. Then she points out the mistakes her husband had made to date. She enumerates the mistakes which her husband had committed in choosing his advisors. The method of her juxtaposing the faults of her husband and criticizing him is the same as that of the Wife of Bath. She lists the faults of women by quoting the words of her husband in order to retaliate by strengthening her own case; while Prudence admonishes her husband for the errors that he had committed in order to control him for her own purpose. Although their causes and effects are different, they exhibit curious contrasts and similarities. The one becomes a parody of the other. Constant logical attack, however, is no different from the irrational chiding of "wykked wyves."

The Wife of Bath and Prudencce are similar in the way they use Authorities. The Wife justifies her remarriages by taking advantage of biblical authority. Prudence uses a chain of authority and makes her assertion, her attack with words, stronger and more reasonable. Yet as she is faceless, the words she utters are not passionate. She is not a flesh-and-blood person. She is merely a personified concept. She plays a role of allegory as 'prudence.'

What makes Prudence different from the Wife of Bath and Criseyde is that she is an insubstantial and fictitious character. Both the Wife and Criseyde are, on the other hand, realistic women who stand or try to stand against male-dominant society and struggle to survive in a severe world by dint of eloquence. Their logic is sometimes inconsistent and sometimes broken-down because of their selfishness and shrewdness. Yet, they speak with their own words. Though the Wife borrows from the authorities to support her logic, she twists the meaning to suit herself, interpreting favorably for her personal intentions. Criseyde's logic is not broken down but is flexibly transfigured in accordance with the situation. They have many faults; however, they are thereby all the more lively and attractive. They are not only charming as women with strong and weak points, but also attractive as human beings.

202   Chapter VI

Prudence is set up as an allegorical being who makes a 'prudent' speech with a flawless theory and plays a role in guiding her husband to right conduct. She has no characteristics of a living woman. It is as if she were invisible. As she serves as a prototype of an eloquent woman, she is faceless, with no characteristics. She is nobody, and so she can be anyone. The Wife of Bath and Criseyde are the embodied parts of Prudence. If she were a real person, she would never be attractive, either as a woman or a wife; or as a human being. In contemporary Chaucer studies, *Mel* is not always highly admired by modern readers because of its tedious speech with an abundance of allegorical expressions and proverbs. Nevertheless, Chaucer especially chooses to tell this story. From the perspective of eloquence, Prudence plays an important part as a prototype of eloquent women in Chaucer's works.

VI-3   The 'Meaning' of Eloquent Women

In literary works women were conventionally objects to be spoken of and characterized by men. Chaucer had changed the women into subjects who can assert themselves for their own sakes. The poet gives them means to express themselves, deliver their intentions, and assert themselves. Each of them has her own logic. By freely using their own language, as a weapon to attack or as a shield to protect, they make eloquent speeches in order to persuade the men. As Cicero says, the aim of eloquence it to persuade. When Chaucer describes those eloquent women, he stands behind them, fully understands their situations, and sympathetically speaks on their behalf. In this sense, the poet is a great supporter of women. At the same time, however, he discloses an extreme bitterness towards women. Chaucer's double views of women are reflected in the eloquence of these women.

The poet permits the Wife of Bath to speak against anti-feministic thoughts and to protect women. She is talkative, selfish, stubborn, and self-assertive. She takes her eloquence as a weapon and attacks anti-feministic authority which opposes her over the fact that she had married five times in her life. She uses her eloquence to dominate her husbands by chiding, deceiving, lying, and cursing. She repeats that her husbands speak ill of her and exposes frankly her sexual desire without worrying about her reputation. She shamelessly lays bare something which women actually are not supposed to express openly. Her eloquence is not only in powerful support of women but is also a sharp disclosure of women's faults. In this respect, she is described from men's point of view. Himself lurking under the mask of the Wife, Chaucer freely protects as well as criticizes women.

Criseyde is, on the contrary, a humble yet cowardly character, full of pity and mercy. But she knows that she is the most beautiful in Troy. She always worries over what other people think of her. It is no wonder because she lives alone powerlessly, helplessly, socially-isolated and politically-threatened. She has to defend herself. She uses her eloquence to keep herself safe. Her most serious speech is made to persuade Troilus to give up holding her in Troy when she is supposed to be exchanged with Antenor. Although she loves Troilus in truth, her groundless confidence of her return turns out to be a merely over-optimistic view of women. He creates her as very decent and sensible, different from those in his sources, who are more fickle and flippant. Chaucer fully understands and well expresses the psychology of a noble woman who is put in a

204   Chapter VI

weak position. He hesitates to describe her betrayal because he offers special adoration of her as if he is fascinated by her. Yet he narrates how she betrays him by sharply contrasting how Troilus spends the ten days and after in some detail. The narrative is focused on Troilus' sorrow and both the poet and audiences altogether sympathize with Troilus. Chaucer intentionally directs his attention to Troilus and suddenly loses his interest in Criseyde. Though Chaucer feels pity for Criseyde's name lest it be disgraced forever, he does not actually protect her at the fatal moment. Or rather he provokes a hatred of Criseyde. He leaves her forlorn in the last situation when she truly deserves sympathy. Chaucer intends to embody a flesh-and-blood woman in Criseyde. It is especially important for noble women to keep up their reputation and calculate things for their own advantages, and flexibly and cleverly adjust themselves to the situation which keeps changing and is unstable. After all, Chaucer never sympathizes nor protects her at this crucial point.

Prudence is, as her name announces, a prudent and wise wife. She uses her eloquence to perusade her husband to forget his anger and forgive his enemies and reconcile with him. First, like the Wife of Bath, she counters the anti-feministic thinking of her husband who does not want to take counsel from her because he thinks all women are "wykked." Her reason and logic are constantly designed to cast blame on her husband in a way that is not unlike being attacked by "wykked wyves." She tries to play the role of a wise wife; nevertheless, her behavior is in fact nothing but that of a "wykked wyfe." Her flawless speech is too formalistic to touch her husband. Ironically, her purpose is accomplished not by her eloquent speech, but by her anger at her husband because he is not easily compromised. Her great effort with a flood of words and logic are at last all in vain. Although Chaucer never shows his true feelings, the plot, process, and especially the last development of the story imply his bitter view as to the self-righteous and wise wife, who has no charm and causes suffering to the husband.

If in their eloquence, Chaucer shows a friendly face to women, he also turns an unfriendly face towards them. What makes him feel bitter toward women? Chaucer's life records tell of his supposedly unhappy experience with women. His marriage with Philippa is mismatched on account of their difference of birth right: Chaucer is from a rising bourgeois, a prominent merchant class, while Philippa, nobly born in northern France, attends Queen Philippa upon marrying Edward III. The marriage itself between a young unlanded squire and a knight's daughter is unconventional. For Chaucer was it fortunate to marry a woman of higher rank and a better income? There is no knowing if his marriage was loving, happy and enjoyable or not. The biographical records relating to Chaucer, Philippa and their children bear witness to the most convincing explanation of their marriage: that is, John of Gaunt took Philippa, as his mistress, got a child, and forced Chaucer to marry her.

Another episode indicative of Chaucer's involvement with women is the case of Cecily Champain. This is surely the most mysterious and dishonorable enigma in Chaucer's life records. It is impossible to know exactly what had happened between Cecily and Chaucer. What is certainly assumed from the legal documents is that Chaucer tries hard to conceal the inconvenient facts and settle things with money through his agents, whatever the word *raptus* means. Chaucer probably exercised his masculine power and social authority to make this woman keep silent. If this case had happened as a reaction to his marriage with Philippa, his personal life with women would have been displeasing and unsatisfactory.

206   Chapter VI

Chaucer's unhappy experience would not leave him with only a negative view of women. His eloquent women are not so simply and plainly described. His harsh personal experience would enable him to learn more about women and give him second thoughts about their nature, which would then help him in reaching a more positive standpoint in describing the eloquent women. Elaine Tuttle Hansen (1991: 37) points out the similarity between court poets and women, in their ambiguous and subordinate position. Chaucer, as a court poet, does not always occupy in a socially dominant position. He is, in a sense, a marginal being, just as women are in patriarchal society. Sometimes Chaucer replaces himself with a woman and exposes his true feelings and real thoughts to the courtly and patriarchal society.

Because of his profound insight into women, Chaucer presents them on a wider and deeper level. He has the Wife of Bath assert that she wants to hold control over her husband and enjoy her life uppermost just as she wishes. She would be supported and sympathized with by modern readers as well as by a medieval audience. There would be a Criseyde for all ages and in all places, who betrays men with an amiable face by changing her position flexibly and stubbornly so as to survive. Both the Wife of Bath and Criseyde are marred by faults and weaknesses, but they are thereby all the more charming. Prudence, on the contrary, is faultless, but it is clear that even complete perfection leads her to failure in persuading her husband. She is an allegorical figure without the substance of a living creature and she aims to maintain herself by her pointed logic; yet her logic finally sounds hollow and fails in persuading her husband. She is, so to speak, a 'learned fool.'

Geoffrey Chaucer stands as one of the most imaginative creators in the history of English literature. He produces his works mostly within the framework of literary conventions and Christian traditions of the Middle Ages. His creativity is rather focused on the description of women. When his imagination transcends the binding of medieval traditions and historical conventions, Chaucer produces outstanding personalities. The three women discussed in this dissertation represent the poet's foremost characters. They are given words to assert themselves, protect themselves, and excuse themselves. Approaching women from the vantage point of eloquence makes it possible for Chaucer to establish his universality. He explores the nature of women over the entire range from the standpoint of their eloquence. He achieves a profound grasp of human nature which goes beyond gender, time and space. In recent Chaucer studies, there is almost no approach that casts a fuller light on human beings.

In sum, Chaucer's eloquent women are examined as to their thoughts, actions and passions via an analysis of what they say and how they say it. In their loquacity they reveal his deliberate intention to create them exactly as they are. The reason why Chaucer's characters attract modern readers, beyond "time and space," just as surely as they appealed to a medieval audience, is that his sharp-eyed insight can be universally shared. His characters in general and in particular invite reader-participation, empathy, sympathy and, it may even sometimes be, condemnation, for in them we uncover questionable aspects of ourselves.

Conclusion

This thesis examined three women characters whom Geoffrey Chaucer develops from the perspective of their 'eloquence': the Wife of Bath, Criseyde, and Prudence. In all of Chaucer's work these three stand alone as eloquent women. In the literary convention of the medieval ages, women were generally objects characterized by men. Among the many different women Chaucer describes in his works, those three are distinctly eloquent in their fluent speech. He gives them their own words which enable them to express themselves, deliver their intentions, and freely assert themselves. By discussing what and how Chaucer makes each of them say, his intention of developing them as eloquent and his hidden view of women and true feeling are revealed.

Past studies have neither paid adequate attention to Chaucer's most eloquent three women nor clarified the universality revealed through their characterization and portrayals. There have been few approaches to explore possible connections between Chaucer's life records and his works and characters so as to examine a hint of his view of women. Chaucer the medieval English poet is clearly descended from the European tradition of rhetoric. Women, seen from the perspective of eloquence, reveal Chaucer's profound insight into human beings such that they transcend gender. They are not bound by narrow time and space. This dissertation aims to reconfirm aspects of Chaucer's literary genius.

The origin of rhetoric is traceable to ancient Greece during and after which it was transmitted to Rome and highly developed by the Romans. Just before and then into the 1st century in Rome, Cicero developed a sustained approach to the study of rhetoric, turning it into the art of language. By 'rhetoric' he intended 'the sophisticated language of oratory for purposes of persuasion' as well as 'the use of elegant adornment in poetry.' His main focus was on the art of oratory. Education consisted in part of a study of the *trivium*; that is, of grammar, logic and rhetoric, the three subjects that were meant to strengthen critical thinking. These subjects were studied throughout medieval Europe.

As noted earlier, the very five-part framework of the *CT* is itself traceable to Roman orator and scholar Cicero. There is, then, a cross-breeding of disciplines—poetic with rhetoric. Just as rhetorical technique loaned itself to imaginative poetic fiction, fiction absorbed rhetoric.

One study relevant to eloquent speech would seem very inviting to pursue; namely, a line-by-line or even phrase-by-phrase identification of the techniques that fall from the lips of the Wife of Bath. Irony, simile, allusion, alliteration and repetition, for instance, are among the common ones; while in fact techniques carried over and in use from Greek and Latin into the present day are voluminous and can be found in abundance in words spoken by characters such as Criseyde, Prudence and the Wife of Bath. Such a study would quickly and overwhelmingly reveal how literature ancient and modern is indebted to rhetoric.

Chaucer earnestly describes these women and completes their words in each story. They are different types of women in their positions as widow, lover and wife. They express themselves with a plethora of words which surely, directly or indirectly, represent Chaucer's true intentions or feelings. Sometimes he offers objections to religious and social authorities through their words, or sometimes he attacks husbands or wives straightforwardly and mercilessly through their sharp speech, and sometimes he makes women speak to protect themselves as powerless and helpless beings. He is sometimes very friendly to women, but his judgment of women is clearly double-edged and is sometimes severe and bitter. Such a negative point of view toward women could possibly, at least in part, be rooted in his unhappy experience with women in his actual life, including his marital life with Philippa. He subtly reveals his true feeling for and against women, or toward patriarchal and courtly society under cover of his women characters. His ingenious devices underline the exquisite touch of their eloquence.

As far as contemporary feminist criticism is concerned, Chaucer comes in for precious little defense. He is on the whole regarded as the characteristic misogynist who can be found in any age. In truth, as is virtually true in all rebellions, the case against Chaucer as misogynist tends to be at least somewhat overstated. He is, in short, a literary whipping boy; one who is forefront and available, and one against whom the more impatient feminists are eager to raise their voices.

In view of this state of affairs, perhaps a demurrer is in order. *CT* is not a sociological treatise. It is first and foremost an imaginative work and should not be viewed as a social critique. Just as the Wife of Bath 'used' authorities to excuse herself, critics should not forget that very little is known about the private Chaucer. *CT* is not biography or autobiography. It is imaginative literature.

Chaucer observes and comprehends them not only just as women but also as human beings. These eloquent women brilliantly expose the truth of living creatures at all times and in all places. That is why they remain attractive and appealing. They transcend time and space; that is to say, their universality is exposed through Chaucer's characterization and portrayals.

It has been said that fictional universality begins in a specific place. In realistic fiction the setting is always local and the characters are ordinary

212   Conclusion

people, who are not unlike ourselves. When characters are developed in depth, readers everywhere understand that these are not just isolated characters, but that they rise above their local setting. The particular gives rise to the universal. The characters and social conditions of any successful piece of fiction achieve universality to the extent that readers all across the world's cultures find their lives powerfully mirrored there. 'Literature is a mirror of life,' as the old saying goes.

Chaucer, just so, in recreating his English 'locale,' has struck at the very heart of universal human experience such that in reading *CT* a reader is drawn up short and is apt to say, 'Yes. I recognize that. For I have had that very same experience.' Chaucer's characters and their experiences are universal not only in that sense but they are also timeless. That they achieve 'universality' must be granted.

Seen from the perspective of 'eloquence' these three women are the most notable characters in Chaucer's works. In describing their eloquence, he brings out not only their virtuous qualities but also wicked aspects of women. He skillfully represents the double-facedness of women by his excellent elocution: women are sometimes obedient and sometimes offensive; while they are indeed loving, how cruel they also are! When he astutely discusses the nature of women, he achieves a central insight into human nature which goes beyond the parameters of gender. This is Chaucer's intention in creating female eloquence. He describes the very nature of human beings through the use of 'eloquence.' By giving women eloquent speech and trenchant words to express and assert themselves, Chaucer's keen understanding of human nature escapes the limited social framework of the Middle Ages. Because of this universality, his works have been read for over 600 years and there is no end in sight.

Notes

1 G. L. Kittredge, *Chaucer and his Poetry* (Cambridge, MA: Harvard University Press, 1951), 2.

2 D. W. Robertson, Jr., *A Preface to Chaucer* (New Jersey: Princeton University Press, 1962), 321.

3 All quotations of Chaucer's works are from L. D. Benson, ed., *The Riverside Chaucer*, 3rd ed. (Boston: Houghton Mifflin, 1987).

4 James. J. Murphy, *Latin Rhetoric and Education in the Middle Ages and Renaissance* (Aldershot: Ashgate, 2005), 1–2.

5 F. N. Robinson, ed., *The Complete Works of Geoffrey Chaucer*, 2nd ed. (Oxford: Oxford University Press, 1957), 545.

6 John H. Fisher, ed., *The Complete Poetry and Prose of Geoffrey Chaucer* (New York: Holt, Rinehart and Winston, 1977), 958–59; Donald R. Howard, *Chaucer: His Life, His Works, His World* (New York: Dutton, 1987), 342–43.

7 Martin M. Crow and Clair C. Olson, eds., *Chaucer Life-Records* (Oxford: Clarendon Press, 1966), 343.

De scripto irrotulato.

Noverint universi me Ceciliam Chaumpaigne filiam quondam Willelmi Chaumpaigne et Agnetis uxoris eius remisisse relaxasse et omnino pro me et heredibus meis imperpetuum quietum clamasse Galfrido Chaucer armigero omnimodas acciones tam de raptu meo tam [*sic*] de aliqua alia re vel causa cuiuscumque condicionis fuerint quas unquam habui habeo seu habere potero a principio mundi usque in diem confeccionis presencium. In cuius rei testimonium presentibus sigillum meum apposui. Hiis testibus domino Willelmo de Beauchamp tunc camerario domini regis domino Johanne de Clanebowe domino Willelmo de Nevylle militibus Johanne Philippott et Ricardo Morel. Datum Londonie primo die Maii anno regni Regis Ricardi secundi post conquestum tercio.

Et memorandum quod predicta Cecilia venit in cancellaria regis apud Westmonastrium quarto die Maii anno presenti et recognovit scriptum predictum et contenta in eodem in forma predicta.

(Close R., 219, 3 Ric. II, m. 9 d.; cf. *L-R*, Pt. IV, No. 134.)

All the English translations from the Latin documents are translated by Dr. Hitoshi Yoshikawa.

8 Crow and Olson, 344.

[213]

214   Notes

Chaucer.—Ultimo die Junii anno regni Regis Ricardi secundi secundo Ricardus Goodchild et Johannes Grove armurer recognovernut subsequens scriptum esse factum suum in hec verba:

Noverint universi nos Ricardum Goodchild coteler et Johannem Grove armurer cives Londonie remisisse relaxasse et imperpetuum pro nobis heredibus et executoribus nostris quietum clamasse Galfrido Chaucer armigero omnimodas acciones querelas et demandas quas versus dictum Galfridum unquam habuimus habemus sec aliquo modo habere poterimus vel aliquis nostrum habere poterit in futurm racione alicuius transgressionis convencionis contractus compoti debiti vel alterius rei cuiuscumque realis vel personalis inter nos et predictum Galfridum vel aliquem nostrum inite vel facte a principio mundi usque in diem confeccionis presencium. In cuius rei testimonium presentibus sigilla nostra apposuimus. Datum Londonie vicesimo octavo die mensis Junii anno regni Regis Ricardi secundi a conquestu quarto.

(City of London, Plea and Momo. R., A23, m. 5 d.; cf. *L-R*, Pt. IV, No. 137.)

9 Crow and Olson, 344.

Goodchild, Grove. Eodem die venit hic Celcilia Chaumpaigne et cognovit subsequens scriptum esse factum suum in hec verba:

Noverint universi me Ceciliam Chaumapigne filiam quondam Willelmi Chaumpaigne et Agnetis uxoris eius remisisse relaxasse et omnino pro me heredibus et executoribus meis imperpetuum quietum clamasse Ricardo Goodchild coteler et Johanni Grove armurer civibus Londonie omnimodas acciones querelas et demandas tam reales quam personales quas versus dictos Ricardum et Johannem vel eorum alterum unquam habui habeo seu quovis-modo in futurum habere potero racione cuiuscumque cause a principio mundi usque in diem confeccionis presencium. In cuius rei testimonium presentibus sigillum meum apposui. Datum Londonie vicesimo octavo die Junii anno regni Regis Ricardi secundi post conquestum quarto.

(City of London, Plea and Momo. R., A23, m. 5 d.; cf. *L-R*, Pt. IV, No. 137.)

10 Crow and Olson, 345.

C. Chaumpaigne. Vacat quia solvit.

Secundo die Jilii anno regni Regis Ricardi secundi quarto Johannes Grove armurer venit hic coram maiore et aldermannis et recognovit se debere Cecilie Chaumpaigne filie quondam Willemi Chaumpaigne et Agnetis uxoris eius decem libras sterlingorum solvendas ad festum Sancti Michaelis proximo futurum etc. Et nisi fecerit concedit etc.

(City of London, Plea and Momo. R., A23, m. 5 d.; cf. *L-R*, Pt. IV, No. 137.)

11 See also D. W. Robertson, Jr. "'And For My Land Thus Hastow Mordred Me?': Land Tenure, the Cloth Industry, and the Wife of Bath," *Chaucer Review* 14 (1980): 409.

12 John M. Manly, *Some New Light on Chaucer* (Gloucester, MA: Peter Smith, 1959), 227–29; Robertson, 410–16.

13 Laura D. Kellogg, *Boccaccio's and Chaucer's Cressida* (New York: Peter Lang, 1995), 6–7. See also Benson, 1021–22.

14 All quotations of Shakespeare's works are from G. Blakemore Evans, ed., *The Riverside Shakespeare* (Boston: Houghton Mifflin, 1974).

15 B. A. Windeatt, *Geoffrey Chaucer: Troilus and Criseyde* (New York: Longman, 1984), 104.

16 Windeatt (1984: 93); Benson (1987: 1026).

17 All quotations from the Bible are from Herbert G. May and Bruce Metzger, eds., *The Oxford Annotated Bible with the Apocrypha, Revised Standard Version* (New York: Oxford University Press, 1965).

18 Corinne Saunders, *Rape and Ravishment* (Cambridge: D. S. Brewer, 2001), 302.

19 Priscilla Martin, *Chaucer's Women: Nuns, Wives and Amazons* (London: Macmillan, 1990), 183.

20 Benson, 1033.

21 Windeatt, 487.

22 Robert William, and Chainani Soman eds. "Summary and Analysis of Chaucer's *Tale of Melibee*," The Canterbury Tales *Study Guide* (November 2008), under GradeSaver, http://www.gradesaver.com/the-canterbury-tales/study-guide/summary-chaucers-tale-of-melibeein MLA Format (accesses November 13, 2014).

Bibliography

Aers, David. *Chaucer*. Brighton: Harvester, 1986.

Askins, William R. "*The Tales of Melibee.*" In *Sources and Analogues of* The Canterbury Tales, edited by M. Correale and Mary Hamel, 321-408. Cambridge: D. S. Brewer, 2002.

Baldwin, Charles Sears. *Medieval Rhetoric and Poetic*. Gloucester, MA: Peter Smith, 1959.

Barney, A. Stephen, ed. *Chaucer's* Troilus*: Essays in Criticism*. Connecticut: Archon Books, 1980.

Baum, Paull F. *Chaucer: A Critical Appreciation*, 1958. Reprint, New York: Octagon Books, 1982.

Benson, C. David. *Chaucer's Drama of Style: Poetic Variety and Constrast in the* Canterbury Tales. Chapel Hill and London: University of North Carolina Press, 1986.

———. *Chaucer's* Troilus and Criseyde. London: Unwin Hyman, 1990.

Blamires, Alcuin. *Chaucer, Ethics, and Gender*. Oxford: Oxford University Press, 2006.

Bishop, Ian. *The Narrative Art of the* Canterbury Tales. London: Everyman's University Library, 1987.

Boccaccio, Giovanni. *Il Filostrato*. Edited by Vincenzo Pernicone. Translated by Robert P. apRoberts and Anna Bruni Seldis. The Garland Library of Medieval Literature. Vol. 53. New York and London: Garland, 1986.

Boitani, Piero and Jill Mann, eds. *The Cambridge Companion to Chaucer*. 2nd ed. Cambridge: Cambridge University Press, 2003.

Bornstein, Diane. "Chaucer's *Tale of Melibee* As an Example of the *Style Clergial.*" *Chaucer Review* 12 (1978): 236–54.

Bowden, Muriel. *A Reader's Guide to Geoffrey Chaucer*. New York: Octagon Books, 1987.

Braddy, Haldeen. "Chaucer and Dame Alice Perres," *Speculum* 21 (1946): 222–28.

———. *Geoffrey Chaucer: Literary and Historical Studies*. New York: Kennikat Press, 1971.

——. "Chaucer, Alice Perrers, and Cecily Chaumpaigne." *Speculum* 52 (1977): 906–11.

Brewer, Derek. *Chaucer and His World*. London: Methuen, 1978.

Brown, Peter, ed. *A Companion to Chaucer*. Oxford: Blackwell, 2000.

Cannon, Christopher. "*Raptus* in the Chaumpaigne Release and a Newly Discovered Document Concerning the Life of Geoffrey Chaucer." *Speculum* 68 (1993): 74–79.

——. "Chaucer and Rape: Uncertainty's Certainties." *Studies in the Age of Chaucer* 22 (2000): 67–92.

Chaucer, Geoffrey. *The Complete Works of Geoffrey Chaucer: Romaunt of the Rose, Minor Poems*. 2nd ed. Edited by W. W. Skeat. Oxford: Clarendon Press, 1899.

——. *The Complete Poetry and Prose of Geoffrey Chaucer*. Edited by John H. Fisher. New York: Holt, Rinehart and Winston, 1977.

——. *The Complete Works of Geoffrey Chaucer*. 2nd ed. Edited by F. N. Robinson. Oxford: Oxford University Press. 1986.

——. *The Riverside Chaucer*. 3rd ed. Edited by L. D. Benson. Oxford: Oxford University Press, 1987.

Collet, Carolyn P. "Heeding the Counsel of Prudence: A Context for the *Melibee*." *Chaucer Review* 29 (1995): 416–33.

Cooper, Helen. *The Structure of* the Canterbury Tales. London: Duckworth, 1983.

——. *Oxford Guide to Chaucer:* The Canterbury Tales. Oxford: Clarendon Press, 1989.

——. "The Classical Background." In *Chaucer: An Oxford Guide*, edited by Steve Ellis, 255–71. Oxford: Oxford University Press, 2005.

Correale, Robert M. and Mary Hamel, eds. *Sources and Analogues of* The Canterbury Tales. 2 vols. Cambridge: D. S. Brewer, 2002–05.

Cowgill, Jane. "Patterns of Feminine and Masculine Persuasion in the *Melibee* and the *Parson's Tale*." In *Chaucer's Religious Tales*, edited by C. David Benson and Elizabeth Robertson, 171–83. Cambridge: D. S. Brewer, 1990.

Crane, Susan. *Gender and Romance in Chaucer's* Canterbury Tales. New Jersey: Princeton University Press, 1994.

Crow, Martin M. and Clair C. Olson, eds. *Chaucer Life-Records*. Oxford

Clarendon Press, 1966.

Curry, Walter Clyde. *Chaucer and the Medieval Sciences*. 2nd ed. New York: Barnes & Noble, 1960.

Dahlberg, Charles. "The Narrator's Frame for Troilus." *Chaucer Review* 15 (1980): 85–100.

Delany, Sheila. *The Naked Text: Chaucer's* Legend of Good Women. Berkeley: University of California Press, 1994.

Dickinson, Lynne. "Deflection in the Mirror: Feminine Discourse in *The Wife of Bath's Prologue and the Tale*." *Studies in the Age of Chaucer* 15 (1990): 61–90.

Dinshaw, Carolyn. *Chaucer's Sexual Poetics*. Madison: University of Wisconsin Press, 1989.

Donaldson, E. Talbot. *Speaking of Chaucer*. London: Athlone Press, University of London, 1970.

Eberle, Patricia J. "Commercial Language and the Commercial Outlook in the *General Prologue*." *Chaucer Review* 18 (1983): 161–74.

Ellis, Steve, ed. *Chaucer: An Oxford Guide*. Oxford: Oxford University Press, 2005.

Evans, Ruth. "Chaucer's Life." In *Chaucer: An Oxford Guide*, edited by Steve Ellis, 9–25. Oxford: Oxford University Press, 2005.

Fisher, John H., *The Importance of Chaucer*. Carbondale: Southern Illinois University Press, 1992.

Frank, Robert Worth, Jr. *Chaucer and* The Legend of Good Women. Cambridge, MA: Harvard University Press, 1972.

Fyler, J. M. *Chaucer and Ovid*. New Haven: Yale University Press, 1979.

Gardner, John. *The Life and Times of Chaucer*. New York: Alfred A. Knopf, 1977.

Goddard, Harold C. *Chaucer's* Legend of Good Women. Illinois: Norwood Editions, 1978.

Gordon, Ida L. *The Double Sorrow of Troilus: A Study of Ambiguities in* Troilus and Criseyde. Oxford: Clarendon Press, 1970.

Green, Richard Firth. "Women in Chaucer's Audience." *Chaucer Review* 18 (1983): 146–54.

Gray, Douglas, ed. *The Oxford Companion to Chaucer*. Oxford: Oxford University Press, 2003.

220   Bibliography

Halliday, F. E. *Chaucer and his World*. London: Thames and Hudson, 1968.

Hamel, Mary. "The Wife of Bath and a Contemporary Murder." *Chaucer Review* 14 (1979) : 132–39.

Hansen, Elaine Tuttle. *Chaucer and the Fictions of Gender*. Berkeley: University of California Press, 1992.

Howard, Donald R. *Chaucer: His Life, His Works, His World*. New York: Dutton, 1987.

Huppe, Bernard F. *A Reading of* the Canterbury Tales. New York: University of New York, 1964.

Hussey, S. S. *Chaucer: An Introduction*. London: Methuen, 1981.

Jones, Terry, et al. *Who Murdered Chaucer? A Medieval Mystery*. London: Methuen, 2003.

Kellogg, Laura D. *Boccaccio's and Chaucer's Cressida*. New York: Peter Lang, 1995.

Kittredge, George Lyman. *Chaucer and his Poetry*. Cambridge, MA: Harvard University Press, 1951.

———. "Chaucer's Discussion of Marriage," 1911–12. Reprint in *Chaucer Criticism*. Vol. 1, edited by Richard Schoeck and Jerome Taylor, 130–59. Notre Dame: University of Notre Dame Press, 1982.

Knight, Stephen. *Geoffrey Chaucer*. Oxford: Basil Blackwell, 1989.

Laskaya, Anne. *Chaucer's Approach to Gender in* The Canterbury Tales. Cambridge: D. S. Brewer, 1995.

Lenaghan, R. T. "Chaucer's Circle of Gentlemen and Clerks." *Chaucer Review* 18 (1983): 155–60.

Lerer, Seth. *Chaucer and His Readers: Imagining the Author in Late-Medieval England*. New Jersey: Princeton University Press, 1993.

Lucas, Angela, M. *Women in the Middle Ages: Religion, Marriage and Letters*. Sussex: Harvester, 1983.

Lumiansky, R. M. *Of Sondry Folk: The Dramatic Principle in* the Canterbury Tales. Austin: University of Texas Press, 1980.

Lynch, Kathryn L, ed. *Chaucer's Cultural Geography*. New York: Routledge, 2002.

Manly, John M. "Chaucer and the Rhetoricians." *PBA* 12 (1926): 95–113.

———. *Some New Light on Chaucer*. Gloucester, MA: Peter Smith, 1959.

Mann, Jill. "Troilus' Swoon." *Chaucer Review* 14 (1980): 319–35.

——. *Feminizing Chaucer*. 2nd ed. New York: D. S. Brewer, 2002.

Martin, Priscilla. *Chaucer's Women: Nuns, Wives and Amazons*. London: Macmillan, 1990.

Matheson, Lister M. "Chaucer's Ancestry: Historical and Philological Re-Assessments." *Chaucer Review* 25 (1991): 171–89.

Matsunami, Tamotsu. "Chaucer's Mortal Coil." *The Journal of Social Science and Humanities* 178 (1985): 1–27.

McAlpine, Monica. *The Genre of* Troilus and Criseyde. Ithaca: Cornell University Press, 1978.

McCall, John P. *Chaucer among the Gods: The Poetics of Classical Myth*. University Park and London: Pennsylvania State University Press, 1979.

Miller, Robert P. *Chaucer Sources and Backgrounds*. New York: Oxford Univer-sity Press, 1977.

Morse, Ruth and Barry Windeatt, eds. *Chaucer Traditions*. Cambridge: Cambridge University Press,1990.

Murphy, James J. *Rhetoric in the Middle Ages*, 1974. Reprint in *Medieval and Renaissance Texts and Studies* 227. Arizona: Arizona State University, 2001.

——. *Latin Rhetoric and Education in the Middle Ages and Renaissance*. Aldershot: Ashgate, 2005.

Owen, Charles A., Jr. "*The Tale of Melibee*." *Chaucer Review* 7 (1973): 267–80.

Palomo, Dolores. "What Chaucer Really Did to *Le Livre de Melibee*." *Philological Quarterly* 53 (1978): 304–20.

——. "The Fate of the Wife of Bath's 'Bad Husbands'," *Chaucer Review* 9 (1975): 303–19.

Patterson, Lee. " 'For the Wyve's Love of Bath': Feminine Rhetoric and Poetic Resolution in *the Roman de la Rose and the Canterbury Tales*." *Speculum* 58 (1983): 656–95.

——. *Negotiating the Past*. Wisconsin: University of Wisconsin Press, 1987.

——. *Chaucer and the Subject of History*. Madison: University of Wisconsin Press, 1991.

Pearsall, Derek. *The Life of Geoffrey Chaucer*. Oxford: Blakwell, 1992.

Pitcher John A. *Chaucer's Feminine Subjects: Figures of Desire in* The Canterbury Tales. New York: Palgrave Macmillan, 2012.

222   Bibliography

Prendergast, Thomas A. *Chaucer's Dead Body: From Corpse to Corpus*. London: Routledge, 2004.

Pugh, Tison and Marcia Smith Marzec, eds. *Men and Masculinities in Chaucer's* Troilus and Criseyde. Cambridge: D. S. Brewer, 2008.

Richmond, Velma Bourgeois. *Geoffrey Chaucer*. New York: Continuum, 1992.

Robertson, D. W., Jr. *A Preface of Chaucer: Studies in Medieval Perspectives*. New Jersey: Princeton University Press, 1962.

——. "'And For My Land Thus Hastow Mordred Me?': Land Tenure, the Cloth Industry, and the Wife of Bath." *Chaucer Review* 14 (1980): 403–20.

Robertson, Elizabeth, and Christine M. Rose, eds. *Representing Rape in Medieval and Early Modern Literature*. New York: Palgrave, 2001.

Rowland, Beryl. "On the Timely Death of the Wife of Bath's Fourth Husband." *Archiv* 209 (1972–73): 273–82.

Saunders, Corinne, ed. *Chaucer*. Oxford: Blackwell, 2001a.

——. *Rape and Ravishment*. Cambridge: D. S. Brewer, 2001b.

Shakespeare, William. *The Riverside Shakespeare*. Edited by G. Blakemore Evans. Boston: Houghton Mifflin, 1974.

Stone, Brian. *Chaucer*. London: Penguin Group, 1987.

Strohm, Paul. "The Allegory of the *Tale of Melibee*." *Chaucer Review* 2 (1967): 32–42.

——. "Chaucer's Audience(s): Fictional, Implied, Intended, Actual." *Chaucer Review* 18 (1983): 137–45.

Thompson, N. S. *Chaucer, Boccaccio, and the Debate of Love: A Comparative Study of* The Decameron *and* The Canterbury Tales. Oxford: Clarendon Press, 1996.

Turner, Marion. *Chaucerian Conflict: Languages of Antagonism in Late Fourteenth-Century London*. Oxford: Clarendon Press, 2006.

Traversi, Derek. *Chaucer: The Earlier Poetry*. Newark: University of Delaware Press, 1987.

Weisl, Angela Jane. *Conquering the Reign of Femeny: Gender and Genre in Chaucer's Romance*. Cambridge: D. S. Brewer, 1995.

Weissman, Hope Phyllis. "Why Chaucer's Wife is from Bath." *Chaucer Review* 15 (1980): 11–36.

Wetherbee, Winthrop. *Geoffrey Chaucer:* The Canterbury Tales. Cambridge:

Cambridge University Press, 1989.

Whittock, Trevor. *A Reading of* the Canterbury Tales. Cambridge: Cambridge University Press, 1968.

Williams, George. *A New View of Chaucer*. Durham, NC: Duke University Press, 1965.

William, Robert and Soman Cahinani, eds. "Summary and Analysis of Chaucer's *Tale of Melibee*." The Canterbury Tales *Study Guide*. GradeSaver (November, 2008). http://www.gradesaver.com/the-canterbury-tales/study-guide/summary-chaucers-tale-of-melibee in MLA Format (accessed November 13, 2014).

Wilson, Katharina and Elizabeth M. Makowaski. *Wykked Wyves and the Woes of Marriage*. New York: State University of New York Press, 1990.

Windeatt, Barry. "'Love That Oughte Ben Secree' in Chaucer's *Troilus*." *Chaucer Review* 14 (1979): 116–31.

——. *Geoffrey Chaucer:* Troilus and Criseyde. New York: Longman, 1984.

Wood, Chauncey. *The Elements of Chaucer's* Troilus. Durham: Duke University Press, 1984.

Afterword

In completing my doctoral dissertation (the original title is *Eloquence and Chaucer's Women: The Wife of Bath, Criseyde and Prudence*), I am indebted to many people who guided me through this difficult but attractive field of study. I would like to express my cordial gratitude to them.

First of all, I would like to offer my special thanks to Emeritus Professor Kazuo Misono, who occasionally advised his former student to pursue a Ph.D. Without his encouragement, I would not have dared to make a start on my dissertation. Next, I need to express deepest gratitude to my academic supervisor, Professor Yuko Tagaya, who was the first person to introduce me to the fascinating world of medieval literature when I was an undergraduate student. She gladly accepted me as a graduate student and gave me numerous suggestions and valuable academic support. Then I should express my superlative appreciation to Emeritus Professor William I. Elliott, who kindly and patiently read my paper and made stylistic suggestions. He regularly spared time for me in his busy schedule. I cannot thank him enough. I also would like to give sincere thanks to Dr. Hitoshi Yoshikawa, who helped me to translate the legal documents written in Medieval Latin. Finally, I would like to thank my family and friends who have persistently supported me for a long time.

Last but not least genuine gratitude from the bottom of my heart is to both Mr. Takashi Yamaguchi snd Mr. Shoichi Honjo for my publication.

It goes without saying that the responsibility for shortcomings and errors in this dissertation is entirely upon my shoulders.

Index

Achilles 47, 104, 149

Adam 91

Adversus Jovinianum→Epistola adversus Jovinianum

Aeneid 42

Aers, David ii

Aesop 164

Agamemnon 47

Albertanus of Bresica 61

Antenor 101, 120–22, 203

anti-feminism 90

anti-feministic viii, 31, 66, 80, 203–04

Aristotle iv, 67, 156

Aureolus liber Theophrastti de nupitiis 80

Ball, John 122

Benoit de Saint-Maure 42–43, 45, 52, 54–55, 57, 122

Benson, C. David 109–10

Benson, Larry D. 13, 20, 37–38, 52, 54–55, 61, 98–99, 122, 131, 175

Bible

  Colossians 76

  Corinthians 73, 76

  Ephesians 76

  Eve i, 91, 157

  Samaritan 70–72

Black Prince 10

Blanche vii, 10

Blessed Virgin, the→Mary, the Virgin

Boccaccio, Giovanni vii, 42, 44–45, 51–52, 55, 57, 122, 139

Boethius 98

Briseida 42–43, 45

Calchas 47

Calkas 55, 57, 121, 127–29

Cannon, Christopher 21, 26–28

Cassandra 149

Cato, Marcus Porcius 164, 181

Champain, Cecily vii–viii, 2, 4, 12, 18–26, 28–29, 205

Chaucer, Geoffrey

  A Treatise on the Astrolabe 12–14, 19, 24

  Boece v

  Pilgrim-Chaucer 62–63

  Sir Thopas 62–63

  The Book of the Duches vii

  The Canterbury Tales [*CT*] iii, vii, 31, 61, 156, 188, 210–12

  The Clerk's Tale v

  The Franklin's Prologue v

  The Friar's Tale 34

  The General Prologue [*GP*] 31–33, 35–36, 38, 41–42, 51, 69, 77

  The House of Fame v

  The Legend of Good Women 152

  The Merchant's Tale 75, 160

  The Nun's Priest's Tale v

  The Pardoner's Tale 35

  The Romaunt of the Rose [*RR*] vii, 52–53, 56, 116–18

  The Shipman's Tale 75

The Squire's Tale v

The Tale of Melibee [*Mel*] 61, 64–
67, 153, 155, 157–58, 160–63,
165–67, 169–74, 178–87, 189,
191, 202

The Wife of Bath's Prologue [*WBP*]
32, 36–41, 69–75, 77–79, 81–92,
159, 169

The Wife of Bath's Tale [*WBT*] v,
viii, 92–99

Troilus and Criseyde [*TC*] vii,
34, 43, 49–51, 54–56, 58–59,
103–16, 119, 121–23, 125–26,
128, 131–35, 137–39, 141–43,
145–46, 149–50, 197

Chaucer, John (le) 3–5

Chaucer, Lewis 3–4, 11–14, 19, 24–
25

Chaucer, Philippa vii, 2, 4, 9–18, 20,
205, 211

Chaucer, Robert (le) 3–7

Chaucer, Thomas 3–4, 6–8, 11–13,
15

Cicero, Marcus Tullius iii, v, 164,
174–75, 177, 199, 202, 209–10

Constance of Castile 11

Cooper, Helen 63, 188, 190

Copton, Agnes 3–4, 8

Cresseid 45

Cressida 44, 46–48, 57

Criseida 42, 44–45, 139

Criseyde iii, vii–viii, 42–43, 45, 48–
50, 52–61, 67, 101–20, 122–33,
135–37, 139–40, 142–44, 146–51,
195–204, 206, 209–10

Crow, Martin M. 1, 9–10, 13–15, 17

Curry, Walter Clyde 36, 38

Dante Alighieri vii, 98

Dares the Phrygian 42

De officiis 175

De excidio Toroiae historia 42

Deiphebus 144

Deschamps, Eustache vii

Dickinson, Lynne 77, 79

Dictys of Crete 42

Delany, Sheila ii

Dinshow, Carolyn iii

Diomede 45, 101, 136, 139–45, 149–
50, 198

Diomedes 46–48

Douglas, Gavin ii

Edward III vi, 9–10, 25, 205

Elizabeth, Countess of Ulster vi, 9–
10

Ephemeridos belli Troiani libri 42

Epistola adversus Jovinianum 70, 80

Evans, Ruth 1

Fisher, John H. 9, 11, 20

Frigii Daretis Ylias 42

Froissart, Jean vii, 26

Gawain 1, 93–95

God of Love 117–18

Guido delle Colenne 42

Guillaume de Lorris vii, 53

Guinevere 94–95

Hamel, Mary 86

Hansen, Elaine Tuttle iii, 206

Hector 55, 114, 120–21, 196

Helen 55

Henry II 15

Henry IV 16, 20
Henryson, Robert 45–46
Hercules 91
Heyron, John 3–6
Heyron, Thomas 3–4, 6
Historia Trojana 42
Homer 43
Host 62, 190, 192
Howard, Donald H. 6–8, 15–16, 22, 24–26

Il Filostrato vii
Iliad 42

Jesus Christ i, 39, 64, 70–72, 74, 76, 98, 157, 171, 178, 182
John of Gaunt vii, 9–11, 14–19, 205
Joseph of Exeter 42, 52

Kellogg, Laura D. 44
King Arthur 93–94
King Midas 96
Kittredge, G. L. ii

Le Roman de la rose vii
Lady Reason 117, 118, 120
Laskaya, Anne iii
Liber consolationis et consilii 61
Livre de Melibee et de Dame Prudence 61
Ludwig Gomph 42

Machaut, Guillaume de vii
Madonna, the→Mary, the Virgin
Makowaski, Elizabeth M. 80
Malyn, Agnes 3–4, 6–7
Manly, John M. 15, 32

Martin, Pricilla iii, 57, 60, 151
Mary, the Virgin i, 5, 39, 157
Matheson, Lister M. 5–7
Matsunami, Tamotsu 8
Melibeus 63–66, 153, 155–56, 158–61, 163–92, 200
Menelaus 47
Miroir de Mariage 80
misogamy i
misogyny i, 79, 157,
Murphy, James J. iii

Olson, Clair C. 1, 9–10, 13–15, 17

Pallas 57, 104, 122, 141, 196
Palomo, Dolores 85
Pandaro 42
Pandarus 59, 101–07, 118, 144, 147, 195, 197
Pasiphae 92
Patroclus 47
Patterson, Lee 99
Pearsall, Derek 5, 7, 12, 20, 25–26
Peasant Revolt 122
Petrarca, Francesco vii
Priam 121–22
Prioress 38, 51, 62
Prudence iii, vii–viii, 61, 63–67, 137, 153, 155–62, 164–79, 181–93, 199–202, 204, 209–10

Queen Philippa 10, 16, 205

Remedie of Love 65
Renaud de Louens 61
Richard II vi, 14
Robertson, D. W. ii, 70–71

Robinson, F. N. 15, 109
Roet, Giles de 10, 16
Roman de Troie 42, 45
Rowland, Beryl 85

Samson 91
Saunders, Corinne 94
Seneca, Lucius Anneaus 65, 98, 157, 164, 181, 199
Shakespeare, William 45–48
Sir Degare 93
Skeat, W. W. 5–8, 19–20, 24, 109
Socrates 91
Solomon 67, 90. 157, 164, 181, 199
Sophie 63–64, 153
Speght, Thomas 12
Stace, Geoffrey 3–4, 6–7
Straw, Jack 122
Strode, Ralph 13–14
Swynford, Hugh 10, 17
Swynford, Joan 16
Swynford, Katherine 9, 16–17

The Marriage of Sir Gawain 93
The Wedding of Sir Gawain and Dame Ragnell 93
Theophrastus 80, 90
Thersities 46–47
Troilo 42
Troilus vii, viii, 42–43, 45–48, 56–60, 101–12, 114, 116, 118–20, 123–26, 128–51, 195–98, 200, 203–04
Tyler, Wat 122

Ulysses 46–47

Valerius 90, 98
Virgil 42

Weisl, Angela Jane iii
Weissman, Hope Phyllis 34–35
Westhale, Joan 3–4, 6
Westhale, Walter de 3–4, 6
Williams, George 14, 17
Wilson, Katharina M. 80

Eloquence of Chaucer's Women:
The Wife of Bath, Criseyde, and Prudence

2017年9月30日　初版発行

著　者　野地　薫

発行者　本城　正一

発行所　ほんのしろ

〒 343–0838　埼玉県越谷市蒲生 2–13–22–506
☎ 048–987–4863

発売所　音羽書房鶴見書店

〒 113–00033　東京都文京区本郷 4–1–14
☎ 03–3814–0491

印刷・製本／岩佐印刷所

ISBN978–4–7553–0405–7
Copyright © 2017 by NOJI Kaoru
All rights reserved

落丁・乱丁本はお取り替えいたします

About the Author

Kaoru Noji took her undergraduate work at Kanto Gakuin University and postgraduate work at Meiji Gaikuin University. She received her doctorate in literature from Kanto Gakuin University in 2015, specializing in Middle English literature. Her major articles include "Chaucer's View of Women: Dorigen, Griselda, the Wife of Bath" (2000), "Reconsideration of Chaucer's 'raptus'" (2007) and "Eloquence of the Wife of Bath" (2014). Having served on the faculty of Yamamura Gakuen College for 26 years. She currently holds part-time positions at Kanto Gakuin University, Komazawa University and Kokugakuin University. She has read papers widely both in Japan and abroad and is regarded as among the leading Chaucerians in contemporary Japan.